Learn ENGLISH with NEWS

讀力報導：看新聞學英文

編著者簡介

朱嬿婷
學歷／英國倫敦國王學院應用語言學與英語教學碩士
經歷／新北市立北大高中英文教師

李秀玲
學歷／國立清華大學外語教學所碩士
經歷／桃園市立壽山高中應英科教師

巫沂璇
學歷／國立交通大學英語教學研究所碩士
經歷／臺中市立文華高中英文教師

審訂者簡介

Graeme Todd
學歷／英國赫瑞瓦特大學英語教學所碩士
經歷／國立臺灣師範大學英語學系講師

蘇文賢
學歷／國立臺灣師範大學教育研究所碩士
經歷／國立基隆高中英文教師

葉秋菊
學歷／美國紐約聖約翰大學東亞研究所碩士
經歷／桃園市立武陵高中英文教師

三民書局

給讀者的話

在現今資訊爆炸時代，具備理解與識讀新聞媒體能力至關重要。閱讀新聞英文如同擁有一把智慧鑰匙，它能帶領讀者穿越不同文化和觀點，打開通往全球資訊的大門。

《讀力報導：看新聞學英文》非常適合做為讀者踏上這趟全球之旅的入門指南。本書取材新聞最核心的六大主題：文教育樂、身心健康、社會觀察、生態環境、科技要聞、政治財經，共十八個單元引導讀者進入新聞英文世界。而每單元可分為五個面向：

一、情境主題跨頁

補充新聞主題關鍵字詞與 Fun Facts 知識問答，延伸新聞主題學習，擴增各新聞領域的趣味知識。

二、新聞文章（含獨家新聞播報影音檔）

每單元依據主題精選三篇新聞文章，提供外師新聞播報影音檔，透過多樣化的新聞報導，了解國內外大小事，一併培養閱讀、聽力、口說技能，增進英語能力。

三、混合題型練習

閱讀文章最重要的莫過於能夠真正理解文意，並歸納其重點，因此作者們精心編寫了多樣化的混合題型，協助讀者自我檢核是否能夠精確理解新聞文章的文意，同時備戰學測。

四、精選字彙片語

貼心整理文章重要字彙、慣用語和片語，提供詞性、字義以及字級（參考學測大考中心公布之「111學年度起適用之高中英文參考詞彙表」），方便讀者背誦重要字彙。搭配例句及中譯，進一步了解字彙用法，強化學習記憶，拓展英文字彙量。

五、解析夾冊：

解析夾冊提供 Fun Facts 知識問答的說明、新聞文章翻譯以及混合題翻譯與解析，協助讀者理解文意與解題要領。

相信讀者能夠透過本書，學會如何閱讀、理解和分析新聞文章。不論你是對新聞英文有興趣卻還不敢跨出第一步，或想提升英文閱讀、聽力與口說技能，本書將是你學習新聞英文的最佳利器。

審訂團隊專業推薦 Graeme Todd 蘇文賢 葉秋菊

使用說明

Step 1 情境主題跨頁

補充新聞主題關鍵字詞，輕鬆延伸學習

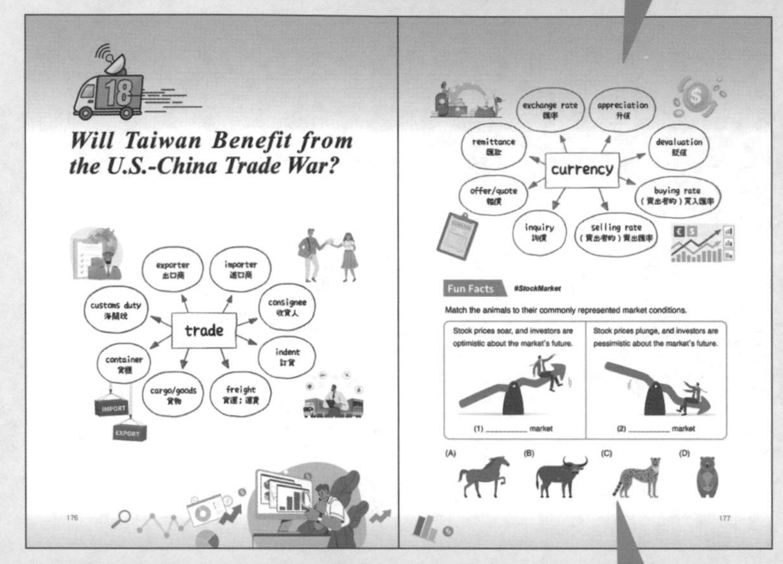

Fun Facts 知識問答，介紹主題相關趣味知識，增添學習樂趣

Step 2 閱讀新聞文章

The presence of refugees, or displaced persons, is not a rare **occurrence**. Throughout history, regular people have borne the brunt of conflicts and wars. Many have thus been **compelled** to **flee** their **homelands**, driven by violence or persecution, in search of safety and sanctuary in foreign countries. Unfortunately, now there are even more refugees in the world.

The growing global refugee crisis can be traced back to the events of 2011 and 2012 in the Middle East and Africa. The "Arab Spring" began as a peaceful pro-democracy movement but eventually **transformed** into terrible wars in Syria and Libya. Additionally, civil

158

數位學習有效又便利

1. 掃描音檔 QR code，聽外師朗讀文章，訓練英文聽力！
2. 掃描影音檔 QR code，觀看外師播報影片，模仿口音與語調，強化口說能力！

Step 3 混合題型練習

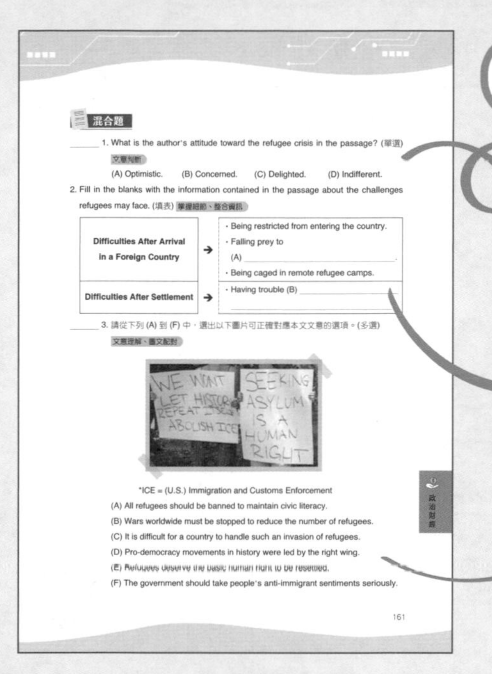

混合題

_____ 1. What is the author's attitude toward the refugee crisis in the passage? (單選) 文意判斷

(A) Optimistic. (B) Concerned. (C) Delighted. (D) Indifferent.

2. Fill in the blanks with the information contained in the passage about the challenges refugees may face. (填表) 掌握細節、整合資訊

Difficulties After Arrival in a Foreign Country	→	· Being restricted from entering the country. · Falling prey to (A) ______________. · Being caged in remote refugee camps.
Difficulties After Settlement	→	· Having trouble (B) ______________

_____ 3. 請從下列 (A) 到 (F) 中，選出以下圖片可正確對應本文文意的選項。(多選) 文意理解、圖文配對

*ICE = (U.S.) Immigration and Customs Enforcement

(A) All refugees should be banned to maintain civic literacy.
(B) Wars worldwide must be stopped to reduce the number of refugees.
(C) It is difficult for a country to handle such an invasion of refugees.
(D) Pro-democracy movements in history were led by the right wing.
(E) Refugees deserve the basic human right to be resettled.
(F) The government should take people's anti-immigrant sentiments seriously.

政治財經

161

閱讀完文章後，利用混合題檢測文章理解程度

單選題

手寫題

多選題

多樣化的混合題題型，引導你精確理解文章文意，訓練文章訊息歸納以及分析等解題能力

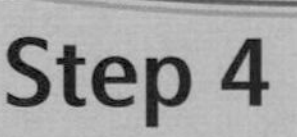

Step 4 精選字彙片語

重要字彙提供 a. 詞性、b. 字義、c. 字級、d. 例句與中譯，學習字彙實際用法，更有效加深單字記憶

Words for Production

1) **refugee** *(n.)* 難民 ❹ (a: 詞性, b: 字義, c: 字級)

d · The **refugees** in the camp lack food and clean water.
營區裡的難民缺乏食物與乾淨的水。

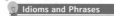

Idioms and Phrases

1) **bear the brunt of sth** 承受⋯的衝擊 同 也作take/suffer the brunt of sth
· The tall tree in the forest had **borne** the full **brunt of** the lightning.
森林裡這棵高大的樹承受了閃電的所有衝擊。

2) **welcome sb with open arms** 熱烈地歡迎⋯ 同 也作greet sb with open arms
· The host family **welcomed** the Japanese exchange student **with open arms**.
寄宿家庭熱情地歡迎這名日本籍交換學生。

適時補充慣用語和片語的替換用法，懂得換句話説，提升寫作實力

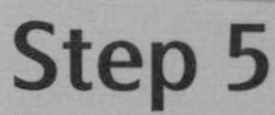

Step 5 解析夾冊

解析提供豐富的說明與補充，有助於理解文意與解題要領。

新聞文章翻譯

混合題精闢解析

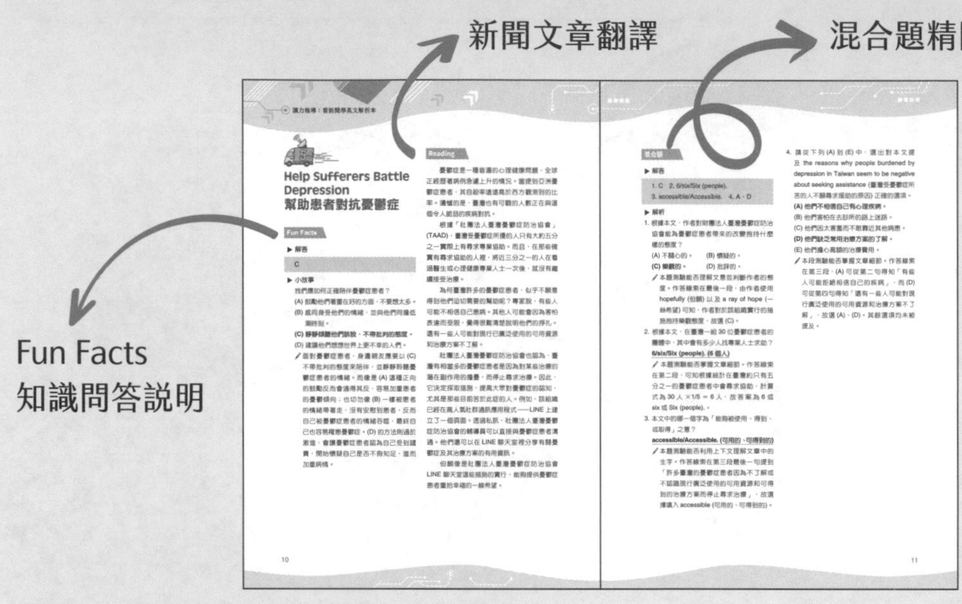

Fun Facts
知識問答說明

電子朗讀音檔下載說明

請先輸入網址或掃描 QR code 進入「三民・東大音檔網」
https://elearning.sanmin.com.tw/Voice/

❶ 輸入本書書名即可找到音檔。請再依提示下載音檔。

❷ 也可點擊「英文」進入英文專區查找音檔後下載。

❸ 若無法順利下載音檔，可至「常見問題」查看相關問題。

❹ 若有音檔相關問題，請點擊「聯絡我們」，將盡快為你處理。

❺ 更多英文新知都在臉書粉絲專頁。

三民東大外文組-英文	若有音檔相關問題，歡迎聯絡我們 ④ 服務時間：週一-週五，08:00-17:30 臉書粉絲專頁：Sanmin English - 三民英語編輯小組 ⑤

Table of Contents

Picture Credits:
All pictures in this publication are from Shutterstock and Wikimedia Commons.

Japanese Collectors of Cambodian Art Do the Right Thing

Famous Museums Around the World

1
2
3
4
5
6
7
8
9

Fun Facts

#Combodia #RollsRoyce #AngkorWat

Which three of the following statements about Cambodia are correct?

(A) Cambodia has the highest number of Rolls-Royce cars in the world.

(B) The most widely practiced religion in Cambodia is Islam.

(C) Visitors to Angkor Wat are required to wear clothing with sleeves and knee-length skirts or pants.

(D) McDonald's stores in Cambodia offer the cheapest food compared to those in other countries.

(E) Cambodians consider the left hand unclean, and the right hand clean.

Reading

In the 1970s, Cambodia was in the grip of a bloody civil war that plunged the country into **chaos**. The Khmer Rouge finally **seized** power and **executed** many of the country's brightest and best citizens. Many others were sent to prison camps for reeducation. The remaining population was forced to participate in large-scale public **labor** projects in the countryside.

During this dark time, countless Cambodian cultural **relics** went missing. Statues of Buddha, as well as other carvings and art objects, were stolen from temples and sold for profit. Most of these stolen

▲ Democratic Kampuchea, aka the Khmer Rouge regime (1975–1979), and its flag.

▲ The Kingdom of Cambodia (1993–) and its flag, featuring Angkor Wat in the center.

cultural treasures were **smuggled** out of the country and found their way into the hands of private art **collectors** like Fumiko Takakuwa and her husband. Over the years, the Japanese couple **purchased** nearly a hundred Cambodian cultural relics and displayed them in their home. Although they enjoyed the beauty of these objects, they felt **guilty**. They knew these artworks had most likely been stolen, which is why they decided to return the objects to the National Museum of Cambodia in 2019.

The museum expressed its **gratitude** to the Takakuwas, who had **volunteered** to do the right thing by returning the statues, jars,

▲ The National Museum of Cambodia located in Phnom Penh, the capital of Cambodia. It is a renowned historical and archaeological museum of the country.

and jewelry they had in their **possession**. These ancient objects date from the 8th to 14th centuries and are **undoubtedly** priceless to Cambodians. Now that Cambodia has regained peace and **prosperity**, its government is **desperate** to recover its lost cultural **heritage**. Besides showing appreciation, the Ministry of Culture and Fine Arts is hopeful that other art collectors will follow Cambodian laws, international agreements, and the example set by the Takakuwa family by returning any treasures they have purchased. This way, these treasures may be valued and appreciated by all.

▲ Angkor Wat, a historic relic of the Khmer Empire, is now a significant symbol of Cambodia.

混合題

1. 請從文章第一段和第三段中各找出一個最適當的單詞 (word)，分別填入下列句子空格中，並視語法需要做適當的字形變化。**每格限填一個單詞 (word)**。(填充) 掌握脈絡、字形變化

After the Khmer Rouge seized power, the country's brightest and best citizens faced (A) ______________ while many others were sent to prison camps for reeducation.

The Cambodian government hopes that there will be more collectors like the Takakuwa family who are willing to give up their right to (B) ______________ the treasures and return them to Cambodia.

2. Match the correct background and result according to the passage. (單選)

掌握細節、分析資訊

Background	Result
Cambodia was thrown into chaos because of a civil war.	Many citizens of Cambodia were put into prison camps.
Thieves stole cultural treasures from many Cambodian temples.	(A) ______________
(B) ______________	They returned the missing treasures of Cambodia to its museum.

① The citizens of Cambodia were forced to sell cultural treasures to other countries for profit.

② The Japanese art collectors were guilty because they knew their collections were stolen from Cambodia.

③ Most of the items were smuggled out of the country and purchased by art collectors.

______ 3. According to the passage, which of the following best describes the Cambodian government's attitude toward the Japanese art collectors? (單選) 引申推論

(A) Grateful. (B) Disagreeing. (C) Neutral. (D) Indifferent.

Words for Production

1) **chaos** *(n.)* 混亂 ❺
   - After the earthquake, the whole country was in complete **chaos**.
     地震發生後，全國一片混亂。

2) **seize** *(v.)* 奪取 ❹
   - The enemy **seized** control of the airport at the beginning of the war.
     敵軍在戰爭開始時就奪取機場的控制權。

3) **execute** *(v.)* 將…處死 ❺
   - The prisoner has been **executed** because he committed murder.
     該名囚犯因為犯了謀殺被處死。

4) **labor** *(n.)* 勞動 ❹
   - The workers were paid fairly for their **labor**.
     工人的勞動得到了公平的報酬。

5) **relic** *(n.)* 文物；遺跡 ❻
   - The castle, built over 300 years ago, is now considered a historic **relic**.
     這座建於300多年前的城堡現在被視為歷史遺跡。

6) **smuggle** *(v.)* 走私 ❻
   - The criminal gang is planning to **smuggle** illegal drugs into the country.
     該犯罪集團正計劃將非法毒品走私到該國。

7) **collector** *(n.)* 收藏家，收集者 ❺
   - Diana is a crazy **collector** whose house is full of art from all over the world.
     Diana是個瘋狂的收集者，她的房子裡堆滿了來自世界各國的藝術品。

8) **purchase** *(v.)* 購買 ❺
   - Customers who **purchase** goods in large quantities usually get special discounts.
     大量購買商品的顧客通常可以得到特別折扣。

9) **guilty** *(adj.)* 愧疚的 ❹

- Samuel should have felt **guilty** about cheating on the math exam.

  Samuel應該要為他在數學考試作弊感到愧疚。

10) **gratitude** *(n.)* 感激之情 ❹

- The lady sent the police officer some homemade cookies to express her **gratitude**.

  這位女士送了警察一些自製的餅乾以表達她的感激之情。

11) **volunteer** *(v.)* 自願⋯，主動⋯ ❹

- Those citizens **volunteered** to clean the streets on weekends.

  那些市民自願在週末清掃街道。

12) **possession** *(n.)* 持有，擁有 ❹

- Andrew was arrested by the police after he was found in **possession** of the stolen goods.

  Andrew在被發現持有贓物後就被警方逮捕了。

13) **undoubtedly** *(adv.)* 毫無疑問地 ❺

- The Louvre Museum is **undoubtedly** one of the most famous museums in the world.

  羅浮宮無疑是世界上最著名的博物館之一。

14) **prosperity** *(n.)* 繁榮 ❹

- It is believed that the **prosperity** of a country depends on its educational system.

  人們相信一個國家的繁榮取決於其教育體制。

15) **desperate** *(adj.)* 非常想要的 ❹

- These students are **desperate** to know the exam results.

  這些學生非常想知道考試結果。

16) **heritage** *(n.)* 遺產 ❺

- Visitors can enjoy Chinese cultural **heritage** at the National Palace Museum.

  遊客可以在故宮博物院欣賞中國文化遺產。

Words for Recognition

1) **Cambodian** *(adj.)* 柬埔寨的；*(n.)* 柬埔寨人

Cambodia *(n.)* 柬埔寨

2) **Khmer Rouge** *(n.)* 紅色高棉

3) **reeducation** *(n.)* 再教育　補 也作re-education

4) **large-scale** *(adj.)* 大規模的

5) **Buddha** *(n.)* 佛像

6) **carving** *(n.)* 雕刻品

7) **artwork** *(n.)* 藝術品

8) **Ministry of Culture and Fine Arts** *(n.)* (柬埔寨) 文化藝術部

Idioms and Phrases

1) **be in the grip of . . .** 處於 (不利局勢) 中

- Many countries **are in the grip of** water shortages because of global warming.

  因為全球暖化，許多國家都面臨缺水的問題。

2) **plunge . . . into . . .** (突然) 陷入…

- The affair between the two singers **plunged** their musical careers **into** darkness.

  這兩位歌手之間的緋聞使他們的音樂生涯陷入黑暗。

NOTE

The Olympic Games

Summer Olympic Games

cycling road
公路自行車

swimming
游泳

athletics
田徑運動

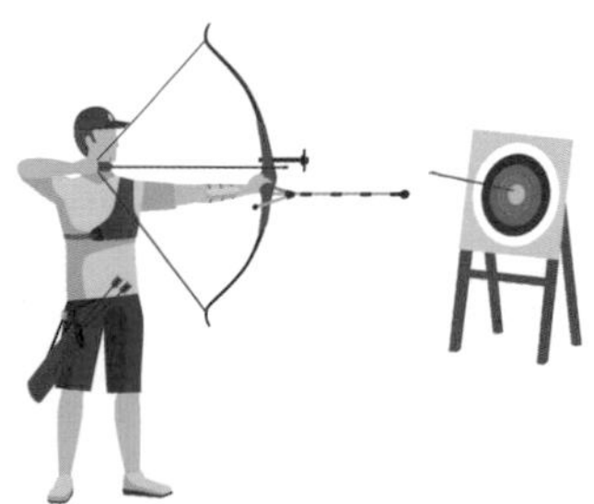

archery
射擊

fencing
西洋劍(擊劍)

rhythmic gymnastics
韻律體操

Winter Olympic Games

skeleton
空架雪車

figure skating
花式滑冰

bobsleigh
雪車

alpine skiing
高山滑雪

curling
冰壺

biathlon
冬季兩項

Fun Facts

#TheOlympicRings

1. What do the five colors of the Olympic rings symbolize?
   (A) Five element theory. (B) Five Oceans.
   (C) Five continents. (D) Five days a week.
2. Currently, how long is the period between the Summer Olympics and the Winter Olympics?
   (A) 1 year. (B) 2 years. (C) 3 years. (D) 4 years.

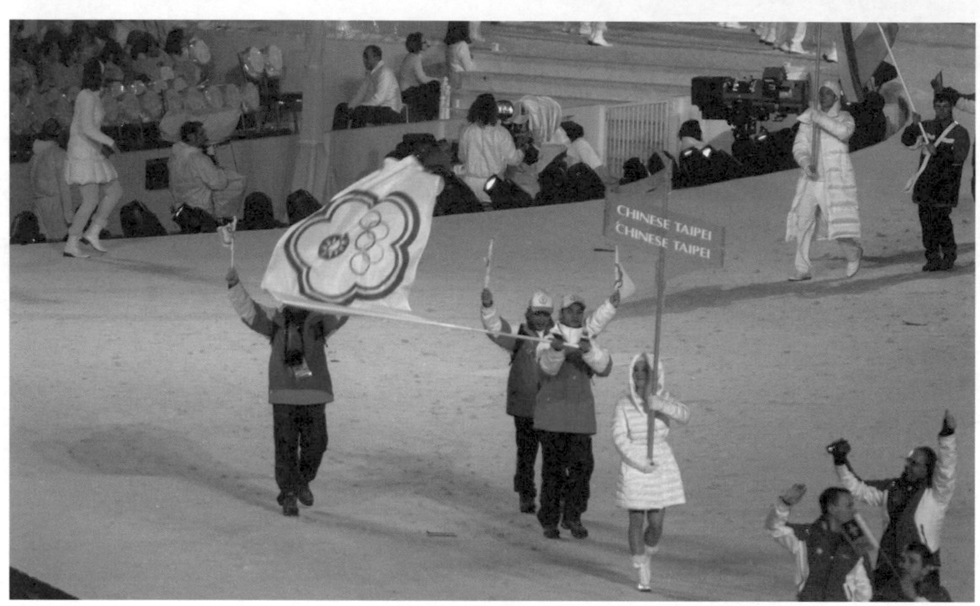

▲ Team Chinese Taipei carried its Olympic flag when entering the opening of the Winter Olympics.

The Olympic Games are one of the most important sporting events in the world. They bring the best athletes from different countries together to take part in the hope of winning medals. Countries also compete for the honor of hosting the Olympics, as it attracts international attention. The International Olympic Committee has the final say on the city where the Games are held.

The host city opens the Olympics with an exciting **ceremony**. Then, the **athletic competitions** get **underway**. Athletes compete in a variety of events, including sprints, **relays**, the **marathon**, the long jump, and **wrestling**.

Spectators are eager to see the athletes perform. Will **legendary** Olympic athletes add to their medal count or be beaten by younger **rivals**? Some athletes strike a **trademark** pose after each victory. Others may get off to a slow start but **eventually** come back to finish with a gold, silver, or **bronze** medal. Still others can be so good that they win in both team and individual events, creating more **highlights**

▲ The "Our Heroes! Team Taiwan Victory Party" was held to celebrate the 2 gold medals, 4 silver medals, and 6 bronze medals won at the 2020 Tokyo Olympics.

of the Games. Another focus of attention is the national medal race. People are **enthusiastic** about which country wins the most medals overall.

Finally, at the closing ceremony, the Olympic flame is extinguished. Immediately, the **organizers** of the next Olympic Games work hard to get ready, aiming to match the fun and excitement of the Games which have just closed. Normally, the Olympic Games take place every four years, the few **exceptions** being because of the World Wars and the COVID-19 pandemic.

All in all, the Olympic Games encourage a spirit of peaceful, friendly competition between nations. The most important thing is not to win, but to participate.

1st 1896 Athens, Kingdom of Greece	2nd 1900 Paris, France	3rd 1904 St. Louis, USA
30th 2012 London, UK	31st 2016 Rio de Janeiro, Brazil	32nd 2021 Tokyo, Japan
33rd 2024 Paris, France	34th 2028 Los Angeles, USA	34th 2032 Brisbane, Australia

混合題

_______ 1. According to the passage, which of the following best describes "Others may get off to a slow start but eventually come back to finish with a gold, silver, or bronze medal" in the third paragraph? (單選) 引申推論

(A) Great oaks from little acorns grow. (B) Every cloud has a silver lining.

(C) A leopard can't change its spots. (D) Better late than never.

_______ 2. 請從下列 (A) 到 (F) 中，選出對countries all over the world和the audience of the Olympics都正確的選項。(多選) 掌握細節、資訊關係

(A) In the hope of winning medals.

(B) Competing to host the Olympics.

(C) Sponsoring athletes for their trademark.

(D) Participating to fulfill the spirit of peace.

(E) Beating the spectators from rival countries.

(F) Deciding which city can host the Olympics.

3. Fill in the blanks with the information contained in the passage about the Olympic Games. (填充) 掌握細節、整合資訊

Facts About the Olympic Games

- Cities in the world fight for the right to host the Olympics.
- The Olympic Games are held every (A) _______________.
- Athletes can compete in both team and (B) _______________ events.
- The extinguishment of the Olympic flame marks the closing of the Olympic Games.

Words for Production

1) **ceremony** *(n.)* 儀式；典禮 ❺

• The principal spoke for thirty minutes without interruption at the opening **ceremony**.

校長在開幕式中不間斷地講了三十分鐘的話。

2) **athletic** *(adj.)* 運動的 ❹

• The boy's excellent **athletic** ability makes him the leader of the track and field team.

那男孩出色的運動能力使他成為田徑隊的隊長。

3) **competition** *(n.)* 競賽 ❹

• The athlete put her defeat behind her and entered the **competition** again.

這位運動選手拋開她過去的挫敗，再度參賽。

4) **underway** *(adj.)* 正在進行中的 ❻

• The research is **underway** and has not made much progress so far.

該研究正在進行中，目前沒有太大進展。

5) **relay** *(n.)* 接力賽；接替人員 ❻

• The **relay** race was put off owing to the typhoon. 這場接力賽因颱風而延期。

6) **marathon** *(n.)* 馬拉松 ❹

• The medical team provided the injured **marathon** runners with on-site medical treatment.

醫療團隊為受傷的馬拉松跑者提供現場醫療救治。

7) **wrestling** *(n.)* 角力，摔角 ❻

• No one believed the shy girl was capable of winning this **wrestling** game.

沒人相信這害羞的女孩有能力贏得這場角力比賽。

8) **spectator** *(n.)* 觀眾 ❺

• The players can feel the excitement of the **spectators** during their sporting competitions.

選手們在運動賽事進行時可以感受到觀眾的興奮。

9) **legendary** *(adj.)* 傳奇的；著名的 ❺

• Johnny is a **legendary** actor whose autobiography is selling like hot cakes.

Johnny是位傳奇的演員，他的自傳十分暢銷。

10) **rival** *(n.)* 對手 ❺

• Danny's harsh words added fuel to the fire and made his **rival** angrier.

Danny尖酸的話語火上加油，使他的對手更生氣了。

11) **trademark** *(n.)* (某人的) 特徵；商標 ❻

• Wearing a blue jacket and a yellow baseball cap became Bob's **trademark**.

穿著藍色外套和戴黃色棒球帽成為Bob的特徵。

12) **eventually** *(adv.)* 最終，最後 ❹

• After months of fierce competition, Dana **eventually** defeated the other opponents.

經過數個月的激烈競爭，Dana最終戰勝了其他對手。

13) **bronze** *(adj.)* 青銅色的；*(n.)* 銅牌 ❺

• The **bronze** statue of the Queen will be built in the square before her memorial service.

女王的銅像將在她的追悼會前被建造在廣場上。

14) **highlight** *(n.)* 亮點；精采部分 ❺

• The **highlight** of the New Year celebration is the fireworks show.

新年慶典的亮點就在煙火秀。

15) **enthusiastic** *(adj.)* 熱衷的 ❺

• After the show, the actors received an **enthusiastic** response from the audience.

表演結束後，演員們得到了觀眾的熱烈回響。

16) **organizer** *(n.)* 籌辦者 ❻

• Being the **organizer** of the big event, Zoe has been under a lot of stress lately.

身為那場盛大活動的籌辦者，Zoe最近倍感壓力。

17) **exception** *(n.)* 例外 ❹

• Everyone has to pay an entrance fee, with the **exception** of children under twelve.

除了十二歲以下的孩童，每個人都必須支付入場費。

Words for Recognition

1) **the Olympics Games** *(n.)* 奧運 (奧林匹克運動會) 補 也作 the Olympics

2) **sprint** *(n.)* 短跑

3) **extinguish** *(v.)* 熄滅

4) **COVID-19** *(n.)* 新冠肺炎

5) **pandemic** *(n.)* 疫情、大流行病

Idioms and Phrases

1) **take part in** 參與⋯

• The professor likes to invite her students to **take part in** the discussion.

這位教授喜歡邀請她的學生參與討論。

2) **strike a pose** 擺出姿勢 補 也作strike an attitude

• The photographer asked the model to **strike a** dramatic **pose**.

攝影師要求模特兒擺出引人注目的姿勢。

3) **get off to a(n) . . . start** 有⋯的開始 補 常用good、bad、slow、impressive等形容詞

• Ariel usually drinks a cup of coffee to **get off to a** good **start** every morning.

Ariel通常會喝一杯咖啡來讓她每天早上有個美好的開始。

4) **take place** 舉辦

• Jane and John's wedding will **take place** at noon next Saturday.

Jane和John的婚禮將於下週六中午舉行。

5) **all in all** 整體來說，總而言之

• It rained a lot, but **all in all**, it was a good journey.

下了大雨，但整體來說，這是一次愉快的旅程。

NOTE

Learn to Identify Facts and Fake News

Well-known News Media

U.S.A

1.	**Cable News Network (CNN)** 有線電視新聞網 · A prominent U.S. cable news network covering global events and current affairs.	CNN
2.	***The New York Times* (*NYT*)** 《紐約時報》 · It delivers comprehensive news and analysis in many fields. "All the News That's Fit to Print" is its famous slogan.	The New York Times
3.	***USA Today*** 《今日美國》 · It provides diverse news coverage, sports, tech, etc. The paper features colorful graphics and brief stories.	USA TODAY
4.	***The Washington Post*** 《華盛頓郵報》 · It reports coverage, investigations, worldwide news, etc. "Democracy Dies in Darkness" is its official slogan.	The Washington Post
5.	***The Wall Street Journal*** 《華爾街日報》 · A respected financial and business-focused news media.	THE WALL STREET JOURNAL.

U.K.

	Media	Logo
1.	**BBC News** 英國廣播公司新聞部 · A public service broadcaster that delivers world and UK news about entertainment, business, science, technology, and health news.	BBC NEWS
2.	**Sky News** 天空新聞 · A free-to-air broadcaster that delivers breaking news from business, politics, entertainment, and more in the UK and worldwide.	sky news
3.	***The Guardian*** 《衛報》 · A daily media that releases world news, opinions, sports, cultures, and lifestyle reports.	The Guardian
4.	***The Sun*** 《太陽報》 · A popular tabloid, a newspaper with small pages, and media which provides news, particularly about showbiz and other entertaining news.	THE Sun
5.	***Financial Times* (*FT*)** 《金融時報》 · A media and daily newspaper which mainly focuses on business, finance, and global economics.	FT .com FINANCIAL TIMES

Fun Facts

#MediaLiteracy #EuropeanUnion

"Media literacy" is an important skill for modern people. According to an EU report, which of the following abilities are considered important to practice as part of media literacy?

① action/agency	⑤ publicity
② examination and certification	⑥ access
③ reflection	⑦ challenge
④ creation	⑧ analysis and evaluation

(A) ①, ②, ③, ④, ⑤　　(B) ①, ③, ④, ⑥, ⑧　　(C) ①, ④, ⑤, ⑦, ⑧

Nowadays, news uses more and more sensational headlines to **lure** people into reading it. However, many of these stories are nothing but "fake news," stories that are dramatic but untrue. They can be found in the press, on TV, on social media, and even on chat apps.

With easy **access** to the Internet, people receive **vast** amounts of information every day. Misinformation and rumors spread like wildfire, influencing people's opinions and leading to misunderstandings. "There's more information than ever before," said James Harding, the former director of BBC News, "some of it is old news. Some of it is half-truths. Some of it is just downright lies. And it's harder than ever when you look at those information feeds to discern what's true and what's not." So, it's necessary to **filter** out false information and fabricated news in order to avoid being **deceived**.

Many have realized the importance of **tackling** fake news and have started to take action. For example, the government of Taiwan has set up a fact-checking office to identify false news stories and shut them down. The British Broadcasting Corporation (BBC) has also **launched** an educational program that aims to teach students how to tell which news stories are real and which are fake.

James Harding (1969–)

Founder
Tortoise Media (2019–)

Director of News & Current Affairs
BBC News (2013–2018)

Editor
The Times (2007–2012)

Actually, people can use certain skills to identify fake news. First of all, determine the source. Sources with good **reputations** are more reliable. Next, **evaluate** the tone. A story making **exaggerated** statements or using rude words to **criticize** something is probably not factual.

Fake news also takes advantage of people's **ignorance**. Therefore, people should **equip** themselves with the ability to better filter news and make informed choices about the information they **consume**. In doing so, they can more easily separate the truth from lies!

混合題

_______ 1. According to the passage, which of the following statements is true? (單選)

掌握細節

(A) News in newspapers is not to be trusted by BBC News.

(B) Exaggerated content is a necessity for a good news story.

(C) News with dramatic and scary headlines is likely to be identified as fake.

(D) The press won't release fake news on social media or on TV.

2. Fill in the blanks with the information contained in the passage about Taiwan's and the U.K.'s responses to fake news. (填表) 掌握細節

Countries	Responses to Fake News
Taiwan	establish a(n) (A) ______________
the U.K.	start a(n) (B) ______________

3. 請從文章中第四段與第五段中各找出最適當的單詞 (word)，分別填入下列句子空格中，並視語法需要做適當的字形變化。**每格限填一個單詞 (word)**。(填充) 掌握脈絡、字形變化

It is very important for people to (A) ______________ on information from credible sources.

People should be (B) ______________ to identify whether the information they are given is true or not.

Words for Production

1) **identify** *(v.)* 辨認 ❹

- Although the witness was terrified, he tried hard to **identify** the murderer.

  儘管目擊者很害怕，他還是努力試著指認兇手。

2) **nowadays** *(adv.)* 現今 ❹

- **Nowadays**, people often contact each other by sending direct messages on social media.

  現今，人們經常透過社群媒體傳私訊來彼此聯繫。

3) **lure** *(v.)* 誘導，引誘 ❻

- Luna was **lured** into the private company by a high salary.

  Luna被高薪引誘進了這間私人公司。

4) **access** *(n.)* 方式，途徑；使用某物的權利 ❹

- Users who post insulting comments will be denied **access** to the website.

  發表侮辱性評論的使用者將會被拒絕造訪該網站。

5) **vast** *(adj.)* 大量的 ❹

- The capitalist invested a **vast** sum of money in real estate.

  這位資本家投資鉅款於房地產。

6) **filter** *(v.)* 過濾 ❺

- The R&D team developed a piece of software that can **filter** spam.

  該研發團隊開發了一款可以過濾垃圾郵件的軟體。

7) **deceive** *(v.)* 欺騙，矇騙 ❺

- Anna **deceived** many people into believing she was a millionaire.

  Anna欺騙了很多人，讓他們相信她是百萬富翁。

8) **tackle** *(v.)* 處理；與…交涉 ❺

- It is challenging to **tackle** water shortages in Taiwan.

  要解決臺灣的缺水問題是很艱鉅的。

9) **launch** *(v.)* 發起 ❹

• The company **launched** a marketing campaign to increase its market share.

這間公司發起了行銷活動以增加它的市場占有率。

10) **reputation** *(n.)* 名譽 ❹

• The reported food safety issue ruined the brand's good **reputation**.

被舉報的食品安全問題毀掉了該品牌的良好名譽。

11) **evaluate** *(v.)* 評估 ❹

• Before making a crucial decision, we have to **evaluate** the situation first.

在做出關鍵的決定前，我們必須先評估情況。

12) **exaggerated** *(adj.)* 誇大的，誇張的 ❹

• The press often reports news in an **exaggerated** way to catch people's attention.

媒體經常以誇大的方式報導新聞來吸引人們的注意。

13) **criticize** *(v.)* 批判 ❹

• Some of the activities done by this religious group are **criticized** for violating animal rights.

這個宗教團體從事的一些活動因侵犯動物權利而受到批評。

14) **ignorance** *(n.)* 無知，愚昧 ❹

• The salesman took advantage of the old lady's **ignorance** to persuade her to buy his products.

這名推銷員利用老太太的無知，說服她買下他的產品。

15) **equip** *(v.)* 具備… ❹

• The latest model is **equipped** with an automated driving system.

最新車款配備了自動駕駛系統。

16) **consume** *(v.)* (從媒體中)取得資訊 ❹

• People nowadays spend a lot of time **consuming** posts and short videos on social media.

人們現在花很多時間從社群媒體上的貼文和短影音獲得資訊。

Words for Recognition

1) **sensational** *(adj.)* 聳動的

2) **app** *(n.)* 應用程式 補 也作application

3) **misinformation** *(n.)* 假消息

4) **wildfire** *(n.)* 野火

5) **misunderstanding** *(n.)* 誤解

6) **downright** *(adj.)* 十足的

7) **discern** *(v.)* 辨識，辨別出⋯

8) **fabricated** *(adj.)* 捏造的

9) **fact-checking** *(n.)* 事實查核

10) **factual** *(adj.)* 真實的

Idioms and Phrases

1) **lead to sth** 引起⋯，導致⋯
   - Human activities are to blame for the increase of greenhouse gases, which **lead to** global warming.

     人類活動是導致全球暖化的溫室氣體增加的罪魁禍首。

2) **set up** 建立，設立
   - The monument was **set up** in memory of the victims of the war.

     這座紀念碑是為了紀念戰爭中的罹難者而建立的。

3) **shut down** (使) 停止運作
   - Calvin **shut down** his computer upon hearing his mother's footsteps.

     Calvin一聽到他媽媽的腳步聲就把他的電腦關機了。

NOTE

The Rise of Phubbing–How Are Smartphones Affecting People?

Learn More English Blend (Portmanteau) Words!

screen

+

teenager

=

screenager
離不開螢幕的青少年

pedestrian

+

text

=

petextrian
邊走路邊滑手機的人

emotion

+

icon

=

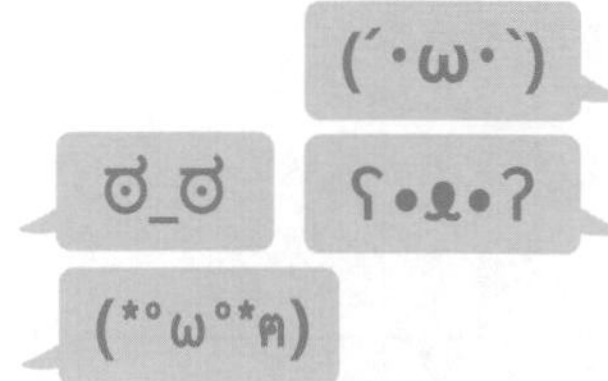

emoticon
顏文字

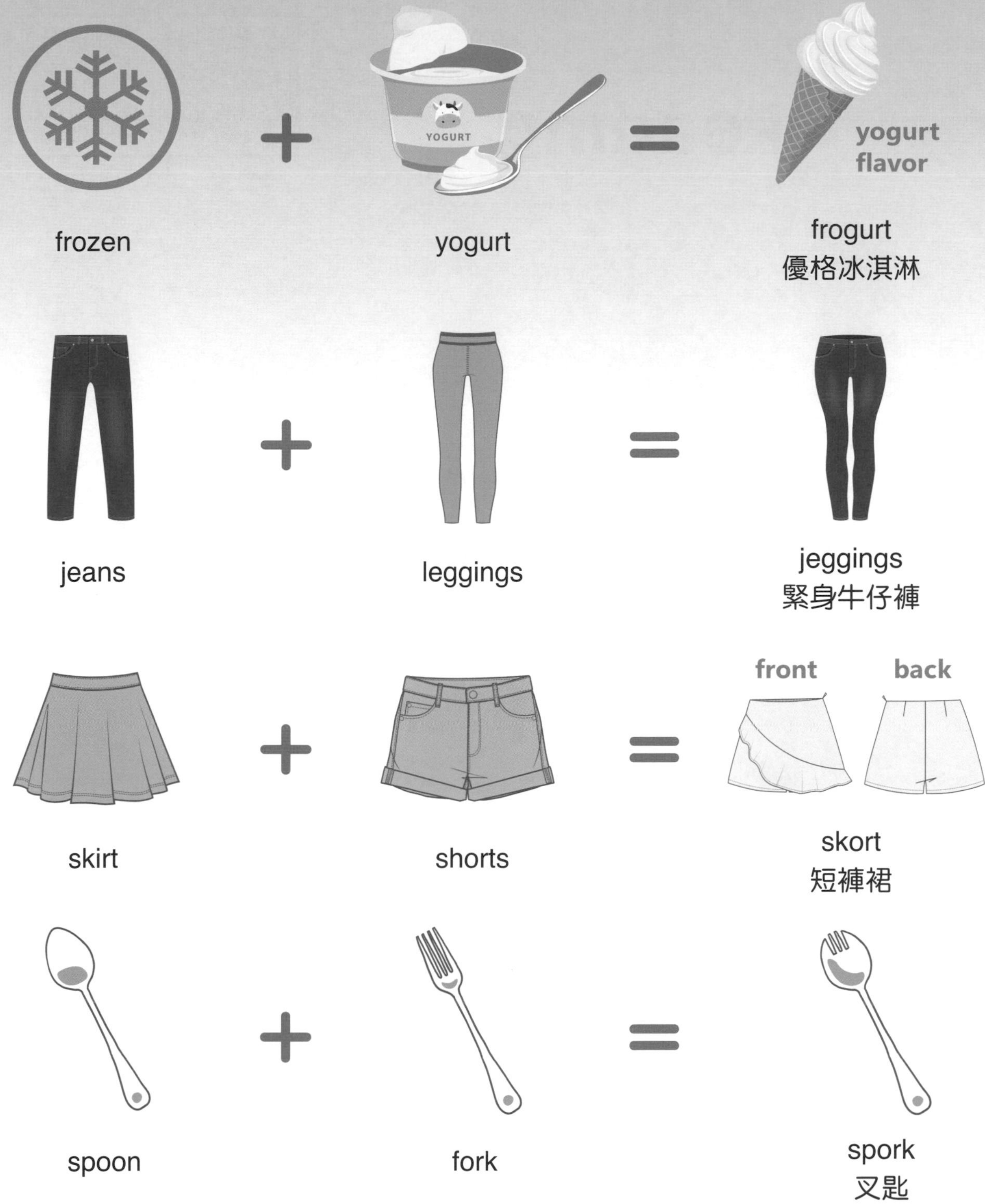

Fun Facts

#TheFirstCellphone #3CProducts

1. Which company invented the world's first mobile phone?

   (A) Nokia. (B) Motorola. (C) Sony Ericsson. (D) BlackBerry.

2. Which of the following is **NOT** one of the three Cs in "3C products"?

   (A) Cellular Phone. (B) Communication.

   (C) Consumer Electronics. (D) Computer.

In this modern world, "phubbing" happens all the time. The term "phubbing" combines the words "phone" and "snubbing" and means ignoring others by looking at one's smartphone. Those who engage in this **behavior** are called "phubbers." It has become increasingly common for us to see phubbers everywhere, even in places like restaurants and coffee shops. Nowadays, friends and family members often sit together in silence as they stare mindlessly at their phones.

❶ Many people have become so **accustomed** to phubbing that they consider it normal, rather than recognizing it as problematic. ❷ However, some **observers** regard phubbing as antisocial and believe it may mark the end of politeness and civility as we know it. ❸ Teachers worldwide are also noticing a change in students' behavior. ❹ In the past, most students could pay attention during classes and **lectures**. ❺ But now, even **diligent** students are **tempted** to steal a glance at their smartphone from time to time. ❻ This not only leads to poor learning but also shows no respect for teachers.

What's more, phubbing might negatively affect relationships. Though smartphones are an excellent way to connect with others, phubbers can easily **neglect** others and gradually become **alienated** from those people around them.

Being glued to screens for hours can also cause health problems, such as stiffness and pain in the shoulders, neck, and upper back. Headaches, **blurred** vision, and dry eyes are also common **issues associated** with staring at screens for **extended** periods. Additionally, the fingers and thumb can become inflamed and even get **cramps**, which cause pain and make phubbers unable to move with ease.

Phubbing has become an issue to think **thoroughly** about. Instead of letting smartphones control us, it is **essential** to **exert** control over our smartphone **usage**. By reducing screen time, we can pay more attention to those around us and enjoy a better life.

混合題

1. Which word in the passage means "a painful muscle tightening that restricts movement"? (簡答) 單字理解

____

2. The sentences in paragraph 2 are numbered ❶ to ❻. Which sentence best demonstrates why some people don't see phubbing as something worth public attention? Write down the **NUMBER** of the sentence. (簡答) 文意理解、因果分析

____

3. In the passage, many aspects affected by phubbing are mentioned. Fill in the blanks with the words contained in the passage. There's only ONE word for each blank. (填表) 掌握細節

Affected Aspects	Possible Consequences
students' (A) ________	• bad academic achievement • a lack of respect for teachers
relationships	• ignoring others easily • becoming (B) ________ from other people
health	• physical pain in the upper body • unclear (C) ________ and a lack of moisture in the eyes • infection and inability to move with body parts

Words for Production

1) **behavior** *(n.)* 行為 ❹

- Celine's recent **behavior** has been strange, so I suspect she's hiding something.

  Celine最近的行為很奇怪，我懷疑她有什麼隱瞞。

2) **accustomed** *(adj.)* 習慣的 ❻

- The senior students are **accustomed** to staying up late studying.

  高三學生習慣熬夜讀書。

3) **observer** *(n.)* 觀察家 ❺

- As a political **observer**, I'm supposed to stay objective.

  作為一名政治觀察家，我應該要保持客觀。

4) **lecture** *(n.)* 課，講座 ❹

- The **lecture** was so boring that most of the audience began tuning out halfway through it.

  這講座十分無聊，大部分聽眾聽到一半就開始放空。

5) **diligent** *(adj.)* 勤奮的 ❹

- Roger has been **diligent** since he decided to become a doctor.

  Roger自從決定要當醫生後就很勤勉用功。

6) **tempt** *(v.)* 想做(某事)，想要(某物) ❺

- Kelly was very **tempted** to be a supermodel.

  Kelly非常想要成為超級名模。

7) **neglect** *(v.)* 忽視 ❹

- The ambitious man pursued fame and wealth, **neglecting** moral values.

  那野心勃勃的人追求名利，忽視了道德觀念。

8) **alienated** *(adj.)* 疏遠的 ❻

- Since Sebastian moved to the north, he felt **alienated** himself from his old friends.

  自從Sebastian搬到北部後，他感覺與他的老朋友疏遠了。

9) **blurred** *(adj.)* 模糊的 ❺

- The photos were **blurred** because I forgot to turn on Vibration Reduction.
  照片會模糊是因為我忘記開防手震。

10) **issue** *(n.)* 問題；議題 ❹

- Censuses will bring **issues** like unemployment and mortality rate to light.
  人口普查會把失業率和死亡率等問題帶上檯面。

11) **associate** *(v.)* 把…連在一起 ❹

- The brand became **associated** with poor quality after its food safety issue broke out.
  在該品牌的食安風暴爆發後，它變得跟劣質聯想在一起。

12) **extended** *(adj.)* 長的 ❹

- Consumers who place orders by the end of the month will receive more discounts and an **extended** warranty. 在月底前下訂的消費者可享更多折扣及保固期延長。

13) **cramp** *(n.)* 抽筋 ❻

- The coach told us to warm up before swimming so as not to get a **cramp**.
  教練告訴我游泳前要暖身以免抽筋。

14) **thoroughly** *(adv.)* 仔細地 ❹

- My parents warned me to read any contract **thoroughly** before signing.
  我父母告誡我，在簽任何合約之前都要仔細閱讀。

15) **essential** *(adj.)* 至關重要的 ❹

- The manager considers it **essential** for his employees to have good communication skills.
  這位經理認為他的員工需要有好的溝通技巧。

16) **exert** *(v.)* 施加…；運用… ❻

- The father **exerted** his authority and set clear boundaries to maintain discipline in the household.
  這名父親運用自己的權威並設定明確的界線來維持家庭紀律。

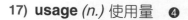

17) **usage** *(n.)* 使用量 ❹

- The **usage** of electricity and water always increases during summer.

  夏季用電量和用水量總是增加。

Words for Recognition

1) **phub** *(v.)* 低頭滑手機 (而不理人)
2) **snub** *(v.)* 不理睬人
3) **phubber** *(n.)* 低頭族
4) **mindlessly** *(adv.)* 不自覺地，無需動腦筋的
5) **problematic** *(adj.)* 成問題的
6) **antisocial** *(adj.)* 反社會的
7) **civility** *(n.)* 文明
8) **inflamed** *(adj.)* 發炎的

Idioms and Phrases

1) **engage in** 做…，從事…；參加

- After graduating from college, Jamie plans to **engage in** international trade.

  Jamie大學畢業後打算從事國際貿易。

2) **rather than** 而不是

- In modern society, people often choose to purchase products online **rather than** in a brick-and-mortar store.

  在現代社會中，人們選擇在網路上購買產品而不是在實體商店購買。

3) **pay attention** 集中注意力

• An athlete tends to suffer injury if he or she does not **pay attention** during a competition.

如果運動員沒有在比賽中集中注意力，就會容易受傷。

4) **steal a glance** 偷瞄… 補 也作steal a look

• Henry couldn't help **stealing glances** at his watch during the class.

Henry上課時忍不住一直偷瞄他的手錶。

5) **what's more** 而且

• In Singapore, gum can only be sold in a drugstore. **What's more**, there is a heavy fine for spitting out gum in public.

在新加坡，只有藥局才能販售口香糖。此外，在公共場所亂吐口香糖將面臨巨額罰款。

6) **be glued to sth** 目不轉睛地看，全神貫注地盯著…看

• Jenny's husband **was glued to** the TV instead of sharing the housework. All her complaints were in vain.

Jenny的丈夫一直盯著電視，不分擔家事。她的抱怨完全無效。

Help Sufferers Battle Depression

Common Mental Illnesses

depression
憂鬱症

· feeling unhappy and anxious for long periods or having persistent thoughts of committing suicide

bipolar disorder
躁鬱症

· often changing from being extremely excited to being extremely depressed

sleep disorder
睡眠障礙

· problems with the quality, timing, and amount of sleep

gender dysphoria
性別不安(性別認同障礙)

· disapproving of their sex at birth

bulimia
暴食症

· eating in uncontrolled ways and amounts

nervosa
厭食症

· too afraid of gaining weight to eat properly

schizophrenia
思覺失調症

· cannot distinguish between reality and fantasy

dissociative identity disorder (DID)
解離性身分障礙

· having two or more distinct identities

Fun Facts

#DepressionAwareness #DepressionSupport

How should we properly accompany people with depression?

(A) Encourage them to focus on the positive aspects and not to overthink.

(B) Empathize with their emotions and share their low moments.

(C) Quietly listen to their thoughts without a judgmental attitude.

(D) Counsel them to think about the more unfortunate people in the world.

Reading

Depression, a **prevailing** mental health problem, is experiencing a global **surge** in cases. When it comes to sufferers of depression in Asia, the suicide rates are considerably higher than those observed in the West. Sadly, a **substantial** number of people in Taiwan are also battling this debilitating condition.

According to the Taiwan **Association** Against Depression (TAAD), only about one-fifth of people burdened by depression in Taiwan actually seek **professional** help. **Furthermore**, of those who do seek **assistance**, nearly one-third do not continue with treatment beyond their first visit to a doctor or mental health **professional**.

Why do so many with depression in Taiwan seem **reluctant** to get the help they **desperately** need? Experts say that some may be in **denial** about their condition. Others may be **restrained** by a fear of talking, finding it difficult to **articulate** their struggle. Still others may lack understanding of **accessible** resources and treatment **options** that are widely in use now.

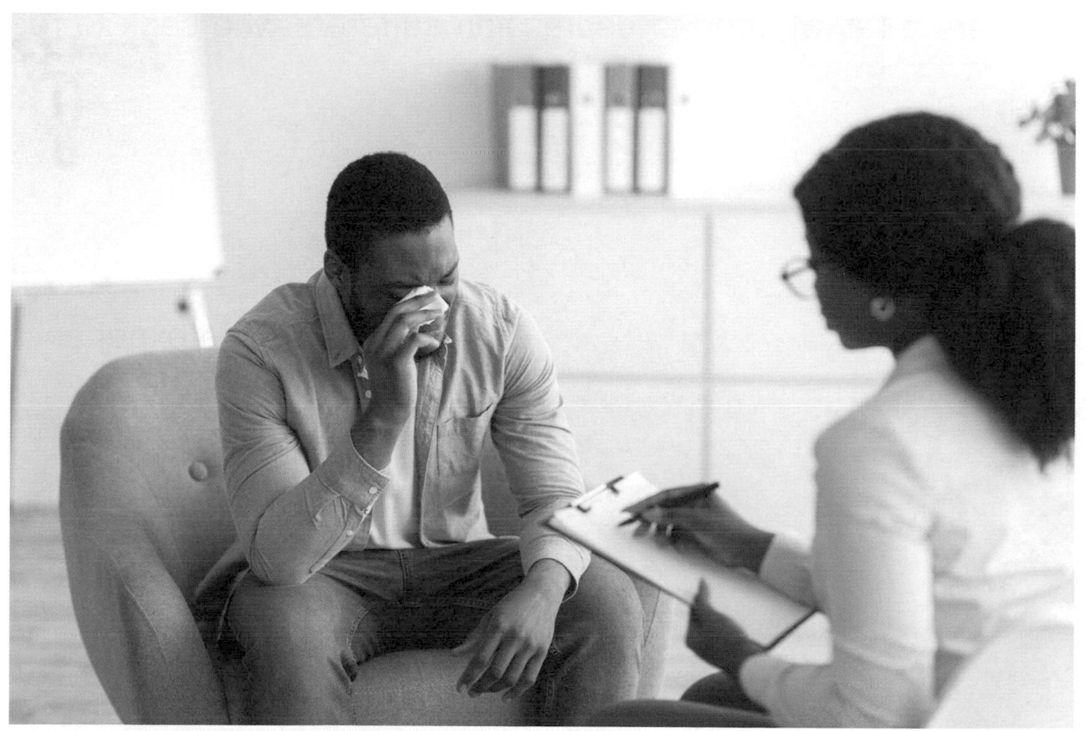

TAAD also believes that a significant number of people with depression in Taiwan **cease** seeking treatment because of concern about the **potential** side effects of some treatments. As a result, it has decided to take steps to raise public awareness about depression, especially among current sufferers. The group, for example, has set up a page on LINE, the popular social messaging app. Through direct messages, TAAD **counselors** can directly communicate with depression sufferers. They can also offer support and share useful information about depression and its treatment options in LINE chat rooms.

Hopefully, the implementation of measures like TAAD's LINE chat rooms offers a ray of hope to depression sufferers who seek to reclaim their well-being.

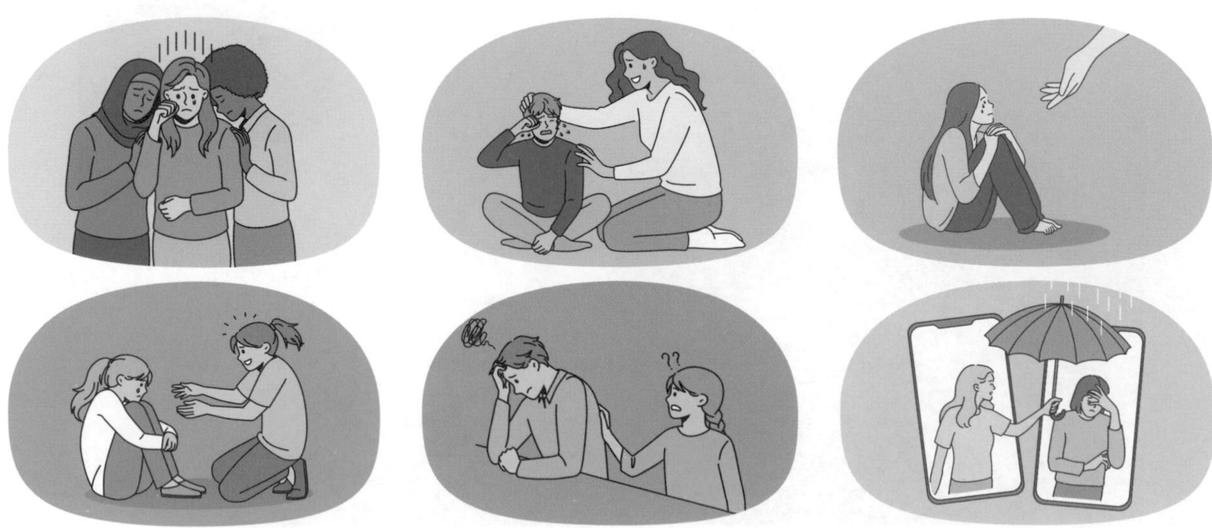

混合題

_______ 1. According to the passage, what is the author's attitude toward the change TAAD can bring to depression sufferers? (單選) 文意判斷

(A) Indifferent. (B) Doubtful. (C) Optimistic. (D) Critical.

2. According to the passage, in a group of 30 depression sufferers from Taiwan, how many of them would ask professionals for help? (簡答) 掌握細節

____

3. Which word in the passage means "being able to be used, reached, got, or obtained"? (簡答) 單字理解

____

_______ 4. 請從下列(A)到(E)中，選出對本文提及the reasons why people burdened by depression in Taiwan seem to be negative about seeking assistance正確的選項。(多選) 掌握細節

(A) They do not believe that they are mentally ill.

(B) They are afraid of getting lost on the way to the clinic.

(C) They are too shy to get close to other patients.

(D) They lack knowledge of frequently used treatment options.

(E) They are worried about the high cost of the treatment.

Words for Production

1) **depression** *(n.)* 憂鬱症 ❹

- Nowadays, people with **depression** are more willing to talk about their conditions because society has encouraged them to do so.

  如今，有憂鬱症的人更願意講述他們的狀況，因為社會鼓勵他們這麼做。

2) **prevailing** *(adj.)* 普遍的 ❺

- The **prevailing** idea of washing hands to maintain personal hygiene did not become popular until approximately two centuries ago.

  洗手以維持個人衛生這個普遍的觀念直到大約兩個世紀前才變得流行。

3) **surge** *(n.)* 急遽上升 ❻

- There has been a **surge** of infections after the government lifted all social restrictions.

  在政府解除所有社交限制後，出現了一波急遽上升的感染潮。

4) **substantial** *(adj.)* 可觀的 ❺

- Josephine inherited a **substantial** amount of money from her late aunt, which she used to establish a school for orphans.

  Josephine從她已故的阿姨那邊繼承了一筆可觀的財產，且她用那筆錢設立了一間給孤兒的學校。

5) **association** *(n.)* 協會 ❹

- The student **association** urged school authority to investigate the alleged sexual harassment by one of the university staff.

  學生會呼籲校方調查其中一位大學職員疑似性騷擾的案件。

6) **professional** *(adj.)* 專業的；*(n.)* 專業人士 ❹

- Students in need of mental support can visit the Student Counseling Room and arrange an appointment with a **professional** therapist there.

  需要心理支持的學生可以前往學生輔導室並與那邊的專業諮商師安排會談。

- Fallon is a **professional** in the field of deep-sea exploration and has collaborated with marine scientists, treasure hunters, and touring companies.

  Fallon是深海探索領域的專業人士，且跟海洋科學家、寶藏獵人和旅遊公司合作過。

7) **furthermore** *(adv.)* 此外 ❹

- Chris denied the accusation that he had made a pass at Vicky, and **furthermore**, said he had never even spoken to her.

  Chris否認他騷擾Vicky的指控，此外，他說他根本沒和她講過話。

8) **assistance** *(n.)* 協助 ❹

- With the **assistance** of social workers, the elderly man who lives alone is finally willing to go out and socialize.

  在社工的協助下，那名獨居老人終於願意外出社交。

9) **reluctant** *(adj.)* 不情願的 ❹

- If you find your children **reluctant** to go to school, try to understand the reasons behind their feelings instead of forcing them.

  如果你發現你的孩子不願意去上學，試著了解他們感受的原因，而不是強迫他們。

10) **desperately** *(adv.)* 迫切地 ❹

- Farmers are pleading with the government for help as it has been three months without rain, and the crops **desperately** need water.

  農民向政府懇求援助，因為已經三個月沒下雨了，作物迫切地需要水。

11) **denial** *(n.)* 拒絕相信 ❺

- When people heard about the sinking of the Titanic, they were initially in **denial** about the news. They simply could not imagine that such a thing would happen.

  當人們聽到鐵達尼號沉沒時，他們起初拒絕相信這則消息。他們簡直無法想像會發生這種事。

12) **restrain** *(v.)* 限制 ❻

- Pet owners should **restrain** their pets when taking them outside to prevent them from frightening or harming others.

  寵物飼主在帶寵物出門時應要限制牠們，以防止牠們嚇到傷害他人。

13) **articulate** *(v.)* 清楚表達 ❺

- The assault victims are still in shock, making it difficult for them to **articulate** what happened during the incident.

  這起襲擊的罹難者仍處於驚嚇之中，使得他們無法清楚表達事件經過。

14) **accessible** *(adj.)* 可得到的 ❺

- In modern urban environments, free Wi-Fi service should be **accessible** in every public space.
  在現代的都市環境裡，免費的無線網路服務應該在每個公共場所都可取得。

15) **option** *(n.)* 方案 ❹

- For users who wish to share your streaming service account with people you live with, we offer a shared-account **option**.
  對於想與同住者分享您的串流服務帳號的用戶，我們有提供共享帳號方案。

16) **cease** *(v.)* 停止 ❹

- Captain Winters ordered his army to **cease** firing when he saw that the enemies had raised their hands to surrender.
  當Winters上尉看到敵人已舉手投降時，他命令他的部隊停火。

17) **potential** *(adj.)* 潛在的 ❹

- Experts warned the drivers about **potential** dangers posed by the submarine's structural problem but were dismissed.
  專家們警告駕駛員有關潛水艇結構問題可能帶來的潛在危險，但被忽視了。

18) **counselor** *(n.)* 輔導員 ❺

- We encourage students to go to the school's **counselors** when they encounter any problems instead of keeping the problems to themselves.
  我們鼓勵學生在遇到問題時去找學校輔導員，而不要自己一個人承擔。

Words for Recognition

1) **sufferer** *(n.)* 患者

2) **debilitating** *(adj.)* 令人衰弱的

3) **Taiwan Association Against Depression (TAAD)** *(n.)* 社團法人臺灣憂鬱症防治協會

4) **messaging app** *(n.)* 通訊應用程式

5) **hopefully** *(adv.)* 但願

6) **implementation** *(n.)* 實施

7) **reclaim** *(n.)* 取回

8) **well-being** *(n.)* 幸福

Idioms and Phrases

1) **when it comes to** 說到…

- **When it comes to** fashion, no one can match Steven. He knows about everything trendy.

  說到時尚，沒人能和Steven相比。他知道現正當紅的一切。

2) **according to** 根據…

- **According to** Google Maps, we have already reached our destination, but it seems like we are in the middle of nowhere.

  根據Google地圖，我們已經抵達了目的地，但我們似乎身在一片荒蕪之中。

3) **in use** 受到使用

- My electric guitar hasn't been **in use** for quite a while. I need to have it checked and maintained.

  我的電吉他已經好一陣子沒使用了。我得把它送去檢查與保養。

The Dangers of Smoking: What You May Not Know About Smoking

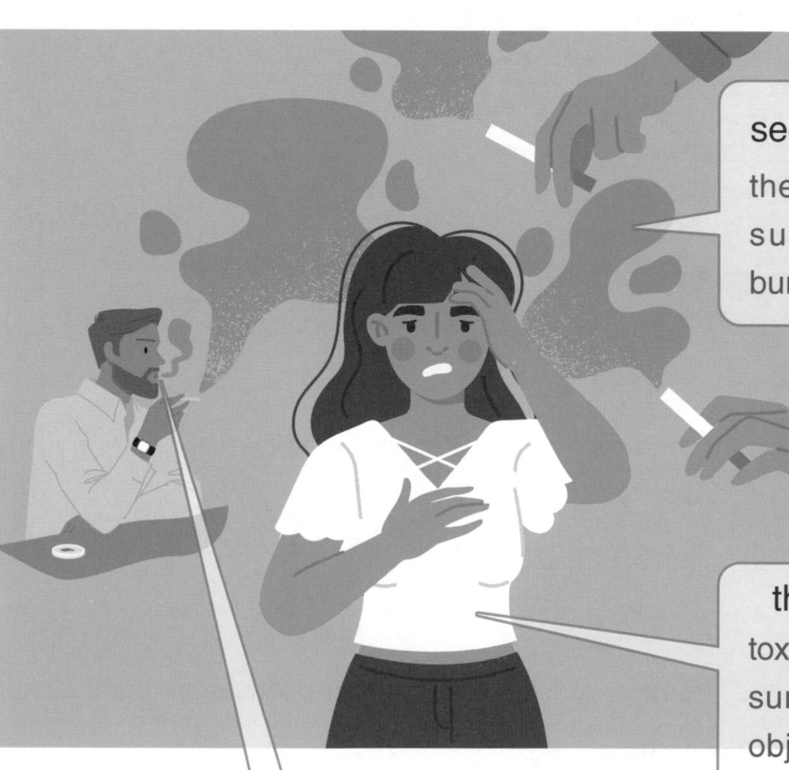

second-hand smoke 二手菸
the exhaled smoke and other substances released from burning tobacco products
third-hand smoke 三手菸
toxic chemicals that stuck to the surfaces of food, bodies, and objects after the second-hand smoke disappeared in the air
*The smoke will become progressively more toxic over time!
first-hand smoke 一手菸
the smoke inhaled by a smoker

tobacco 菸草	
cigarette（紙）香菸	
cigar 雪茄	
pipe 菸斗	
hookah 水煙	
e-cigarette (vape) 電子煙 E-cigarettes were officially banned in Taiwan on March 22, 2023.	

Fun Facts

#CigaretteChemical

1. Please arrange first-hand smoke, second-hand smoke, and third-hand smoke in order of toxicity to the human body.

   ______________ > ______________ > ______________

2. Which of the following ingredients in tobacco products makes people easily addicted to smoking?

   (A) CO. (B) Nicotine. (C) Tar. (D) Arsenic.

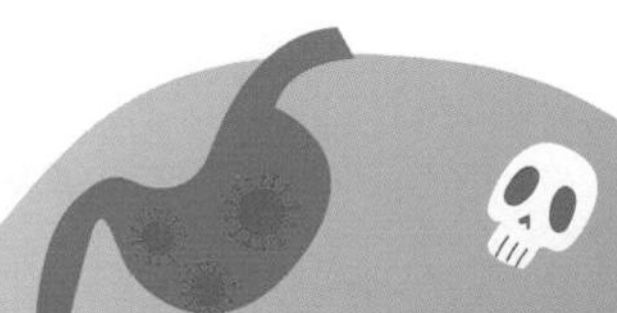

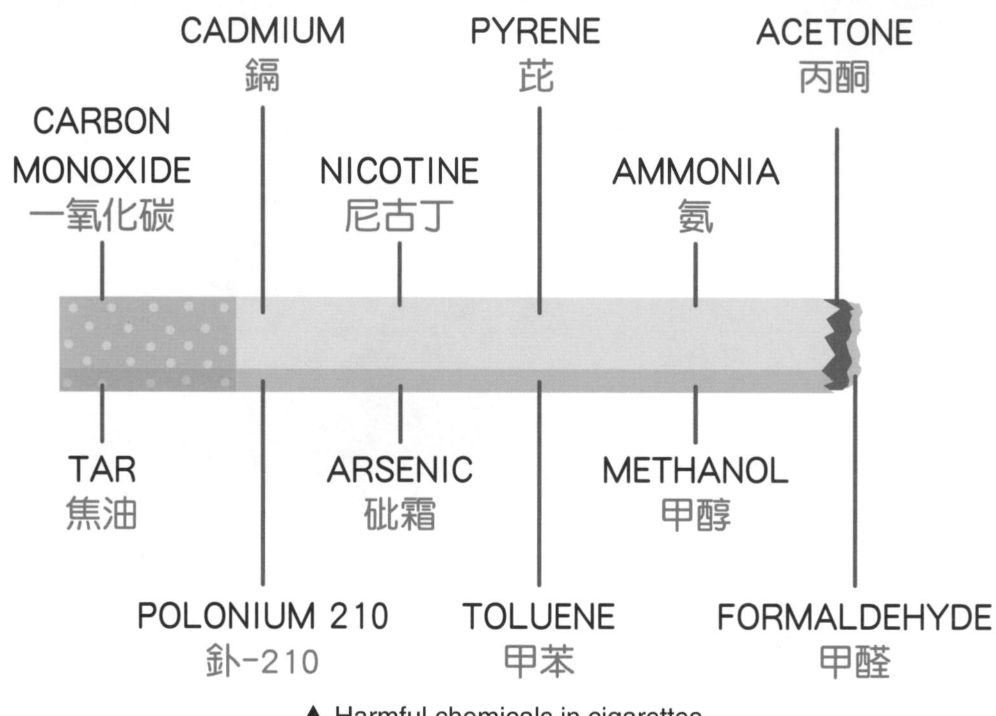

▲ Harmful chemicals in cigarettes

Nowadays, people are aware that smoking is unhealthy. They also know that smoking doesn't only damage the health of those **addicted** to the habit. People who have never put a cigarette in their mouths can also be affected.

Cigarette smoke contains thousands of chemicals, including over 65 substances known to cause cancer. When people smoke, a significant portion of these harmful substances go straight into the lungs, while the rest is released into the air as smokers exhale. **Notably**, **research** has shown that cigarette smoke and its **toxic** chemicals can **linger** in the air for hours, posing risks long after the smell and color have disappeared. This explains why nonsmokers also suffer from illnesses related to smoking.

Furthermore, some studies indicate that smoking affects people of different **genders** differently. For example, people often connect smoking and lung cancer with men, but studies provide a different **perspective**. According to studies, compared to men, women who smoke are actually more likely to get lung cancer at a younger age. Also, women are more **prone** to develop small-cell lung cancer, which spreads quickly. It's been found that **biological** differences between men and women may contribute to the higher possibility of lung cancer in women.

Although people **acknowledge** that smoking is a serious issue, some find it challenging to break free from its **grip**. To reduce the dangers caused by smoking, governments worldwide have passed laws to **ban** it in public places. These policies not only **ensure** the safety of nonsmokers but also **cultivate** awareness among smokers themselves. **Ultimately**, it cannot be denied that chemicals found in cigarettes can be **fatal**. To quit smoking remains a great idea, or, even better, never start in the first place.

混合題

1. 請從文章第二段中找出最適當的單詞 (word)填入下列句子空格中，並視語法需要做適當的字形變化。**每格限填一個單詞 (word)**。(填充) 掌握脈絡、字形變化

Cigarette smokers not only breathe in harmful substances into their lungs but also ______________ poisonous chemicals into the atmosphere.

2. Fill in the blanks with the information contained in the passage about small-cell lung cancer. (填表) 掌握細節

Small-cell Lung Cancer	
Main Cause	The exposure to toxic chemicals from cigarette smoke.
Characteristics	• Small-cell lung cancer (A) ______________ rapidly. • (B) ______________ are more likely to get small-cell lung cancer.

______ 3. 請從下列(A)到(E)中，選出作者於文章內有提及的選項。(多選) 文意理解、掌握細節

(A) The reason why many people find it hard to quit smoking.

(B) The fact that cigarettes contain life-threatening substances.

(C) The negative impact of smoking on people of different ages.

(D) The most effective treatment for people who are diagnosed with cancer.

(E) The effort made by governments around the world to help stop public smoking.

Words for Production

1) **addicted** *(adj.)* 成癮的 ❹

• Manage your screen time if you do not wish to be **addicted** to electronic devices.
如果你不想變得對電子裝置成癮，那就得要管理你的螢幕使用時間。

2) **notably** *(adv.)* 值得注意地 ❻

• Stories of sexual harassment that have been made public have **notably** increased in recent times. 近年來，被公開的性騷擾故事有明顯地增加。

3) **research** *(n.)* 研究 ❹

• More **research** on micro-plastic is needed to determine how it affects us when entering our bodies.
需要更多關於塑膠微粒的研究才能確認它在進入我們的身體後會如何影響我們。

4) **toxic** *(adj.)* 有毒的 ❺

• Carbon monoxide (CO) is a kind of colorless and tasteless **toxic** gas that is capable of killing a person if he or she breathes in too much of it.
一氧化碳(CO)是一種無色無味的有毒氣體，當一個人如果吸入太多時會喪命。

5) **linger** *(v.)* 停留，徘徊 ❻

• We mustn't **linger** in the woods after sunset. We don't know what we might encounter in the dark night.
我們不能在日落之後於樹林中停留。我們不知道在暗夜裡會遭遇什麼。

6) **gender** *(n.)* 性別 ❹

• The **gender** movement aims to liberate both women and men so that women don't have to feel lesser anymore, and men don't have to be tough all the time.
性別運動旨在一起解放女性和男性，這樣女性就不必覺得自己低人一等，而男性不需總是表現得剛強。

7) **perspective** *(n.)* 觀點，看法 ❺

• Sunny and Tom have opposite **perspectives** on love. While Sunny doesn't believe in the concept of the one, Tom heavily believes in true love.
Sunny和Tom對於愛情有相反的觀點。Sunny不相信真愛這個概念，然而Tom卻對此深信不疑。

8) **prone** *(adj.)* 容易遭受(疾病)的 ❺

• Health authorities have urged citizens to get their COVID-19 vaccines, warning that people without vaccination are **prone** to severe symptoms of infections.

衛生當局呼籲民眾去施打新冠疫苗，並警告沒有接種疫苗的人容易出現嚴重的感染症狀。

9) **biological** *(adj.)* 生理的 ❺

• You should develop a regular sleep pattern, or your **biological** clock will be disrupted. 你應該培養規律的睡眠模式，否則你的生理時鐘會被打亂。

10) **acknowledge** *(v.)* 承認 ❺

• In the recent announcement, the management has **acknowledged** that the company has sustained heavy financial losses and will be asking its employees to take unpaid leave.

在近期的聲明中，管理階層已承認公司蒙受巨大的財務損失，並將要求員工放無薪假。

11) **grip** *(n.)* 控制 ❺

• President Sputnik has tightened the **grip** on his regime by eliminating or silencing all his political opponents.

Sputnik總統藉由消滅或噤聲壓制他所有的政治對手來鞏固他對政權的控制。

12) **ban** *(v.)* 禁止 ❺

• A lot of agricultural and fish products from Taiwan have been **banned** by China for absolutely no reason. 許多臺灣的農產品或漁產品被中國毫無理由地禁止輸入。

13) **ensure** *(v.)* 確保 ❹

• To **ensure** your safety during the flight, you should keep your seatbelt fastened at all times while seated. 為了確保你的搭機安全，你應該在就座時全程繫好安全帶。

14) **cultivate** *(v.)* 培養 ❻

• Sophie made a conscious effort to **cultivate** her skills in public speaking by attending multinational workshops and practicing regularly.

Sophie透過參加跨國研討會並且定期練習，努力培養自己的公開演講技巧。

15) **ultimately** *(adv.)* 終究 ❺

- **Ultimately**, when the Sun begins to die in five billion years, it will expand and consume every planet in the solar system, including the Earth.
  最終，當太陽於五十億年後開始死亡之時，它會膨脹並吞噬太陽系內的所有行星，包含地球。

16) **fatal** *(adj.)* 致命的 ❹

- Numerous **fatal** shootings in the U.S. have prompted the American people to plead for stricter gun controls.　數起發生在美國的致命槍擊案促使美國人籲求更嚴格的槍枝管制。

Words for Recognition

1) **smoker** *(n.)* 吸菸者

2) **exhale** *(v.)* 呼氣

3) **nonsmoker** *(n.)* 不吸菸者

4) **small-cell lung cancer** *(n.)* 小細胞肺癌

Idioms and Phrases

1) **contribute to** 導致⋯，促成⋯

- Amity between the two countries will **contribute to** their mutual prosperity.
  這兩國之間的和睦將有助於共榮。

2) **in the first place** 最初⋯，原本⋯

- Andrew keeps complaining about the schedule of the project all day. I cannot understand why he agreed to participate in it **in the first place**.
  Andrew整天都在抱怨專案的排程。我搞不懂他為何當初要答應參與。

NOTE

Taking Action: Standing Up for Others

Bullying Can Happen at . . .

workplace

military

school

Types of Bullying

physical bullying 肢體霸凌

· It is the use of physical force to harm or intimidate the victims, including hitting, kicking, pushing, or any form of physical assault.

---

verbal bullying 言語霸凌

· It is the use of words to hurt or humiliate the victims, including name-calling, insulting, teasing, and verbal threats.

social bullying/relational bullying 關係霸凌

· It aims to harm the victims' social standing or relationships, including isolating them, spreading rumors, and manipulating friendships.

electronic bullying/cyberbullying 網路霸凌

· It occurs through digital platforms such as social media, messaging apps, or online forums, involving threatening and humiliating the victims through the Internet.

counterattack bullying 反擊霸凌

· It refers to the situation where the victims can't stand the bullies anymore and counterattack or turn to bully others weaker than themselves.

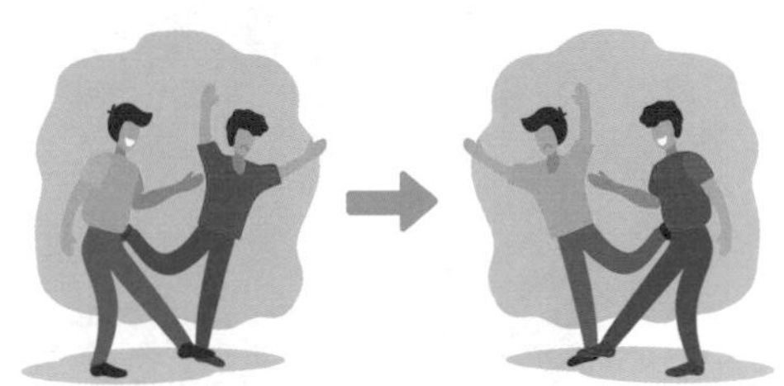

sexual bullying 性霸凌

· It involves unwanted sexual jokes, comments, gestures, or displaying any offensive actions that aim to harass or humiliate the victims.

prejudicial bullying 偏見霸凌

· It refers to the attack based on the victims' race, religion, ethnicity, nationality, sexual orientation, disability, or any characteristic that makes them different.

Fun Facts

#AntiBullyingDay

Which of the following is an alternative name for "Anti-Bullying Day"?

(A) Galentine's Day. (B) World Cotton Day.

(C) Global Love Day. (D) Pink Shirt Day.

Reading

When **witnessing** an accident, most people first **assess** if those **involved** are **injured**, and then maybe call the police. But what about when witnessing someone being **verbally assaulted**? While this may not be **physically** damaging for the victim, it could be equally **distressing**. Would you do anything? For the average person, the answer might be no.

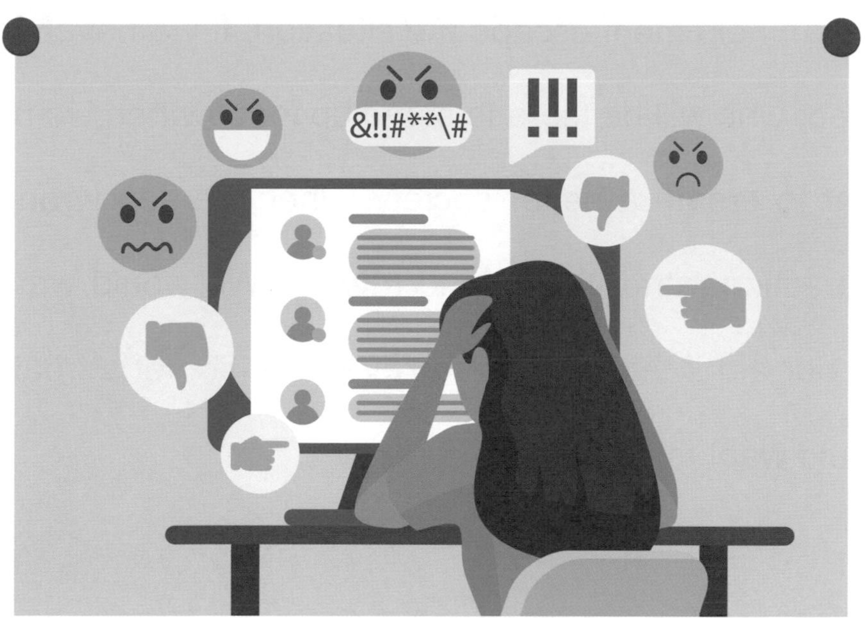

When witnessing **injustice**, the common reaction is to ignore it. It may seem unrelated to us. However, by doing nothing, we are **essentially** enabling the aggressor. This doesn't mean we are bad people, but we do need to put ourselves in the victims' shoes. If we were being attacked either verbally or physically, would we want someone to step in? The answer most **definitely** is yes.

If we come across an injustice being done to someone, we should approach that person instead of turning a blind eye. Mostly, a **bully** aims to scare or **irritate** their victim and is likely to continue if he or she feels that the victim lacks supportive friends. By going over to help, we send a clear message that the bully's actions are unacceptable. We should directly **confront** injustice. When we observe someone being bullied, we can help them escape the situation. If we never stand up for those in need, who will be there to stand up for us when we need help?

In order to create a better society, when we see wrongdoing, we should take action rather than stand **idly** by. We would want someone to come to our aid if the roles were **reversed**, so, let's treat others the way we would want to be treated.

混合題

1. Which word in the second paragraph means "unfair treatment or lack of fairness"? (簡答) 單字理解

____

_____ 2. According to the passage, what does the word "**reversed**" in the last paragraph most likely mean? (單選) 文意理解、字義推論

(A) Changed. (B) Accepted. (C) Overlooked. (D) Bullied.

_____ 3. According to the passage, why is it important for people to take action when they witness bullying? (單選) 文意理解

(A) To avoid getting involved in conflicts.

(B) To protect themselves from potential harm.

(C) To prevent the wrongdoing from continuing.

(D) To gain recognition and support from others.

_____ 4. 根據本文，選出當看到小男孩被霸凌時，應該如何幫助他的正確敘述。(多選)

掌握細節、歸納重點

(A) Turn a blind eye to it.

(B) Step in to rescue him.

(C) Irritate or scare him.

(D) Be his supportive audience.

(E) Get yourself away from the situation.

(F) Come to his aid.

Words for Production

1) **witness** *(v.)* 目擊 ❹

• Lucy **witnessed** a car accident and called an ambulance right away.

Lucy目擊了一場車禍，並馬上打電話叫救護車。

2) **assess** *(v.)* 評估 ❺

• This checklist can help you **assess** your risk of getting cancer.

這份檢核表可以幫助你評估罹患癌症的風險。

3) **involve** *(v.)* 涉及 ❹

• All the officials **involved** in the drug smuggling scandal are now under investigation.

所有涉及毒品走私醜聞的官員現在都在接受調查。

4) **injured** *(adj.)* 受傷的 ❹

• The nurse wound the bandage around my **injured** thigh.

護理人員為我受傷的大腿纏上繃帶。

5) **verbally** *(adv.)* 言語地 ❺

• Having been **verbally** abused by her husband for years, Sylvia decided to get a divorce.

因長年遭受先生言語虐待，Sylvia決定離婚。

6) **assault** *(v.)* 攻擊 ❺

• Officer Taylor was **assaulted** by several gangsters while he was on patrol.

Taylor警官在巡邏途中遭到數名幫派分子攻擊。

7) **physically** *(adv.)* 肢體上地 ❹

• My sister was born **physically** disabled because of genetic defects.

我妹妹因為基因缺陷，一出生就有肢體障礙。

8) **distressing** *(adj.)* 令人痛苦的 ❻

• It must be very **distressing** to lose someone you love.

失去所愛的人，你一定非常痛苦吧。

9) **injustice** *(n.)* 不公不義之事 ❻

• The young lawyer has vowed to fight against social **injustice**.

該名青年律師誓言要對抗社會上的不公不義。

10) **essentially** *(adv.)* 基本上 ❹

• This play is **essentially** a story of revenge.

這齣劇基本上是一個復仇的故事。

11) **definitely** *(adv.)* 絕對地 ❹

• I think fall is **definitely** the best season to visit Kinmen.

我認為秋天絕對是造訪金門的最佳季節。

12) **bully** *(n.)* 霸凌他人的人；*(v.)* 霸凌 ❺

• Ariel reported the incident to the authorities after witnessing a **bully** verbally harassing her friends.

Ariel在目睹一名霸凌者對她朋友言語騷擾後向有關單位報告了這一事件。

• The novel is based on the author's experience of being **bullied** in the workplace.

那本小說是根據作者在職場遭受霸凌的經驗寫成的。

13) **irritate** *(v.)* 激怒 ❻

• John's selfish behavior really **irritates** me.

John自私的行為真的把我激怒了。

14) **confront** *(v.)* 正視 ❺

• Environmental activists urged world leaders to **confront** climate change.

環保人士呼籲世界各國領袖要正視氣候變遷。

15) **idly** *(adv.)* 無行動地 ❹

• We like to sit **idly** on a bench and watch people going by.

我們喜歡無所事事地坐在長椅上，看著行人走過。

16) **reverse** *(v.)* 反轉

• At the end of the movie, the roles of the hunter and the prey are **reversed**.

在這部影片的最後，獵人和獵物的角色反轉過來了。

Words for Recognition

1) **unrelated** *(adj.)* 不相關的

2) **aggressor** *(n.)* 攻擊者

3) **supportive** *(adj.)* 擁護的

4) **unacceptable** *(adj.)* 無法接受的

5) **wrongdoing** *(n.)* 壞事，違法行為

Idioms and Phrases

1) **stand up for** 為…挺身而出

• Sally is too shy to **stand up for** her rights.

Sally太害羞了，不敢為自己的權利挺身而出。

2) **put oneself in sb's shoes** 設身處地

• When you want to criticize other people, please try to **put yourself in his or her shoes**.

當你想批評別人時，請試著站在對方的立場想一想。

3) **step in** 介入

• If the government doesn't **step in**, the conflict between these two peoples will escalate into a war.

如果政府不介入的話，這兩個民族間的衝突會升級成戰爭。

4) **come across** 偶然發現，偶然碰見

• While cleaning the attic, I **came across** an old journal that belonged to my grandmother.

我在打掃閣樓時，偶然發現了一本我祖母的舊日記。

5) **turn a blind eye** 視而不見

• Jason is always late for work, but his supervisor **turns a blind eye** to it.

Jason上班老是遲到，但他的主管對此視而不見。

NOTE

Japanese Women Outraged at Discrimination by Tokyo Medical University

Various Types of Discrimination

age discrimination/ageism 年齡歧視

· It involves treating someone unfairly based on their age. It can limit opportunities or benefits for both younger and older individuals.

disability discrimination 身心障礙歧視

· It refers to the unjust treatment of people with disabilities. It may involve denying them equal access to opportunities and services owing to their impairment.

religious discrimination 宗教歧視

· It occurs when individuals are subjected to biased actions based on their religious beliefs. It can bring about exclusion, prejudice, or bias in various aspects of life.

sexual orientation discrimination 性傾向歧視

· It involves treating people unfairly because of their sexual orientation. Heterosexuality, homosexuality, and bisexuality are several examples of sexual orientation.

---

racial discrimination/racism 種族歧視

· It is the unjust treatment of individuals based on their race or ethnicity. It may result in inequality, bias, and systemic disadvantages in various aspects of society.

Fun Facts

#GenderNeutralPronouns #PreferredGenderPronouns

"Hi, everyone, my name is Simon. My pronouns are they/them."

Have you ever heard someone introducing themselves with their preferred gender pronouns (PGPs)? PGPs are a new trend that allows people who have their own gender identity to choose which pronouns they want to be identified as.

Let's fill in the blanks of the form to learn the new gender pronouns and try to introduce yourself with your PGPs!

Subject Pronouns	Object Pronouns	Possessive Adjectives	Possessive Pronouns	Reflexive Pronouns
I	me	my	mine	myself
you	you	yours	(1) ______	yourself
he	(2) ______	his	his	himself
she	her	her	hers	herself
it	it	its	its	itself
ze/zie/sie	hir/zir	hir/zir	(3) ______	hirself/zirself
xe	xem	xir/xyr	xirs/xyrs	(4) ______
they	(5) ______	their	theirs	themselves

Reading

TRACK-08

影音檔 音檔

Sex discrimination occurs when someone is treated differently because of their sex. It's usually unpleasant and may be a one-off action or caused by some form of rule. While sex discrimination happens all over the world, there was a **notable** example a few years ago in Japan.

In 2018, Japan investigated **evidence** of sex discrimination within its medical universities. Officials at Tokyo Medical University admitted

that they had changed the test scores of female **applicants**, lowering them to prevent too many women from getting into the university. Those officials sought to **exclude** women from the medical **profession** because they believed women would quit their jobs to start a family after getting married. The systemic discrimination unjustly reserved more than sixty **percent** of the available medical training **slots** for men—even those with lower test scores than their female **counterparts**. Not surprisingly, Japanese women and feminists everywhere were **furious** as the scandal finally came to light. All the nation's medical schools were thus investigated, with particular attention to the **ratios** of male and female applicants and their **admission** exam scores.

The reality is that **widespread** sex discrimination exists in Japan and in many other countries. This is true not just in education, but also in the **workplace**, and even within families. The prevailing Japanese attitude is that a man should be the head of the **household** because he is the breadwinner. A woman's role, in **contrast**, is mainly to obey and support her husband. Although this way of thinking is hopelessly out of date, **tremendous** pressure remains on Japanese women to **submit** to their husbands' wishes—to stay home and raise children.

Such traditional attitudes remain deeply rooted, **despite** a growing **recognition** that it's unfair, and often indeed illegal, to **discriminate** against anyone based on their sex.

混合題

1. 請從文章第二段中找出最適當的單詞 (word) 填入下列句子空格中，並視語法需要做適當的字形變化。**每格限填一個單詞 (word)**。(填充) 掌握脈絡、字形變化

After being accused of sex discrimination, Tokyo Medical University ____________ its fault, and then medical schools all over the country were put under the microscope.

______ 2. What does "the scandal" refer to in the second paragraph? (單選) 掌握脈絡、指涉

(A) The fact that widespread sex discrimination exists in Japanese society.

(B) The belief that women would quit medical practice once they are married.

(C) Investigations that were carried out targeting all the medical schools in Japan.

(D) The incident regarding school officials changing the test scores of female applicants.

3. Which word in the passage means "an acknowledgment that something is true or important"? (簡答) 單字理解

____

______ 4. 請從下列(A)到(E)中，選出符合文意的選項。(多選) 文意理解、掌握細節

(A) The word "counterparts" most likely means "applicants" in the passage.

(B) Tokyo Medical University was under investigation because some of the students changed their scores in order to graduate.

(C) Even though sex discrimination is commonly found on campus, it does not exist in the workplace.

(D) Many Japanese women would rather raise children at home than pursue their career, and that is why they cannot obtain their chances of receiving medical training.

(E) During the investigation, the numbers of male and female applicants and their admission exam scores would be the main focus.

Words for Production

1) **outrage** *(v.)* 激怒⋯，使憤怒 ❻
   - People were **outraged** by the news that a student had been mentally abused by his teacher, ultimately leading to his death by suicide.
     人們對一名學生受到老師精神虐待而最終導致他自殺身亡的消息感到很憤怒。

2) **discrimination** *(n.)* 歧視 ❺
   - A progressive society should make every effort to eliminate all forms of **discrimination** within it. 一個進步的社會應該竭盡所能地消除其內部一切形式的歧視。

3) **notable** *(adj.)* 值得注意的 ❻
   - It is **notable** that Cheryl made remarkable improvements in her grades within a short period. 值得注意的是，Cheryl的成績在短時間內取得了明顯的進步。

4) **evidence** *(n.)* 證據 ❹
   - **Evidence** shows that there are no toxic substances inside the children's bodies, thereby ruling out the allegation of drugging.
     證據顯示，孩童的體內並無有毒物質，因此排除了下藥的指控。

5) **applicant** *(n.)* 申請者 ❹
   - **Applicants** for the position must attach their portfolio containing related projects or works.
     此職位的申請者須檢附包含相關計畫或作品的作品集。

6) **exclude** *(v.)* 排除在外 ❺
   - Taiwan has long been **excluded** from participating in many international organizations, such as the UN and WHO.
     臺灣長久以來被排除在聯合國和世界衛生組織等多個國際組織之外。

7) **profession** *(n.)* 行業 ❹
   - Many newly-certified teachers began to wonder if they had chosen the wrong **profession** when they realized the demand for new teachers had shrunk significantly.
     許多剛獲得資格認證的教師在發現對於新教師的需求已大幅萎縮時，他們開始懷疑自己是否選錯職業了。

8) **percent** *(n.)* 百分之… ❹

- A recent survey reveals that more than twenty **percent** of high school students have experienced depressive episodes.
  一份近期的調查揭露，百分之二十以上的高中生有經歷過憂鬱期。

9) **slot** *(n.)* 職位 ❺

- In light of the personnel changes, we'll have to hold an election to fill the **slots** in the committee.
  有鑑於人事異動，我們得舉辦一場選舉來填補委員會裡的職位。

10) **counterpart** *(n.)* 相對應者 ❻

- Our delegate to APEC engages in talks with his **counterparts** every year at the summit.
  我方的亞太經合會代表每年都會在峰會上與其他代表會談。

11) **furious** *(adj.)* 憤怒的 ❹

- Reagan was **furious** to learn that his friend had been arrested again for drunk driving and decided to distance himself from him.
  Reagan得知他朋友又因酒駕被捕後非常憤怒，並決定與他斷絕關係。

12) **ratio** *(n.)* 比率 ❺

- If the sex **ratio** of a region is lower than one, it means that there are more females than males within that region. 若一個區域的性別比低於一，則代表該地的女性多於男性。

13) **admission** *(n.)* 准許進入 ❹

- The security guard asks all customers to present their ID, or they will be refused **admission** to the club. 保全要求所有顧客出示身分證，否則他們將被拒絕進入俱樂部。

14) **widespread** *(adj.)* 普遍的，廣泛的 ❺

- Sparrows and pigeons are **widespread** birds that can be found worldwide.
  麻雀和鴿子是分布廣泛的鳥類，全球皆可見到。

15) **workplace** *(n.)* 工作場所 ❹

- Jamison doesn't talk about his problems in the **workplace** once he clocks out. He draws a clear boundary between work and life.
  Jamison只要打卡下班了就不會談論他在工作場所遇到的問題。他把工作和生活的界線分得很清楚。

16) **household** *(n.)* 一個家庭 ❹

- Running a **household** used to be a necessary part of being an adult, but this idea has now shifted. 經營家庭曾經是作為一位大人的必需之一，但如今這個觀念已經改變了。

17) **contrast** *(n.)* 相反 ❹

- The new electric multiple unit train stands in sharp **contrast** to the old diesel-powered model that is parked beside it.
這款新型電聯列車與停在旁邊的舊型柴電列車形成強烈對比。

18) **tremendous** *(adj.)* 巨大的 ❹

- Bourne didn't realize how **tremendous** the sound of a bullet being fired is until he served in the military. Bourne直到服兵役後才知道子彈發射的聲音有多麼巨大。

19) **submit** *(v.)* 服從 ❺

- Before democracy was established, people lived in a world where they must **submit** to their lords without having a will of their own.
在民主制度建立之前，人們身處於一個必須服從其君主的世界，沒有自己的意志。

20) **despite** *(prep.)* 儘管 ❹

- **Despite** Norah's utmost efforts, she still wasn't able to pass the trial and become a member of the idol group.
儘管Norah盡了最大努力，她還是無法通過選拔，成為偶像團體的成員。

21) **recognition** *(n.)* 認可 ❹

- Lyvia was presented with an award in **recognition** of the years she had contributed to the company. Lyvia被授予獎項，以作為她這些年來為公司做出的貢獻的認可。

22) **discriminate** *(v.)* 歧視 ❺

- A racist is a person who **discriminates** against others based on their race or ethnicity.
種族主義者是一種會因種族或族裔而表現出歧視他人的人。

Words for Recognition

1) **unpleasant** *(adj.)* 令人不快的
2) **systemic** *(adj.)* 全面性的；有系統的
3) **unjustly** *(adv.)* 不公平地
4) **surprisingly** *(adv.)* 意外地
5) **feminist** *(n.)* 女性主義者
6) **breadwinner** *(n.)* 養家活口的人
7) **hopelessly** *(adv.)* 無可救藥地
8) **rooted** *(adj.)* 根深蒂固的
9) **unfair** *(adj.)* 不公平的
10) **illegal** *(adj.)* 違法的

Idioms and Phrases

1) **get into** 錄取入學
   - Students must take a college entrance exam in order to **get into** a university.
     學生必須參加大學入學考試才能錄取大學。

2) **come to light** (真相)被揭露
   - When Professor Lee's immoral deeds **came to light**, Sophie was very disappointed because she had admired him very much.
     當李教授不道德的行為被揭露時，Sophie非常失望，因為她非常仰慕他。

3) **based on** 根據…
   - Most characters in the Marvel movies are **based on** characters that appear in Marvel Comics. 大多數漫威電影的角色都是根據漫威漫畫裡出現的角色而來的。

The Psychology of Panic Buying

Common Product Categories at Supermarkets

Produce 農產品

broccoli 綠花椰菜

beetroot 甜菜根

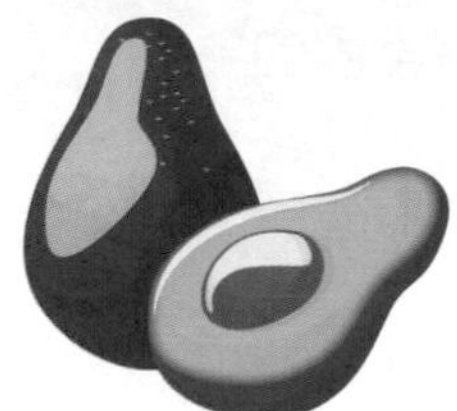
avocado 酪梨

fig 無花果

Dairy 乳製品

milk 牛奶

whipped cream 鮮奶油

butter 奶油

sour cream 酸奶油

Deli (Delicatessen)/Prepared Foods 熟食

sausage 香腸

ham 火腿

cheese 起司

taco 墨西哥夾餅

Bakery 烘焙食品

whole wheat toast 全麥吐司	croissant 可頌	cupcake 杯子蛋糕	baguette 法國長棍

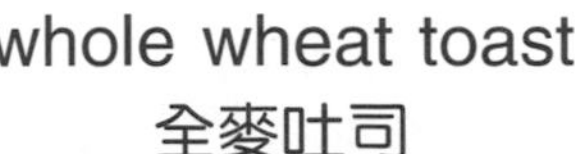

Meat and Seafood 肉類與海鮮

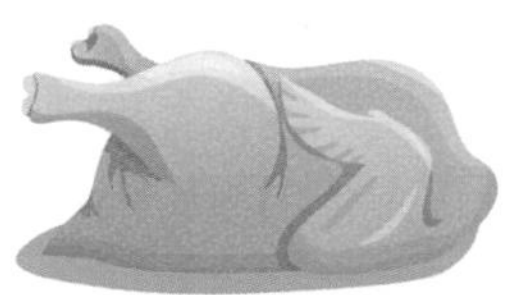	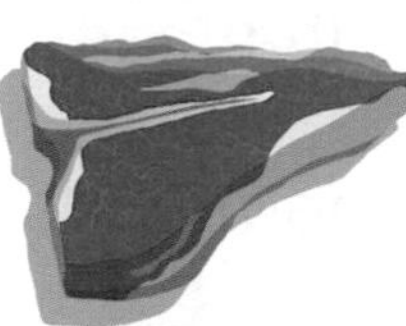		
chicken 雞肉	T-bone steak 丁骨牛排	lobster 龍蝦	salmon steak 鮭魚排

Household Essentials 家庭必需品

toilet paper 衛生紙	towel 毛巾	detergent/cleaner 清潔劑	broom and dustpan 掃把與畚斗

Fun Facts

#PanicBuying

Which of the following factors would **NOT** trigger panic buying?

(A) Statements of price increases or product shortages.

(B) Widespread media coverage concerns about the abundance of some produce.

(C) Wars break out between several major importing countries.

(D) The government suggests the possibility of a lockdown.

Reading

Panic buying is a **phenomenon** that can happen in a **community** hit by a crisis or **disaster**. News reports show empty supermarket shelves and long lines of people desperate to stock up on supplies. Shoppers look **grim**, often waiting hours to buy supplies. When they finally reach the front of the line, many purchase the **maximum** they can carry, even if nothing will be left for others. For example, the COVID-19 pandemic caused panic buying of face masks, rubbing **alcohol**, and toilet paper all over the world.

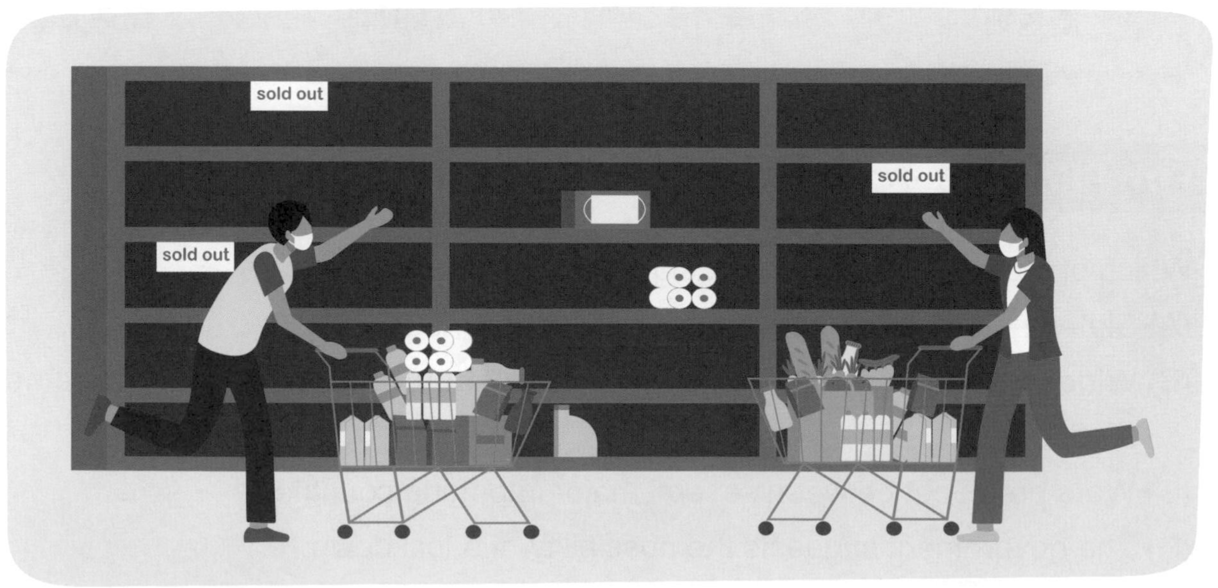

Researchers studying human behavior have explained the psychology of panic buying. The first factor is **anxiety**. People naturally feel worried when facing a war, a natural disaster, or an **outbreak** of a **contagious** disease. Panic buying can also stem from concerns about the rising prices of daily necessities. As a result, the second factor is what **economists** call "loss aversion." Because of a **cognitive bias**, people believe that avoiding losses is more important than making gains. The third factor is a **tendency** called "**herd mentality**." This **refers** to the desire to "follow the crowd" and do what others are doing without thinking for ourselves.

Panic buying causes not only **inconvenience** but also problems. Increased **demand** can make a **shortage** worse. This, in turn, can drive prices up because some suppliers and retailers **seize** the opportunity to charge more. It often turns out that some people have more than they need while others have none, which means it becomes more difficult for **vulnerable** people to survive.

To avoid the problems caused by panic buying, we should stay calm, keep well informed, ignore rumors, and resist the **impulse** to buy more than we need.

混合題

1. According to the passage, what are the 3 causes of panic buying? (簡答) 文意理解、整合資訊

____

_______ 2. What does "others" in the first paragraph refer to? (單選) 掌握脈絡、指涉

(A) Other lines.

(B) Other disasters.

(C) Other shoppers.

(D) Other supplies.

3. The following statements are related to the problems which panic buying can bring about. From (A) to (D) below, put the statements in the correct order of time according to the passage. (填表) 文意理解、因果分析

(A) A typhoon hits the island.

(B) The price of vegetables rises.

(C) The demand for vegetables increases.

(D) The vegetable shortage on the island gets worse.

__A__ → (1) _______ → (2) _______ → (3) _______

社會觀察

Words for Production

1) **psychology** *(n.)* 心理學 ❹
- This novel describes the **psychology** of gamblers in detail.
  這本小說詳細描寫了賭徒的心理狀態。

2) **phenomenon** *(n.)* 現象 ❹
- An earthquake is a natural **phenomenon** which is common in countries like Taiwan and Japan. 地震是一種自然現象，在臺灣和日本等國很常見。

3) **community** *(n.)* 社區 ❹
- Population aging is a problem faced by many rural **communities**.
  人口老化是許多鄉村社區面臨的問題。

4) **disaster** *(n.)* 災難 ❹
- Pripyat is a town that was abandoned after the Chernobyl **disaster**.
  普利皮亞特是一個在車諾比核災之後遭到遺棄的城鎮。

5) **grim** *(adj.)* 哀愁的 ❺
- When we informed Jason that he would be laid off, his face looked **grim**.
  當我們通知Jason他將被解僱時，他看起來愁容滿面。

6) **maximum** *(n.)* 最大量 ❹
- In the experiment, each subject will be given a **maximum** of 20 minutes to answer the questions. 在實驗中，每位受試者會被給予最多20分鐘的時間來回答問題。

7) **alcohol** *(n.)* 酒精 ❹
- My doctor strongly advised me to stop drinking **alcohol**, or my liver would end up failing. 我的醫生強烈建議我別再喝酒，否則我的肝最終會衰竭。

8) **researcher** *(n.)* 研究員 ❹
- Dr. Brown is a leading **researcher** in the field of botany, and he is going to give a talk about tropical plants.
  Brown博士是植物學領域頂尖的研究人員，他即將帶來一場關於熱帶植物的演講。

9) **anxiety** *(n.)* 焦慮 ❹

• David likes jogging because it helps to relieve **anxiety** and stress.
David喜歡慢跑，因為這有助於舒緩焦慮和壓力。

10) **outbreak** *(n.)* 爆發 ❻

• Many things have changed since the **outbreak** of the COVID-19 pandemic.
自從新冠肺炎疫情爆發以來，許多事情都變得不同了。

11) **contagious** *(adj.)* 有傳染性的 ❺

• Good personal hygiene can reduce the risk of getting **contagious** diseases.
良好的個人衛生可以降低得到傳染性疾病的風險。

12) **economist** *(n.)* 經濟學家 ❹

• Some **economists** are predicting that the country's GDP growth will slow down this year.
有些經濟學家預測，該國的GDP成長今年將會放緩。

13) **cognitive** *(adj.)* 認知的 ❺

• After taking the drug, the patient's brain activity and **cognitive** functions will be inhibited. 服用該藥物後，病人的腦部活動與認知功能會受到抑制。

14) **bias** *(n.)* 偏見 ❺

• The YouTuber was heavily criticized for his **bias** against women.
那位YouTuber因對婦女的偏見而遭到強烈批評。

15) **tendency** *(n.)* (行為)傾向 ❹

• My ex-girlfriend has a **tendency** to make a fuss over everything. That's why we are no longer together. 我的前女友有每件事都要大驚小怪的傾向。那就是為什麼我們沒有在一起了。

16) **herd** *(n.)* 群 ❹

• From here, you can see a **herd** of goats grazing beside the river.
從這裡，你可以看到一群山羊在河邊吃草。

17) **mentality** *(n.)* 心態 ❻

• I really cannot understand the **mentality** of those who bully others.
我真的無法理解那些霸凌別人的人是什麼心態。

18) **refer** *(v.)* 指出 ❹

- In this report, the interviewees are not **referred** to by their real names.
  這份報告不會提及受訪者的真實姓名。

19) **inconvenience** *(n.)* 不便 ❹

- The general manager of the airline apologized for the **inconvenience** caused by the flight delay. 航空公司的總經理為了航班延誤造成的不便致歉。

20) **demand** *(n.)* 需求 ❹

- The **demand** for IT professionals has been increasing over these years.
  對於資訊科技專業人才的需求這幾年不斷在增加。

21) **shortage** *(n.)* 短缺 ❺

- Our research project was terminated because of a **shortage** of funds.
  我們的研究計畫因為經費短缺而終止。

22) **seize** *(v.)* 抓住 ❹

- The police officer **seized** the robber by the arm so that he couldn't run away.
  警察抓著搶匪的手臂，好讓他無法逃跑。

23) **vulnerable** *(adj.)* 脆弱的 ❺

- According to a recent study, children are particularly **vulnerable** to this disease.
  一份近期研究顯示，孩童對這種疾病特別沒有抵抗力。

24) **impulse** *(n.)* 衝動 ❺

- After a quarrel with his girlfriend, Charles booked a plane ticket to Okinawa on **impulse**. 和女友爭吵後，Charles在衝動之下訂了一張飛往沖繩的機票。

Words for Recognition

1) **aversion** *(n.)* 厭惡

2) **supplier** *(n.)* 供應商

3) **retailer** *(n.)* 零售商

Idioms and Phrases

1) **stock up** 囤貨，大量購買

• We had better **stock up** on some food and water before the typhoon hits.

我們最好在颱風來襲之前，先囤積一些食物和飲水。

2) **stem from** 源自於…

• The conflict between these two villages **stems from** an argument over land.

這兩個村莊之間的衝突源自於一起土地糾紛。

3) **follow the crowd** 隨波逐流

• Kevin has his own opinion about everything, and he never **follows the crowd**.

Kevin對每件事都有自己的看法，從來不隨波逐流。

4) **in turn** 因此

• The severe drought caused a lack of food, and this **in turn** caused turmoil all over the country.

嚴重的旱災造成糧食短缺，而這又因此導致全國各地發生動亂。

5) **drive up** 抬升(價格)

• Experts warn that a ban on the import of Russian natural gas will **drive up** energy prices.

專家警示，禁止俄羅斯天然氣的進口將造成能源價格上漲。

6) **turn out** 結果是…

• I thought we could complete the task in a couple of days, but it **turned out** that we spent a week on it.

我以為我們一兩天就能完成這項任務，但結果我們卻花了一個星期。

Dengue Fever Spreads to Nepal's High Mountains

Steps to Prevent Yourself from Suffering Dengue Fever

Eliminate standing water

➔Since mosquitoes lay their eggs in stagnant water, it's important to regularly empty or cover water containers, including flower pots, buckets, bird baths, and gutters.

Apply mosquito repellents

➔Use mosquito repellents over exposed skin and clothing when outdoors, especially during the time period from dawn to dusk, when mosquitoes are most active.

Wear protective clothes

➔Wear long sleeves, pants, and socks to minimize exposed skin and reduce the risk of mosquito bites.

Install screens on windows and doors

→Install screens on both windows and doors, ensuring that they are free of any holes to keep mosquitoes out of your living spaces.

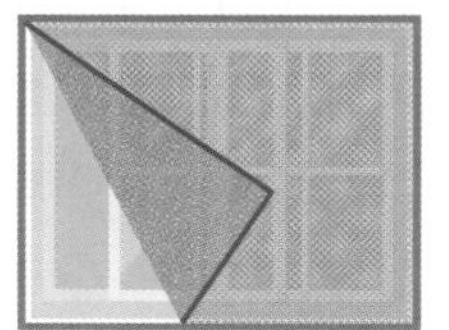

Sleep under a mosquito net

→Sleeping under the mosquito net offers you dual protection against mosquito bites.

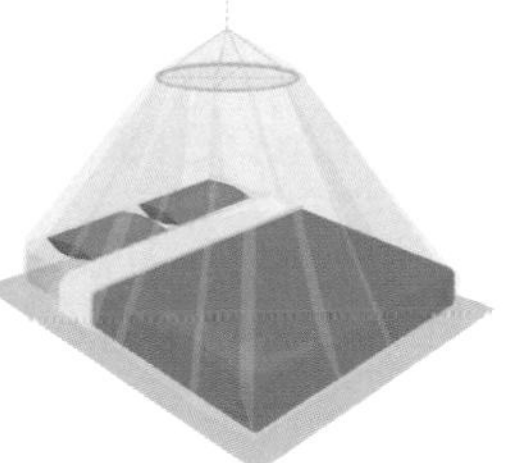

Fun Facts

#DengueFever #MosquitoBorneDiseases

1. Which of the following is **NOT** a symptom of dengue fever?
   (A) Joint pain.
   (B) Vomiting.
   (C) Loss of taste or smell.
   (D) Rash.
2. Which of the following is **NOT** a mosquito-borne disease?
   (A) Malaria.
   (B) COVID-19.
   (C) West Nile Fever.
   (D) Zika virus infection.

A southern Asian country known as one of the coldest and most remote places in the world is struggling with an unwanted visitor more commonly associated with warm tropical climates: Dengue fever has come to Nepal.

This **inland** country lies between the southern border of Tibet and the northern edge of India. Tourists wishing to explore Nepal's natural beauty and rich culture must **adjust** to an average **altitude** of nearly 3,300 meters, though the **renowned** peaks of the Himalayas **soar** to heights more than

double that. Even the low-lying capital, Kathmandu, sits at about 1,350 meters above sea level. The thin air can leave visitors **gasping** for breath.

Yet despite Nepal's northern **latitude** and relatively cold average temperatures, dengue fever, spread by mosquitoes, has **emerged** as a threat. Public health experts are pointing the finger at climate change as the culprit. Nepal has experienced warmer-than-average temperatures in recent years. Coupled with heavy **rainfall**, this creates perfect conditions for mosquitoes to **breed**. Previously, cold temperatures at high altitudes acted as a natural **barrier**, preventing mosquitoes from

reproducing. However, the warmer weather means the **pests** are now able to live up to 2,000 meters above sea level. Carried by cars and trucks, they can travel even

higher to **infect** people in the Himalayas, where mosquitoes were once uncommon.

While **symptoms** of dengue fever, such as high fever, headache, pain behind the eyes, muscle and joint pain, and **rash** are treatable, Nepal's healthcare system is struggling to keep up with the rising number of **infections**. Other countries around the **globe** have also seen recent rises in cases of dengue fever. Shorter winters and longer, hotter summers are enabling mosquitoes to **thrive** and spread the disease across a wider and wider area.

The arrival of dengue fever in Nepal serves as a sharp **reminder** that no corner of the globe is **immune** to the far-reaching **impact** of climate change. Immediate measures are needed to mitigate its effects and protect vulnerable populations from the health risks brought on by changing environmental conditions.

混合題

1. 請根據選文內容，從第三段中選出二個單詞 (word) 填入下列句子的空格中，使句子語意完整、語法正確，且符合全文文意。**每格限填一個單詞**。(填充) 文意理解、資訊歸納

   The two conditions, warmer weather and ________ ________, enable mosquitoes to breed in Nepal.

2. Which verb phrase in the passage means "to blame or accuse someone"? Write down its present simple tense. (簡答) 文意理解、字義推論

   ____

______ 3. 請從下列(A)到(E)中，選出符合文意的選項。(多選) 文意理解、掌握細節

(A) Nepal's health care system has difficulty handling fast-growing dengue fever cases.

(B) Mosquitoes can travel to higher places by hiding in visitors' clothing and belongings.

(C) Dengue fever will spread wider if global warming keeps worsening.

(D) Dengue fever broke out because our planet is mostly covered in tropical climates.

(E) The recent dengue outbreak is an exception that is rarely seen outside of Nepal.

______ 4. According to the passage, which of the following line chart is true? (單選) 圖表判讀

(A)

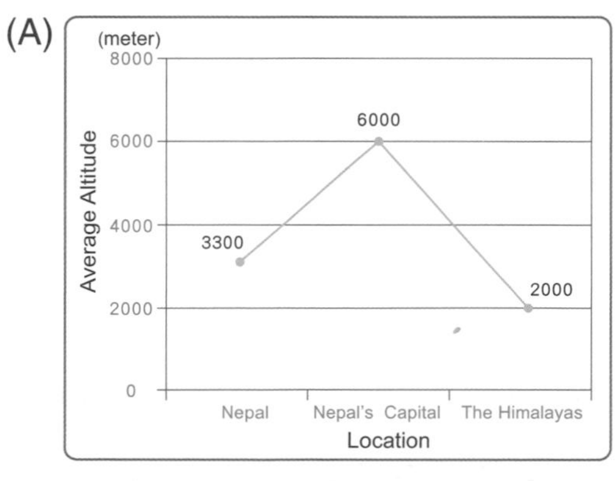

(B)

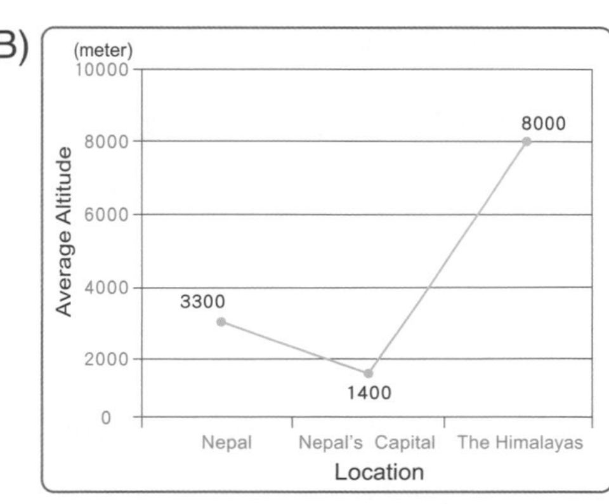

(C)

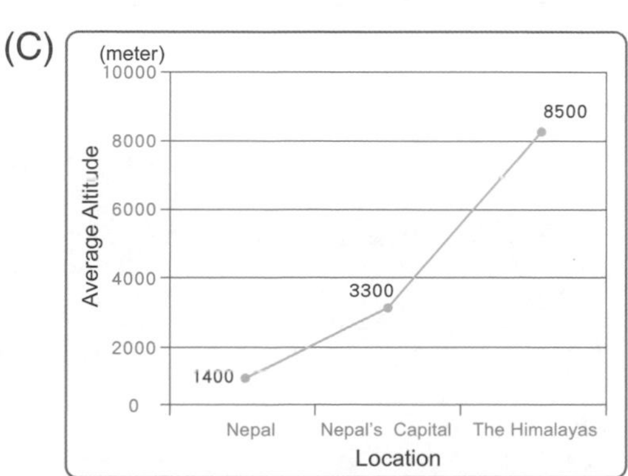

(D)

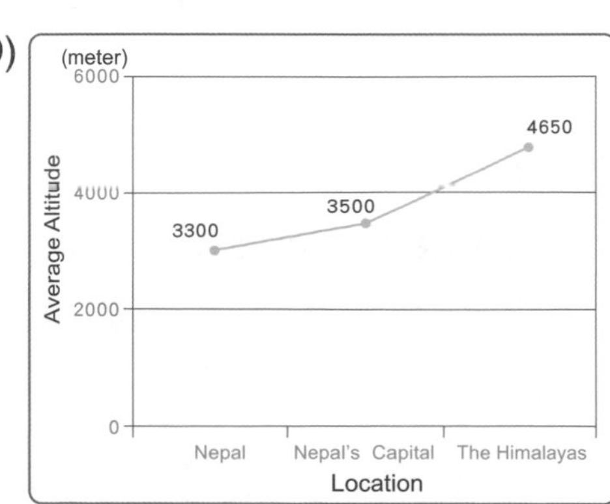

生態環境

Words for Production

1) **inland** *(adj.)* 內陸的 ❻

• Nanzhuang, an **inland** town in Miaoli County, is a popular tourist destination.
南庄，苗栗縣的一個內陸小鎮，是個熱門的旅遊景點。

2) **adjust** *(v.)* 適應 ❹

• It took Jasmine two months to **adjust** to the cold weather in Russia.
Jasmine花了兩個月適應俄羅斯寒冷的天氣。

3) **altitude** *(n.)* 海拔 ❻

• Taiwan's mountainous regions are particularly suitable for tea cultivation because of their high **altitudes** and significant temperature variation.
臺灣山區因其高海拔和氣溫變化大而特別適合茶葉種植。

4) **renowned** *(adj.)* 著名的 ❻

• Thousands of fans crowded into the Taipei Arena to see the **renowned** band perform live. 上千位歌迷湧入臺北小巨蛋看著名樂團的現場表演。

5) **soar** *(v.)* 高達 ❺

• Temperatures in this city **soared** to 45 degrees Celsius because of global warming.
因為全球暖化，這座城市的氣溫高達攝氏45度。

6) **gasp** *(v.)* (困難地)喘氣 ❺

• After completing the marathon, Kurt **gasped** for air as he lay down on the grass.
跑完馬拉松後，Kurt躺在草地上喘氣。

7) **latitude** *(n.)* 緯度 ❻

• This country's high **latitude** and relatively cool average temperatures make crops difficult to grow. 這個國家的高緯度和相對較低的平均溫度讓作物難以生長。

8) **emerge** *(v.)* 出現 ❹

• The prosecutors decided to close the investigation because no further evidence **emerged**. 由於沒有出現更多的證據，檢察官決定結束調查。

9) **rainfall** *(n.)* 降雨(量) ❹

- As the **rainfall** was below average, residents were urged to conserve water.
  由於降雨量已低於平均值，居民們被呼籲要節約用水。

10) **breed** *(v.)* 繁殖 ❹

- It is between October and December that king penguins **breed**.
  十月到十二月期間是國王企鵝繁殖的時候。

11) **barrier** *(n.)* 屏障，障礙物 ❹

- The Taiwan Strait serves as a natural **barrier** between Taiwan and China.
  臺灣海峽是臺灣和中國間的天然屏障。

12) **reproduce** *(v.)* 繁殖 ❻

- Sea turtles face difficulties **reproducing** because of light pollution problems.
  由於光害問題，海龜面臨繁殖困難。

13) **pest** *(n.)* 害蟲 ❹

- Farmers are exploring eco-friendly ways to control **pests** without harmful chemicals.
  農民正在探索對環境友善且不含有害化學物質的方式來控制害蟲。

14) **infect** *(v.)* 傳染給… ❺

- We should take the necessary precautions against some serious diseases that may **infect** humans. 我們應該對一些可能感染人類的嚴重疾病採取必要的預防措施。

15) **symptom** *(n.)* 症狀 ❺

- Joshua had three classic COVID-19 **symptoms**: cough, fever, and loss of taste.
  Joshua有三個典型的新冠肺炎症狀：咳嗽、發燒和味覺喪失。

16) **rash** *(n.)* 疹子 ❻

- Rachel got an itchy **rash** all over her body after eating crabs.
  Rachel吃完螃蟹後全身長滿疹子。

17) **infection** *(n.)* 感染 ❹

- The politician was admitted to the hospital with a severe respiratory **infection**.
  這名政治人物因為嚴重的呼吸道感染入院。

18) **globe** *(n.)* 全球，世界 ❹

- Lisa dreams of traveling around the **globe** one day.
  Lisa夢想有一天能遊遍全世界。

19) **thrive** *(v.)* 茁壯成長 ❺

- Rice cannot **thrive** in a dry climate. 稻米無法在乾燥的氣候下生長。

20) **reminder** *(n.)* 提醒 ❺

- This family photo is a **reminder** of our pleasant stay in Germany.
  這張全家福讓我們想起我們在德國的快樂時光。

21) **immune** *(adj.)* 免疫的 ❺

- Stress can undermine our **immune** system, increasing the risk of disease.
  壓力會破壞我們的免疫系統，增加患病的風險。

22) **impact** *(n.)* (巨大)影響 ❹

- William Shakespeare's writings have had a profound **impact** on literature, theater, and the English language.
  莎士比亞的作品對文學、戲劇和英語留下深遠的影響。

Words for Recognition

1) **dengue fever** *(n.)* 登革熱 補 也作dengue

2) **Nepal** *(n.)* 尼泊爾

3) **Tibet** *(n.)* 西藏

4) **the Himalayas** *(n.)* 喜馬拉雅山脈 補 也作Himalaya

5) **low-lying** *(adj.)* 地勢低窪的

6) **Kathmandu** *(n.)* 加德滿都

7) **culprit** *(n.)* 罪魁禍首

8) **far-reaching** *(adj.)* 波及廣泛的

9) **mitigate** *(v.)* 減輕(危害)

Idioms and Phrases

1) **known as sth** 被稱作…的

• Kaohsiung is **known as** the "Harbor Capital" for its strong connection with maritime transportation.

高雄因其與海上運輸的緊密聯繫而被譽為「港都」。

2) **point the finger at sb** 指責…

• Emily **pointed the finger at** her classmate for stealing her pen.

Emily指責她的同學偷了她的筆。

3) **coupled A with B** 結合A和B

• The singer's beautiful voice, **coupled with** her musical creativity, makes her the Queen of Pop.

這名歌手優美的嗓音加上她的音樂創作能力，使她成為流行音樂天后。

4) **keep up with sth/sb** 跟上…

• To **keep up with** fashion trends, Steve watches fashion shows and reads magazines. 為了跟上時尚趨勢，Steve看時裝秀和閱讀雜誌。

5) **bring on** 引起

• Smog can **bring on** shortness of breath and even lung disease.

霧霾可能會引起呼吸急促甚至是肺部疾病。

From San Francisco to Hualien: What Earthquakes Can Bring

Common Natural Disasters

tsunami
海嘯

downpour/deluge
暴雨

rainstorm
暴風雨

flood
水災

typhoon
颱風

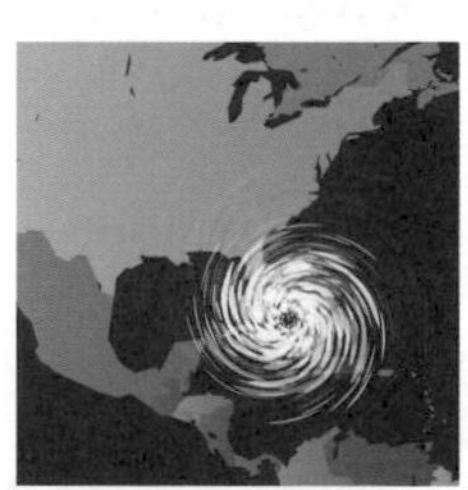

hurricane
颶風

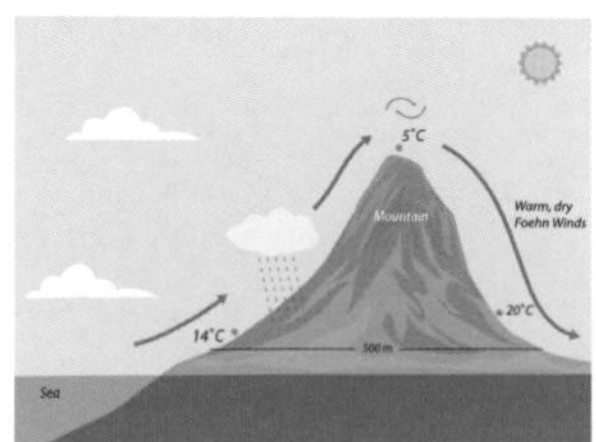

foehn wind
焚風

wildfire
野火

drought
乾旱

landslide
山崩

tornado/twister
龍捲風

volcanic eruption
火山爆發

hailstorm
冰雹 / 雹暴

blizzard
暴風雪

avalanche
雪崩

Fun Facts

#EarthquakeSafety #DropCoverHoldon

Which three of the following statements are **NOT** correct about earthquakes?

(A) When taking cover, stay close to windows and refrigerators to facilitate escape and survival.

(B) People can hide in the Triangle of Life formed by the height differences among the furniture.

(C) People should secure furniture to walls to prevent it from falling over during an earthquake.

(D) When an earthquake strikes, people should avoid using elevators and go outside quickly.

(E) When trapped, it's better to make tapping sounds instead of shouting to ask for help.

Earthquakes often occur along fault lines as can be found on the west coasts of North and South America, along the Pacific coast of Asia, and around the Mediterranean Sea. A well-known example in history is the **deadly** earthquake that struck the San Francisco area in 1906. The most **extensive destruction** resulted from the fires it **sparked**. The city burned for three days, and more than ten thousand buildings were destroyed. Hundreds of lives were lost, and thousands more were left

homeless. In 1989, another earthquake measuring 7.1 on the Richter scale hit Northern California, resulting in the deaths of nearly 70 people.

Taiwan, also located in an earthquake-prone zone, is known to experience frequent earthquakes. For example, a magnitude 6.4 earthquake hit Hualien on February 6th, 2018, with the epicenter located near the **coastline**. A number of smaller **quakes preceded** the mainshock, followed by a **series** of aftershocks. Several buildings were **tilted** and others were **severely** damaged. **Tragically**, there was a great loss of life despite the valiant efforts to **rescue** those trapped in **wrecked**, highly unstable buildings that were **leaning** dangerously

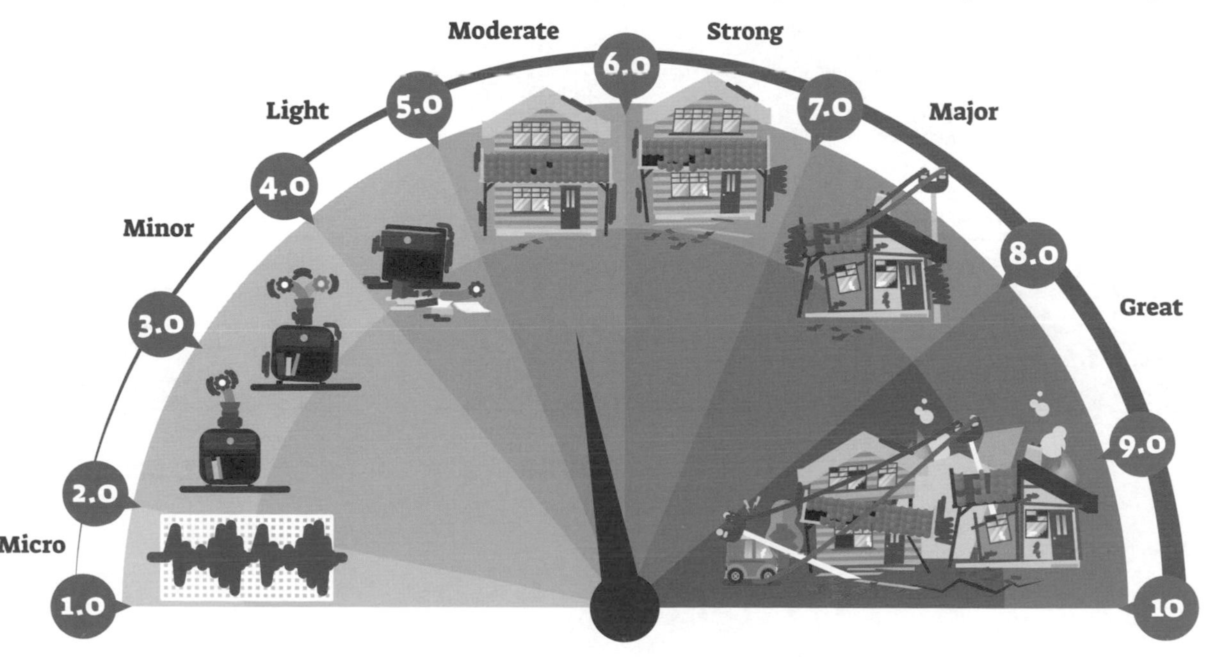

and at risk of complete **collapse**. A significant number of **residents** and tourists were killed and injured.

Earthquakes have the potential to destroy bridges and **freeways**, as well as cutting off water supplies, electricity, and communications. What's worse, earthquakes can **render** many people homeless and cause **casualties**. In order to protect their homes and lives, people who live in earthquake-prone zones must **construct** stronger buildings and roads. Electric power plants and hospitals should be built as far away as possible from earthquake fault lines. When an earthquake strikes, people should **evacuate** to open ground. If that's not possible, they should take protective measures, such as taking **shelter** under **sturdy** tables.

混合題

_______ 1. What is the main idea of the passage? (單選) 歸納主旨

(A) Both Taiwan and America are located in earthquake zones.

(B) There are usually smaller quakes before and after a mainshock.

(C) Most major earthquakes that had happened in history caused tragic deaths.

(D) Earthquakes can lead to the loss of lives and the destruction of property.

_______ 2. According to the passage, which of the following people is **NOT** the witness of the 2018 Hualien earthquake? (單選) 整合資訊

(A)

"It was reported that the epicenter was in the mountain range in eastern Hualien. I didn't know how close it was until I saw the news. Luckily, no one in my family got hurt."

(B)

"I couldn't tell whether it was just my illusion or not. It seemed that there were several quakes that came after the mainshock."

(C)

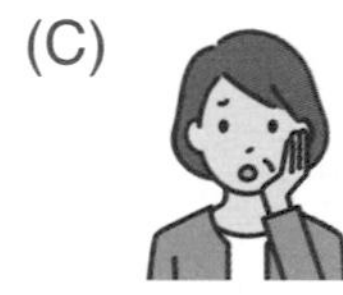

"I was really sorry to hear that there were victims trapped in the damaged buildings and some people killed in the earthquake. What a tragic loss!"

(D)

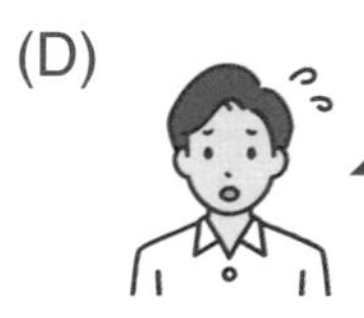

"The rescue teams had done their best. You'd know that if you saw how hard it was to navigate victims inside the seriously tilted buildings."

_______ 3. 請從下列(A)到(E)中，選出文章中未提及的選項。(多選) 文意理解、掌握細節

(A) The damage that earthquakes could cause.

(B) Several earthquake-prone zones in the world.

(C) Appropriate measures one should take after big earthquakes strike.

(D) Major earthquakes that happened in Taiwan and the U.S.

(E) The early warning systems used by earthquake-prone countries.

4. 下圖是Sowa市的地圖。請從文章第三段中選出一個詞組 (phrase) 填入下列句子的空格，使句子語意完整、語法正確，且符合第三段文意。(填充) 圖表判讀

To ensure the safety of the citizens, the mayor of Sowa decided to build the new power plant ____.

Therefore, the mayor chose location B.

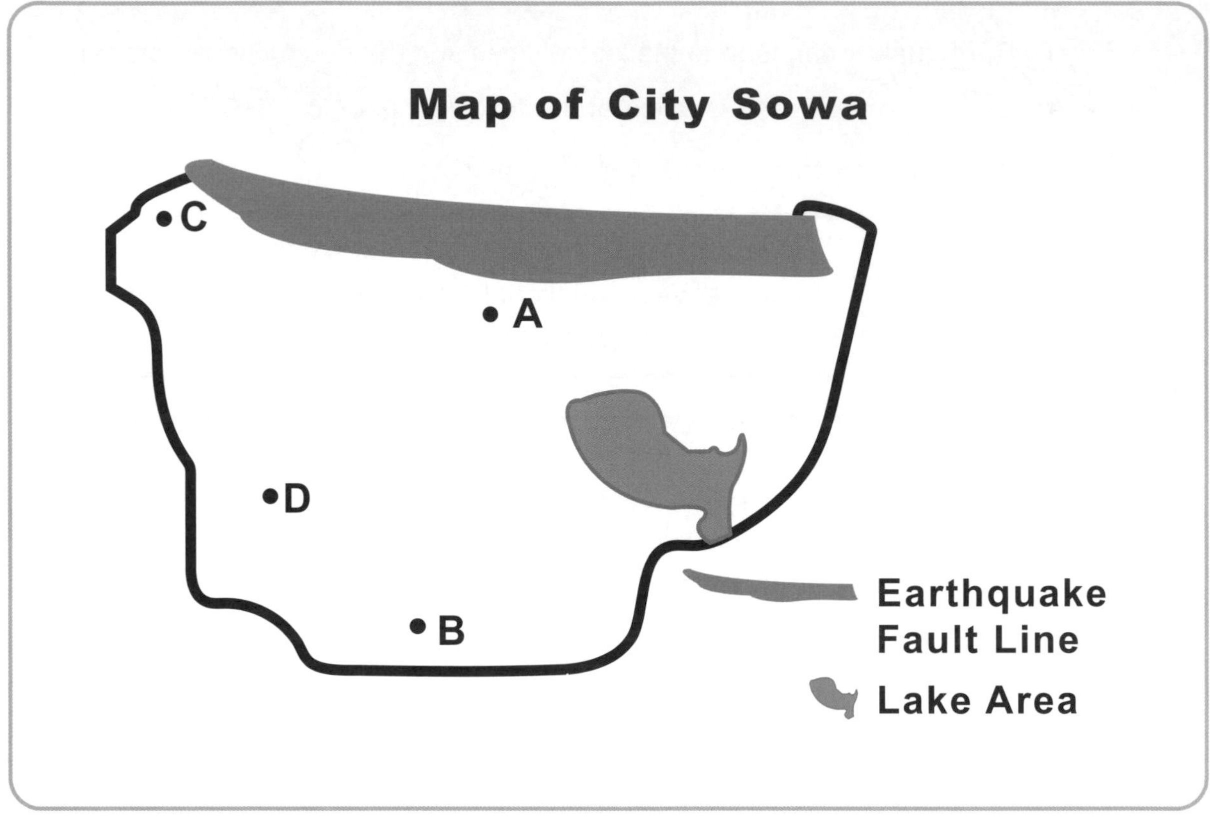

Words for Production

1) **deadly** *(adj.)* 致命的 ❺

• The snake's venom contains a **deadly** toxin that can quickly harm its prey.

這隻蛇的毒液含有可以迅速傷害獵物的致命毒素。

2) **extensive** *(adj.)* 大面積的 ❺

• Julianne sustained **extensive** injuries in the accident, and the doctor said she needs at least six months to recover.

Julianne在事故中受重傷，醫生說她至少需要六個月的時間復原。

3) **destruction** *(n.)* 破壞 ❹

• The oil spill caused by the tanker that ran aground has led to the **destruction** of the nearby coastal ecosystem.

那艘擱淺的油輪所造成的石油外洩導致鄰近海岸生態系的破壞。

4) **spark** *(v.)* 觸發 ❹

• A border conflict **sparked** an all-out war between the two neighboring countries.

一起邊界衝突觸發了兩個鄰近國家的全面戰爭。

5) **coastline** *(n.)* 海岸線 ❻

• Taiwan's **coastline** comprises rocky cliffs, sandy beaches, and coral reef coasts.

臺灣的海岸線包含岩石峭壁、沙灘和珊瑚礁海岸。

6) **quake** *(n.)* 地震 ❻ 補 earthquake的非正式說法

• Regarding the series of **quakes** in the southeast waters during the last few days, the Weather Bureau said that they were a regular release of energy.

關於近日在東南海域的連震，氣象局表示它們為定期的能量釋放。

7) **precede** *(v.)* 在…之前 ❻

• My parents advised me to **precede** my essay with a foreword written by my thesis advisor.

我的父母建議我在論文之前加上指導教授的推薦序。

生態環境

8) **series** *(n.)* 一連串 ❺

• A **series** of poor decisions by the management resulted in the financial crisis and the eventual closedown of the company.
管理層一連串糟糕的決策導致了公司的財務危機，並使公司最終倒閉。

9) **tilt** *(v.)* 傾斜 ❻

• When you feel like taking a nap on the train, you can **tilt** your seat backward.
當你想在火車上小睡一下時，你可以將椅背往後傾斜。

10) **severely** *(adv.)* 嚴重地 ❹

• Water shortages have **severely** affected the agricultural activities of the region.
缺水使得這個地區的農業活動受到嚴重影響。

11) **tragically** *(adv.)* 悲慘地 ❹

• The poor management of the construction site ended up **tragically** killing five innocent pedestrians. 該施工現場管理不善，最終悲慘地導致五名無辜行人的喪生。

12) **rescue** *(v.)* 營救 ❹

• Upon hearing that a group of hikers had lost their way in the mountain, Jack immediately led a team to **rescue** them.
一聽到一群登山客在山裡迷路時，Jack立刻帶領一支隊伍前去營救。

13) **wrecked** *(adj.)* 遭到嚴重破壞的 ❹

• Several train carriages were completely **wrecked** in the rail accident, so the rail company could only have them scrapped.
好幾輛車廂在火車事故中全毀，鐵路公司只得將它們報廢。

14) **lean** *(v.)* 傾斜 ❹

• Don't stand on the old balcony. It has already begun to **lean**.
不要站在老舊的陽臺上。它已經開始傾斜了。

15) **collapse** *(v.)* 倒塌 ❹

• On June 29th, 1995, a department store in Seoul **collapsed** suddenly as a result of a structural failure, killing more than five hundred people.
1995年6月29日，一間位於首爾的百貨公司因結構失效突然倒塌，造成超過五百人喪命。

16) **resident** *(n.)* 居民 ❺

- **Residents** of the war-torn town are forced to leave their homes, as nothing is left for them there.
  飽受戰火摧殘的鎮民被迫離開他們的家園，因為那裡已經什麼都沒有了。

17) **freeway** *(n.)* 高速公路 ❻

- **Freeways** in Germany do not have mandatory speed limits, which means you can drive as fast as you want in certain sections.
  德國的高速公路沒有強制速限，這代表在某些路段上你可以盡情飆速。

18) **render** *(v.)* 使變得 ❺

- The rise of online streaming platforms has **rendered** video rental shops redundant.
  線上串流平臺的興起使得影片出租店不再被需要。

19) **casualty** *(n.)* 人員傷亡 ❻

- As the war in Eastern Europe rages on, **casualties** on both sides continue to mount.
  隨著東歐的戰事激烈地進行，雙方的人員傷亡也持續攀升。

20) **construct** *(v.)* 建造 ❹

- Nowadays, most multi-story buildings are **constructed** of reinforced concrete.
  如今，大部分的多樓層建築都是由鋼筋混凝土建造而成的。

21) **evacuate** *(v.)* 疏散 ❻

- Several seaside settlements received a tsunami warning after the earthquake; residents were then **evacuated** to high ground.
  數座臨海聚落在地震過後收到海嘯警報；居民隨後便被疏散至高處。

22) **shelter** *(n.)* 避難 ❹

- Underground spaces of schools, government facilities, apartment buildings, etc., can provide **shelter** for people when the city is under attack.
  學校、政府機關和公寓建築等的地下空間在城市遭受攻擊時可以提供人們作避難使用。

23) **sturdy** *(adj.)* 堅固的 ❺

- Kyle loved to climb up the **sturdy** old banyan tree and enjoy the view from the top when he was little. Kyle小時候很喜歡爬上那棵結實的老榕樹，並在頂端欣賞風景。

Words for Recognition

1) **the Pacific** *(n.)* 太平洋

2) **the Mediterranean Sea** *(n.)* 地中海 補 也作the Mediterranean

3) **the Richter scale** *(n.)* 芮氏地震規模

4) **magnitude** *(n.)* 規模

5) **epicenter** *(n.)* 震央

6) **mainshock** *(n.)* 主震

7) **aftershock** *(n.)* 餘震

8) **valiant** *(adj.)* 英勇的

9) **unstable** *(adj.)* 不穩固的

Idioms and Phrases

1) **result from** 由於…所導致

- Heatstroke **results from** prolonged exposure to the fierce heat of the sun.
  中暑是由長時間暴露在烈日下所導致的。

2) **result in** 造成…

- Pushing yourself too hard for the sake of productivity is likely to **result in** mental fatigue and burnout. 為了提高生產力而過度逼迫自己很可能導致心理疲勞與過勞。

3) **be known to** 眾所皆知

- It **is known to** all that Wendy is a person of integrity. You can always count on her.
  眾所皆知 Wendy 是一個正直的人。你絕對可以信任她。

4) **cut off** 中斷 (電力供應等)

- The Ukrainian military blew up the Crimean Bridge to **cut off** the Russian supply route. 烏克蘭軍方炸毀克里米亞大橋，以切斷俄羅斯軍方的補給線。

NOTE

Nearly 60% of the Earth's Vertebrate Wildlife Has Gone

IUCN Red List of Threatened Species

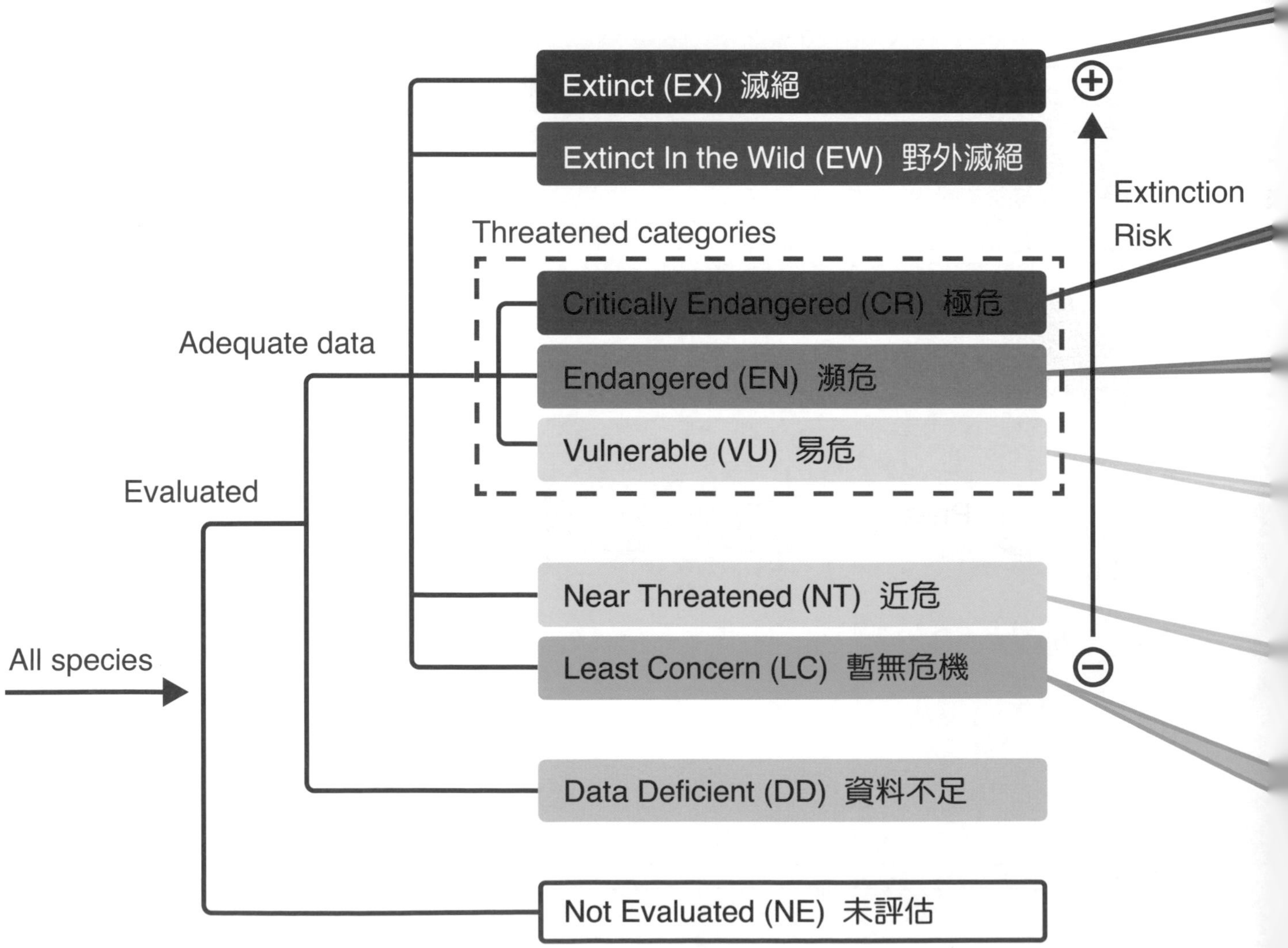

All species

Evaluated

Adequate data

Extinct (EX) 滅絕

Extinct In the Wild (EW) 野外滅絕

Threatened categories

Critically Endangered (CR) 極危

Endangered (EN) 瀕危

Vulnerable (VU) 易危

Near Threatened (NT) 近危

Least Concern (LC) 暫無危機

Data Deficient (DD) 資料不足

Not Evaluated (NE) 未評估

⊕ Extinction Risk ⊖

Fun Facts #LeopardCat

Leopard cats were officially listed as an endangered species in 2008, and there may be fewer than 500 left in Taiwan. Which three of the following actions can people take to conserve leopard cats?

(A) Halt deforestation and habitat destruction to preserve their homes.

(B) Bring adorable cat-like leopard cats home and take good care of them.

(C) Drive through their habitats faster to avoid disturbing them.

(D) Avoid using traps and poisoned baits in order not to threaten their survival.

(E) Don't dump or abandon animals to reduce the risks to leopard cats.

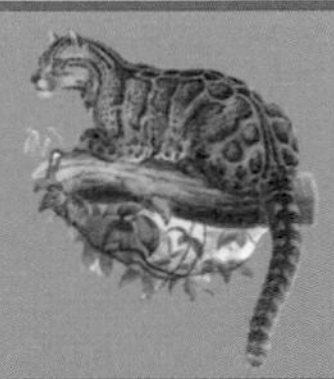

Formosan clouded leopard
臺灣雲豹

Eurasian otter
歐亞水獺

Harpist brown frog
豎琴蛙

Formosan black bear
臺灣黑熊

Formosan landlocked salmon
櫻花鉤吻鮭

Pheasant-tailed jacana
水雉

Formosan pangolin
穿山甲

Black-faced spoonbill
黑面琵鷺

Formosan serow
臺灣長鬃山羊

Hundred-pace snake
百步蛇

Chinese cobra
中華眼鏡蛇

❶ The past decades have been a disaster for wildlife, with many **species** experiencing a population **decline** or even becoming **extinct**, according to a World Wildlife Fund (WWF) report. ❷ The population decline is especially devastating to **mammals**, fish, birds, and other animals with a **backbone**. ❸ **Statistics** indicate that nearly 60% of the Earth's vertebrate wildlife has disappeared since 1970. ❹ Even more alarming, the WWF warns that this trend shows no sign of slowing down.

It's not surprising that human activities are the primary cause of the animals' disappearance. Whether for food or money, hunting kills huge

numbers of animals. Even though the trade in **endangered** animal parts, such as elephant ivory and rhinoceros horn, is **forbidden** by law, black markets continue to feed the demand for such products.

Rapid human population growth also drives a demand for usable land. Clearing forests to make room for **expanding** cities and roads means laying waste to the natural **habitats** of birds, mammals, and **reptiles**. **Deprived** of space to feed and breed, species that cannot **adapt** to changing environmental conditions are **doomed**.

Moreover, the oceans, along with many lakes and rivers, are choked up with pollution, including plastic, chemicals, and other untreated waste. Combined with rising water temperatures, this creates conditions that are no longer suitable for many aquatic species. And even among those that can survive, many populations are rapidly declining because of overfishing.

❺ However, although the situation is grim, there is hope. ❻ **Conservation** efforts have succeeded in saving many endangered species, bringing them back from the **brink** of extinction. ❼ Yet, despite such successes, people still need to take more immediate and **decisive** action to slow down or **reverse** the wildlife population decline. ❽ To **sustain** the environment, we must rethink our **priorities** and patterns of **consumption**.

混合題

______ 1. According to the WWF report, which of the following is **NOT** on the list of disappearing animals? (單選) 圖文配對

(A)  (B)  (C)   (D) 

2. The sentences in the passage are numbered ❶ to ❽. Answer the following questions by writing down the <u>**NUMBER**</u> of the sentence. (填號) 文意理解、文本分析

(A) Which sentence in the first paragraph best indicates the potential development of the wildlife population?

____

(B) Which sentence in the last paragraph is **NOT** the author's opinion on wildlife conservation?

____

3. 請從第三段和第四段各選出一個詞組 (phrase)，分別填入下圖的空格，使下圖語意完整且符合全文文意。請依下表格式適當變化大小寫。(填充) 歸納重點、因果分析

Reasons Why Wildlife Is Disappearing

I. Human Activities

- hunting for food
- hunting for money (e.g. elephant ivory & rhino horn)

II. (A) ______________________

- clearing forests
- expanding cities and roads
- laying waste to natural habitats

III. Water Pollution & Water-related Activities

- plastic, chemicals, and untreated waste
- rising water temperatures
- (B) ____________

Words for Production

1) **wildlife** *(n.)* 野生動植物 ❺

- The charitable organization aimed to raise public awareness of the importance of **wildlife** conservation.

  該慈善機構旨在提高大眾對保育野生動物重要性的意識。

2) **species** *(n.)* 物種 ❹

- Because of marine pollution, some **species** of coral have become endangered.

  由於海洋汙染，一些珊瑚物種已經瀕臨絕種。

3) **decline** *(n.)* 下降 ❺

- There has been a steep **decline** in the population of the town since the 1990s.

  從1990年代以來，該城鎮的人口數急劇下降。

4) **extinct** *(adj.)* 滅絕的 ❺

- Dinosaurs went **extinct** about 65 million years ago.

  恐龍是約在6500萬年前滅絕的。

5) **mammal** *(n.)* 哺乳動物 ❺

- The blue whale, the largest **mammal** in the world, has been listed as an endangered species.

  藍鯨是世界上最大的哺乳動物，已被列為瀕臨滅絕的物種。

6) **backbone** *(n.)* 脊椎 ❻

- Startled by her brother, Shelly fell out of the tree and broke her **backbone**.

  Shelly被她弟弟嚇了一跳，從樹上摔下來並摔斷了她的脊椎。

7) **statistics** *(n.)* 統計數據 ❹

- According to **statistics**, celebrity opinions may significantly influence customers' decisions about what to buy.

  根據統計數據，名人觀點可能會顯著影響顧客的購買決定。

8) **endangered** *(adj.)* 瀕臨滅絕的，瀕危的 ❹

- The government has built several national parks to protect **endangered** plants and animals.

政府建立了幾個國家公園來保護瀕臨滅絕的動植物。

9) **forbidden** *(adj.)* 被禁止的 ❹

- Visitors are **forbidden** to enter the building without showing an ID card.

未經出示身分證件，訪客不得進入此大樓。

10) **expand** *(v.)* 擴大 ❹

- After the conference, the company decided to **expand** its business in the United States.

會議結束後，該公司決定在美國擴展業務。

11) **habitat** *(n.)* 棲息地 ❺

- The tropical forest is an important **habitat** for many creatures.

這座熱帶雨林是許多生物的重要棲息地。

12) **reptile** *(n.)* 爬蟲類 ❻

- Peter has been trying to convince his mother to let him keep **reptiles** as pets.

Peter一直在努力說服他媽媽讓他養爬蟲類當寵物。

13) **deprive** *(v.)* 剝奪 ❻

- Some people think it is unethical to **deprive** someone of his or her life as a punishment.

有人認為剝奪某人的生命作為懲罰是不道德的行為。

14) **adapt** *(v.)* 適應 ❹

- After moving to a foreign country, Bobby had to **adapt** to a new culture and language.

移居國外後，Bobby必須適應新的文化和語言。

15) **doom** *(v.)* 注定 (滅亡、失敗等) ❻

- As the raging storm approached, the sailors knew they were **doomed** to die at sea.

當猛烈的暴風雨逼近時，水手們知道他們注定在海上喪命。

16) **moreover** *(adv.)* 此外 ❹

• Cycling can keep us fit. **Moreover**, it doesn't harm the environment.

騎自行車可以讓我們保持健康。此外，它不會危害環境。

17) **conservation** *(n.)* 保育 ❺

• You can't fish in the **conservation** area without a fishing permit.

如果沒有釣魚許可證，你就不能在該保護區內釣魚。

18) **brink** *(n.)* 邊緣 ❻

• The territorial dispute brought the two countries to the **brink** of war.

領土爭端使這兩個國家瀕臨戰爭邊緣。

19) **decisive** *(adj.)* 明確的 ❻

• Quinn hasn't given me a **decisive** reply to my question about being my girlfriend.

Quinn還沒明確回應我，她要不要成為我女朋友。

20) **reverse** *(v.)* 使 (反向) ❺

• Veronica failed to **reverse** her father's decision to send her abroad to study.

Veronica未能推翻她父親要送她出國讀書的決定。

21) **sustain** *(v.)* 維持 ❺

• The young father's income was not adequate to **sustain** a family of five.

這位年輕爸爸的收入不足以維持一家五口的生活所需。

22) **priority** *(n.)* 優先考慮的事 ❹

• A top **priority** for parents when raising children is keeping them healthy.

父母養育孩子時優先考慮的事情是讓他們保持健康。

23) **consumption** *(n.)* 消耗 ❺

• Using public transportation to commute is a good way to reduce fuel **consumption**.

利用大眾交通工具通勤是個減少燃料消耗的好方法。

Words for Recognition

1) **vertebrate** *(adj.)* 有脊椎的

2) **World Wildlife Fund** *(n.)* 世界自然基金會

3) **devastating** *(adj.)* 破壞性極大的

4) **rhinoceros** *(n.)* 犀牛 補 也作rhino

5) **untreated** *(adj.)* 未經處理的

6) **aquatic** *(adj.)* 水生的

7) **overfishing** *(n.)* 過度捕撈

8) **extinction** *(n.)* 滅絕

9) **rethink** *(v.)* 重新思考

Idioms and Phrases

1) **lay waste to sth** 完全摧毀 補 也作lay sth (to) waste

   • The bomb attack **laid waste to** hundreds of towns and villages overnight.

   那次的炸彈襲擊一夜之間完全摧毀了數百個城鎮和村莊。

2) **choke up** 塞滿，堵塞

   • The drain in the bathroom is **choked up** with hair.

   浴室的排水管被毛髮堵住了。

The Rise of Robot Co-Workers

Various Types of Robots in Human Lives

service robots 服務機器人

· the robots that are used to provide various services such as delivering drinks to customers

medical robots 醫療機器人

· the robots that are used in the medical field

social robots 社交機器人

· the robots that are used for companionship or social interaction with humans

educational robots 教育機器人

· the robots that are used in the field of education and learning

domestic robots 家庭機器人

· the robots that are used in household settings

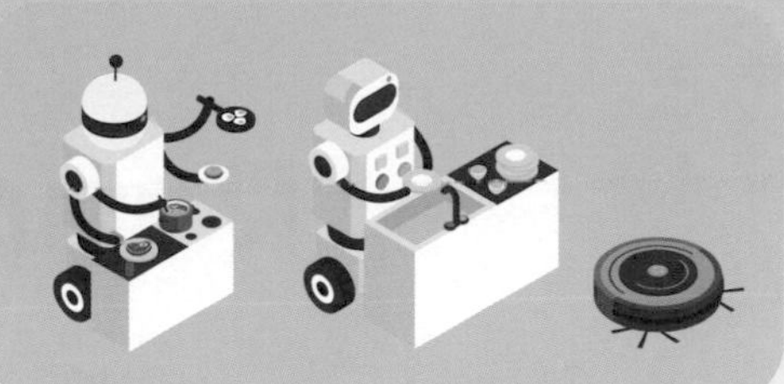

industrial robots 工業機器人

· the robots that are used in manufacturing and production industries

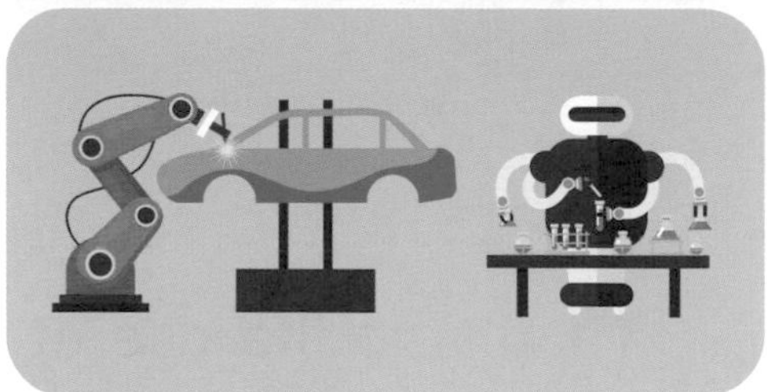

military robots 軍用機器人

· the robots that are used by the military, which are designed to reduce risks to human soldiers

agricultural robots 農業機器人

· the robots that are used to effectively assist in agricultural tasks

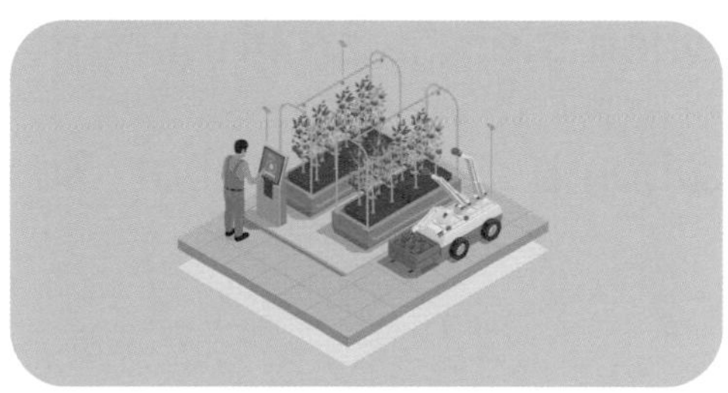

Fun Facts

#TheUncannyValley

The "Uncanny Valley" is a theory proposed by Masahiro Mori, a Japanese robotics professor, in 1970. According to the theory, what kind of emotions will humans experience when a robot closely resembles humans in many respects but is not completely realistic?

(A) People will fear becoming too emotionally attached to the robot.

(B) People will feel uneasy, uncomfortable, or even creeped out.

(C) People will start to doubt and fear their own existence as humans.

(D) People will be afraid of not being able to keep up with the development trends of robots.

Reading

Thanks to the rise of new technology, it's highly probable that we will soon be working **alongside** robots. Though this sounds like something out of a science-fiction movie, experts say that robot co-workers will eventually become an accepted part of the workplace.

In fact, some robots are already working with humans. For example, when there is an **imminent** threat to human life, U.S. soldiers can call in a bomb **disposal** robot. Some soldiers become so close to these robots

that they give them names and even hold **funerals** for them when they are destroyed in bomb **blasts**.

Robots are also becoming increasingly common in **manufacturing facilities**. In recent years, robots in the workplace have increased in North American companies by nearly 50%. Some experts **speculate** that we may soon witness **scenarios** where robots **outnumber** humans in specific industrial **settings**.

While there is a growing concern that people will be replaced by machines, experts say that people should not fear that robots will take over all of their jobs. While it's true that robots **excel** at routine and repetitive tasks, they still **lag** behind in terms of multitasking abilities

and sentience. This means that robots will likely be **assigned** mundane or dangerous tasks, allowing humans to turn their attention to work that requires skills, such as planning, **negotiating**, or empathizing with others.

It's also important to bear in mind that robots **possess** limited **capabilities** and often work best when focused on **singular** tasks. Unlike people, robots will not volunteer to help a co-worker in need unless programmed to do so.

Above all, experts emphasize that people should regard robots as assistants, not as replacements.

混合題

______ 1. 請從下列 (A) 到 (E) 中，選出根據文章內容目前不會被機器人取代的職位。(多選) 引申推論

(A) Factory workers.　(B) Bomb squads.

(C) Public relations consultants.　(D) Sales reps.

(E) Typists.　(F) Healthcare professionals.

______ 2. According to the passage, which of the following graphs best describes the future trend in the number of human workers and robots in manufacturing? (單選) 圖表判讀

(A)

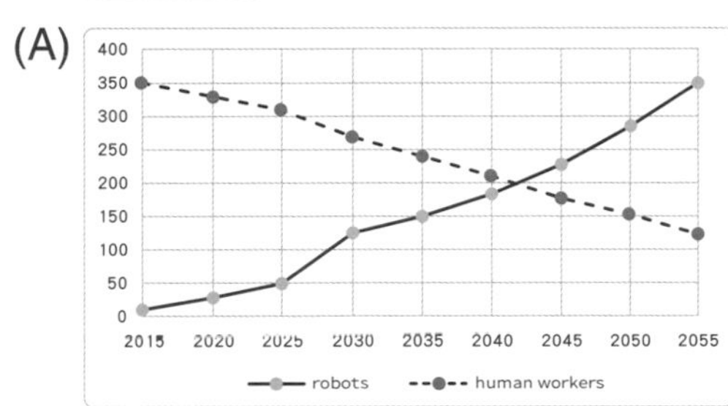

(B)

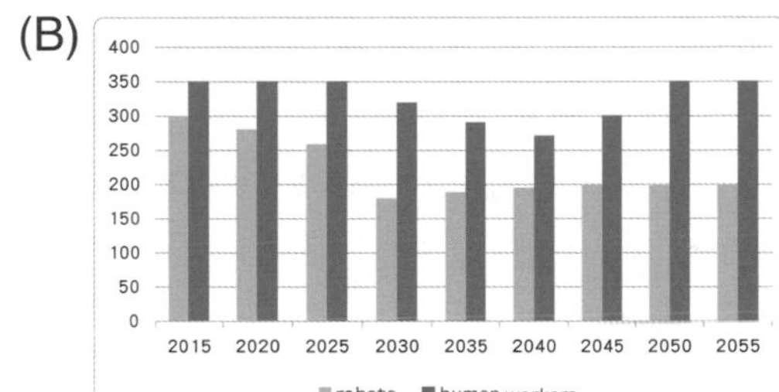

(C)

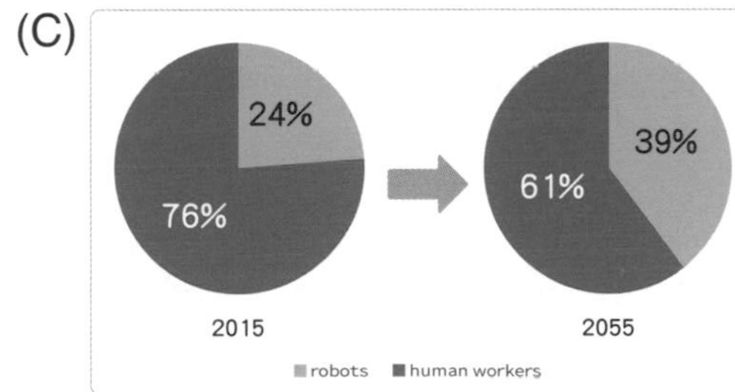

(D)

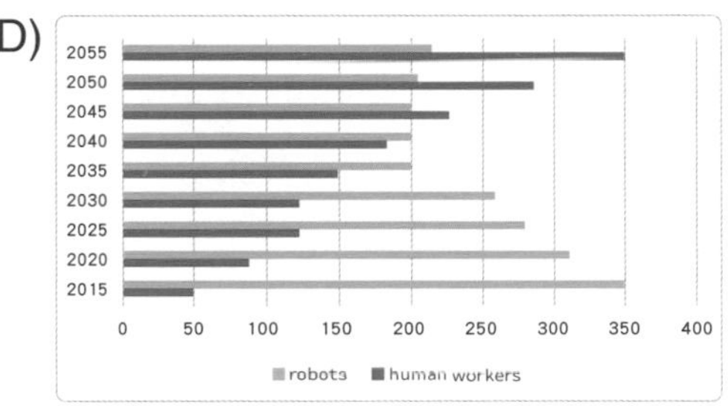

3. Which word in the passage means "likely to be true or likely to happen"? (簡答) 單字理解

____

______ 4. According to the passage, what role are robots most likely to play in the future workplace? (單選) 文意理解

(A) They are threats like bombs to human workers.

(B) They are major risks to human workers.

(C) They are teammates of human workers.

(D) They are replacements for human workers.

Words for Production

1) **alongside** (prep.) 與…一起 ❺
   - The journalist spent a few months living and working **alongside** the locals in order to win their trust.

     那名記者花了幾個月和當地人一起生活與工作，以贏取他們的信任。

2) **imminent** *(adj.)* 迫在眉睫的 ❻
   - The reactor is in **imminent** danger of explosion, and everyone in the power plant must be evacuated immediately.

     反應爐有即將爆炸的危險，發電廠的所有人員都必須立刻疏散。

3) **disposal** *(n.)* 處理 ❻
   - Waste **disposal** has become a major problem in the city because of the increasing population.

     由於人口不斷成長，廢棄物的處理已經成為該城市的一大問題。

4) **funeral** *(n.)* 喪禮 ❹
   - John took a day off to attend his close friend's **funeral** last Friday.

     上週五John請了一天假去參加一個摯友的喪禮。

5) **blast** *(n.)* 爆炸 ❺
   - The **blast** from the missile base resulted in about 300 casualties.

     飛彈基地的爆炸造成約300人傷亡。

6) **manufacturing** *(n.)* 製造(業) ❹
   - The new trade agreement is expected to create millions of jobs in the **manufacturing** sector.

     新的貿易協定預計將為製造業創造數百萬個工作機會。

7) **facility** *(n.)* 場所 ❹
   - My late grandfather was a physicist who worked at a nuclear research **facility** in New Mexico during World War II.

     我已故的祖父是物理學家，二戰時任職於新墨西哥州的一個核子研究中心。

8) **speculate** *(v.)* 推測 ❺

- Political commentators are all **speculating** about whether this business tycoon will run for president. 政治評論家們都在推測這位企業大亨是否會參選總統。

9) **scenario** *(n.)* 情景 ❺

- If we lose the case, the most likely **scenario** is that we will have to pay Mr. Wang a large sum of money.
  如果我們官司打輸了，最可能的情況是我們得要付王先生一大筆錢。

10) **outnumber** *(v.)* 在數量上超過… ❻

- In this small country near the Persian Gulf, immigrant workers **outnumber** native workers. 在這個鄰近波斯灣的小國，移工的數量超過本地勞工。

11) **setting** *(n.)* 場所，環境 ❺

- This national park, with its lush forests, is a perfect **setting** for bird-watching.
  這座國家公園有著茂密的森林，是絕佳的賞鳥地點。

12) **excel** *(v.)* 擅長 ❻

- Lisa has always **excelled** at mathematics, and she is the company's chief accountant now.
  Lisa一直都很擅長數學，且她現在是這間公司的首席會計師。

13) **lag** *(v.)* 緩慢移動 ❹

- Statistics show that we are **lagging** behind our rivals in market share.
  統計數據顯示，我們在市場占有率方面落後競爭對手們。

14) **assign** *(v.)* 分配 ❹

- If you are not happy with the job **assigned** to you, you can tell the manager.
  如果你對分配給你的工作感到不滿，你可以跟經理說。

15) **negotiate** *(v.)* 談判 ❹

- Under diplomatic pressure from the United Nations, the two countries finally agreed to **negotiate** a ceasefire.
  在來自聯合國的外交壓力下，兩國總算同意進行停火談判。

16) **possess** *(v.)* 擁有，具有 ❹

- Susan **possesses** a unique sense of humor, which enables her to see the funny side of things.

  Susan擁有一種獨特的幽默感，讓她能夠看見事物有趣的一面。

17) **capability** *(n.)* 能力 ❺

- Hummingbirds have the **capability** to fly backward.

  蜂鳥具有倒著飛行的能力。

18) **singular** *(adj.)* 單一的 ❹

- The **singular** focus of the project was to increase energy efficiency.

  該專案的唯一重點就是要提高能源效率。

Words for Recognition

1) **co-worker** *(n.)* 同事

2) **science-fiction** *(n.)* 科幻

3) **repetitive** *(adj.)* 重複性的

4) **multitasking** *(n.)* 同時做多件事

5) **sentience** *(n.)* 感知

6) **mundane** *(adj.)* 單調的

7) **empathize** *(v.)* 能感同身受

8) **unlike** *(prep.)* 與…不同

Idioms and Phrases

1) **thanks to** 由於…

- **Thanks to** the support of my family, I was able to recover from depression.

  由於有家人的支持，我得以從憂鬱症中恢復過來。

2) **out of** 形容某事的來歷 (或起源)

- At the Halloween party, Frank was dressed like someone **out of** a Gothic horror novel.

  在萬聖節派對上，Frank打扮得像是哥德恐怖小說中的人物。

3) **call in** 請來，叫來

- As the demonstration escalated into a riot, armed police were **called in** to control the situation.

  由於示威遊行升級成為暴動，武裝警察奉命前往控制局面。

4) **take over** 接手

- Since Ms. Lin **took over** the company, she has radically reformed its management system.

  自從林小姐接手該公司後，她便徹底地改革了它的管理制度。

5) **bear (sth) in mind** 記住…

- I think Vincent's suggestion seems feasible, and I'll **bear it in mind** as I develop the project.

  我認為Vincent的建議似乎可行，我在開發專案時會牢記這一點的。

6) **focus on** 專注於…

- The doorbell rang as Cindy was **focusing on** solving a difficult sudoku puzzle.

  當 Cindy 正在專心解一道數獨難題時，門鈴響了。

A Closer Look at AR and VR

New Technology Trends Nowadays

metaverse 元宇宙

· It's a virtual world where users can interact with each other as if they were in the real world.

self-driving cars 自動駕駛汽車

· It refers to vehicles that can sense their surroundings and operate without human drivers.

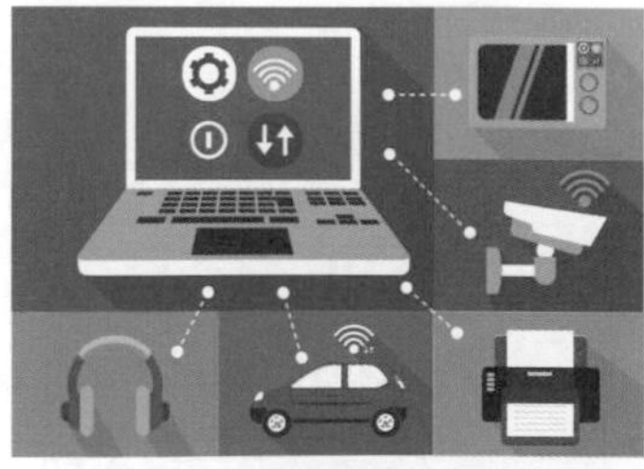

Internet of things (IoT) 物聯網

· It's a network of interconnected devices that can exchange data through the Internet.

3D printing 3D 列印

· It's the process of creating a physical object by layering materials based on a digital model.

digital twin 數位分身

· It's a virtual representation of a physical object, a person, or a system. It uses real-time data and simulation technology to improve monitoring and optimization.

---

blockchain 區塊鏈

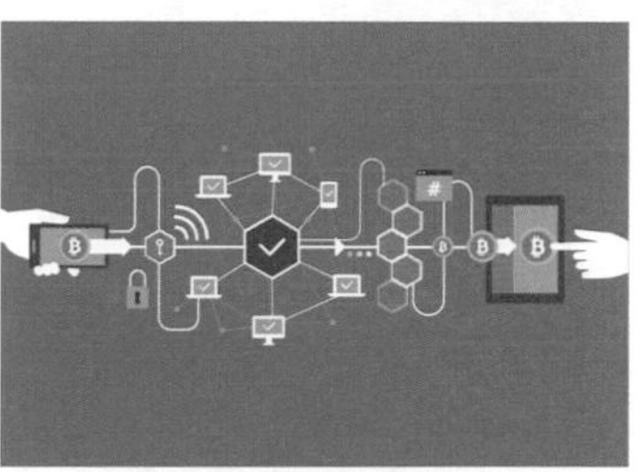

· It's a type of shared database that records transactions across multiple computers, which is the underlying technology for cryptocurrencies like Bitcoin.

---

human genome editing 人類基因編輯

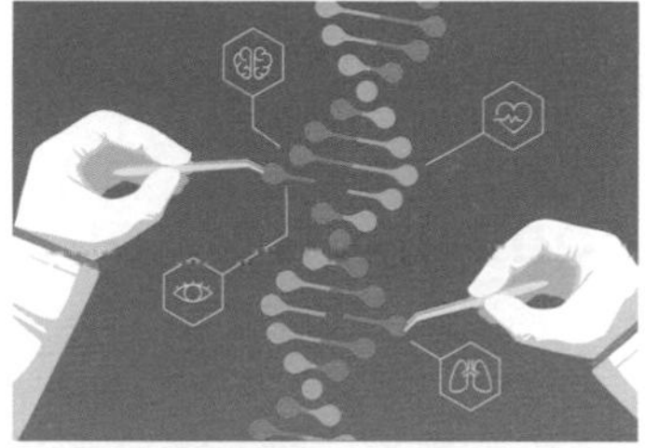

· It's the process of modifying human DNA to correct genetic diseases or enhance certain traits.

---

hyperautomation 超自動化

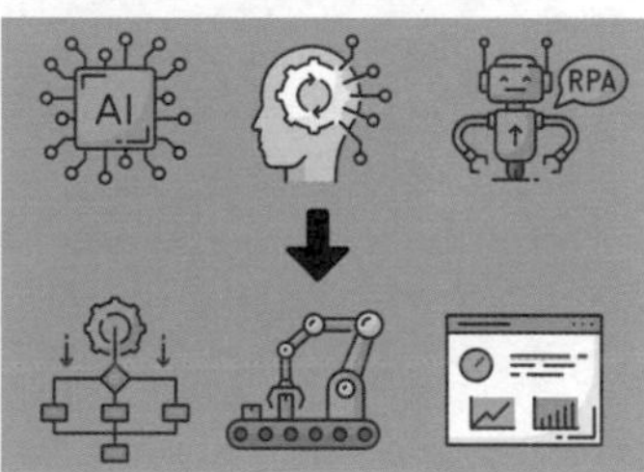

· It combines technologies like AI, machine learning, and robotic process automation (RPA) to automate repetitive tasks without manual or human input.

Fun Facts *#The5thGenerationWirelessSystems*

5G is a new generation of cellular networks that can advance various technologies. Which of the following is **NOT** a benefit of using 5G?

(A) Users can have a better experience when using AR, VR, and even XR.

(B) Users can type over 500 words in a short message.

(C) Doctors can perform remote surgery with the help of its low latency rate.

(D) Compared to 4G, it provides users with faster download and upload speeds.

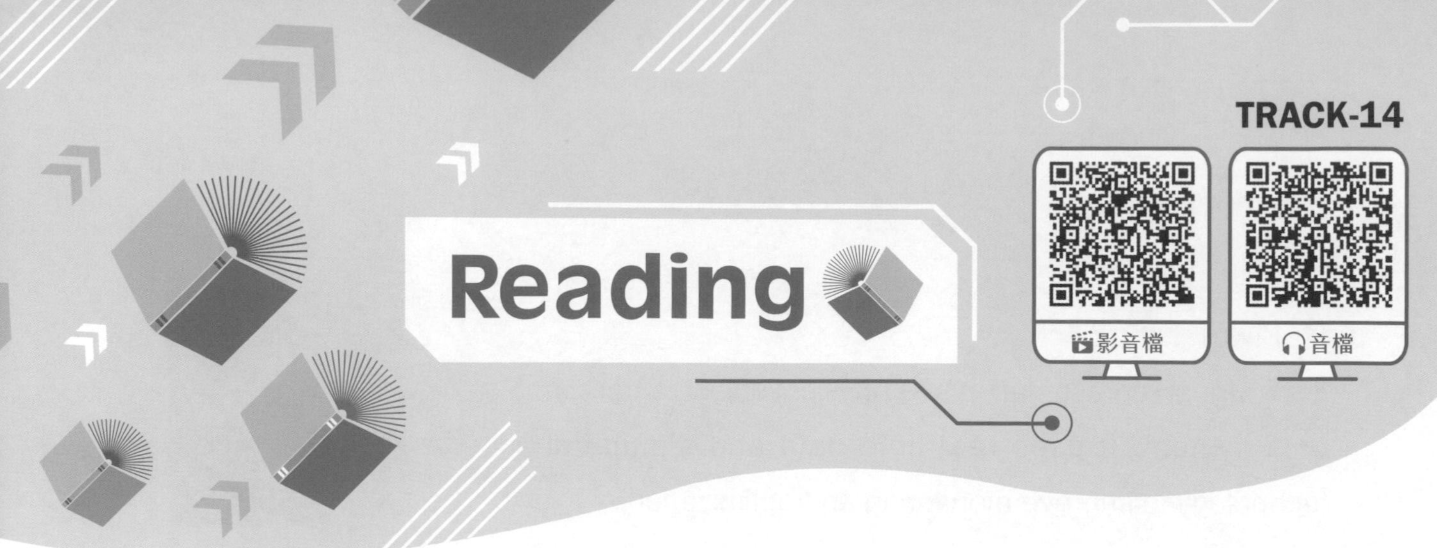

We now live in the Internet age, and technology will undoubtedly play an ever more **prominent** role in our lives. AR (augmented reality) and VR (**virtual** reality) are two good examples of Internet technology.

In VR, users often wear **specialized gear** which looks like a **combination** of an eye mask and glasses. The gear contains a

simulator that projects a highly **realistic** but wholly **synthetic** world. A VR experience is like entering the world of one's favorite anime or game, where users can watch or even **interact** with virtual characters. For instance, a widely praised VR game named *Half-Life: Alyx* takes players on a journey into the dystopian *Half-Life* world. However, a major disadvantage of VR is the **equipment** itself. Some users report that they are not quite satisfied with the **projection**, complaining that it lacks a true sense of reality. There have also been cases in which people feel dizzy after using the VR equipment.

In AR, by contrast, the real world is simply **modified** or **enhanced** by computer-generated elements, all in real time. These elements might include anything from sound to video or **graphics**. A popular example of AR is *Pokémon GO*, an AR game that has enjoyed tremendous global success. In this game, players use AR technology on mobile **devices** to find, capture, and train various Pokémon monsters. These monsters appear in real-world locations, such as parks, **monuments**, and stores.

The **scope** of such Internet technology **extends** beyond games alone, though. Researchers have been exploring diverse avenues for **deploying** it in a variety of other industries, including tourism, **architecture**, and medicine. For example, AR is already being used for several military **applications**. Certainly, Internet technology, such as AR and VR, will help people experience the world in different and interesting ways.

混合題

1. 請從文章第二段與第三段中各找出最適當的單詞 (word)，分別填入下列句子空格中，並視語法需要做適當的字形變化。**每格限填一個單詞 (word)**。(填充) 掌握脈絡、字形變化

   VR equipment allows users to enter a fully simulated yet highly realistic synthetic world. However, some users have reported experiencing (A) ______ after using the equipment. In contrast, AR technology doesn't require users to wear headsets. It enhances the real world with (B) ______ like audiovisual aids that are improved by computers in real time.

2. Fill in the blanks with the information contained in the passage about AR and VR. (填表) 掌握細節、整合資訊

	AR	VR
Equipment	users' mobile devices	specialized gear
Application	games and ______ industries	games
Example	*Pokémon GO*	*Half-Life: Alyx*

3. According to the given information in the passage, match AR or VR to the correct picture. (填表) 圖文配對

The real world

The virtual world

A virtual character

(1) A virtual character in the real world

______

(2) A virtual character in the virtual world

______

Words for Production

1) **prominent** *(adj.)* 重要的 ❹

- Ludwig van Beethoven is widely recognized as one of the most **prominent** musicians of the 19th century.

  貝多芬被廣泛認為是19世紀最重要的音樂家之一。

2) **virtual** *(adj.)* 虛擬的 ❺

- **Virtual** reality technology enables home buyers to remotely tour houses for sale.

  虛擬實境技術使購屋者能夠遠端參觀待售房屋。

3) **specialized** *(adj.)* 專業的 ❺

- After receiving **specialized** flight training, Kevin was certified as a pilot.

  在接受專業飛行訓練後，Kevin獲得了飛行員資格。

4) **gear** *(n.)* 裝備 ❹

- Lydia packed her camping **gear** and headed for the campsite near the lake.

  Lydia 打包好她的露營裝備，前往湖邊的露營地。

5) **combination** *(n.)* 結合 ❹

- The singer's new single is a **combination** of rap and heavy metal.

  這名歌手的新單曲結合了說唱和重金屬。

6) **realistic** *(adj.)* 逼真的 ❹

- The dinosaurs in this 3D movie were so **realistic** that they scared many children.

  這部3D電影中的恐龍太逼真了，嚇壞了許多孩子。

7) **synthetic** *(adj.)* 人造的，合成的 ❻

- Unlike natural fibers, **synthetic** fibers are not always skin-friendly because of the chemicals they contain. 與天然纖維不同，合成纖維由於含有化學物質通常不親膚。

8) **interact** *(v.)* 互動 ❹

- Sylvia **interacts** well with her classmates. They often go out together on weekends.

  Sylvia 和她的同學互動良好。他們週末常一起外出。

9) **equipment** *(n.)* 設備 ❹

- Customers can buy all kinds of kitchen **equipment**, like ovens and pans, in this shop.

  顧客可以在這間店購買各式各樣的廚房用具，例如烤箱和平底鍋。

10) **projection** *(n.)* 投射 ❺

- The little girl was amazed by the **projection** of stars on her bedroom ceiling.

  這名小女孩對臥室天花板上投射的星星感到驚奇。

11) **modify** *(v.)* 修改 ❺

- The manager suggested Helen **modify** the proposal for the new project.

  經理建議Helen修改新專案的提案。

12) **enhance** *(v.)* 增加，增強 ❻

- The food company sponsored the fundraising event to **enhance** its reputation.

  這間食品公司贊助這場慈善捐款活動以提高聲譽。

13) **graphic** *(n.)* 圖像 ❺

- Players can experience movie-like **graphics** and stereo sound effects in this latest game. 玩家可以從這款最新遊戲中體驗電影般的圖像和立體聲音效。

14) **device** *(n.)* 設備 ❹

- The cabin crew asked passengers to turn off all personal electronic **devices** before takeoff.

  機組人員要求乘客在起飛前關閉所有的個人電子設備。

15) **monument** *(n.)* 紀念碑 ❹

- The **monument** was erected in memory of the famous general, who died in the war.

  這座紀念碑是為了紀念戰死的有名將軍而建立的。

16) **scope** *(n.)* 範圍 ❺

- To discover the cause of the incident, the authorities broadened the **scope** of the investigation.

  為了查明事件原因，當局擴大了調查範圍。

17) **extend** *(v.)* 擴展(空間)；延長(時間) ❹

• The department store has **extended** its business hours during the holidays in anticipation of more customers than usual.

由於假期期間顧客預計會比平時更多，百貨公司延長了營業時間。

18) **deploy** *(v.)* 有效運用 ❺

• These fashion designers **deploy** their talents to make comfortable but stylish clothes.

這群時尚設計師有效運用他們的才華製作舒服但優雅的衣服。

19) **architecture** *(n.)* 建築 ❺

• During her trip to England, Gina was deeply fascinated by the style and design of medieval **architecture**.

在英國之旅中，Gina對中世紀建築的風格和設計深感著迷。

20) **application** *(n.)* 用途 ❹

• Artificial intelligence has many **applications** in our lives, such as chatbots and virtual assistants.

人工智慧在我們的生活中有多種用途，例如聊天機器人和虛擬助理。

Words for Recognition

1) **AR (augmented reality)** *(n.)* 擴增實境

2) **VR (virtual reality)** *(n.)* 虛擬實境

3) **simulator** *(n.)* 模擬器

4) **anime** *(n.)* 動畫

5) **dystopian** *(adj.)* 反烏托邦的

6) **computer-generated** *(n.)* 電腦生成的

NOTE

The Pros and Cons of Drones

Various Types of Aircrafts

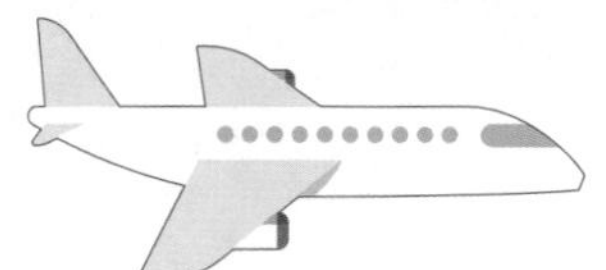

airliner
客機

light aircraft
輕型飛機

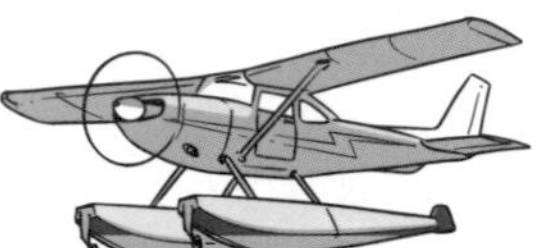

seaplane
水上飛機

hot air balloon
熱氣球

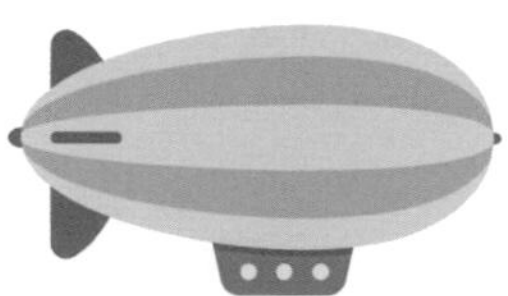

airship
飛船

rocket
火箭

helicopter/chopper
直升機

fighter/combat aircraft
戰鬥機

bomber
轟炸機

jet
噴射機

glider
滑翔機

aerobatic aircraft
特技飛機

Fun Facts

#UAV #AerialPhotography

Which two of the following statements are true about flying a drone in Taiwan for personal use?

(A) A drone that weighs less than 250 grams can be flown without registration.

(B) Operating a remote-controlled drone on a moving vehicle or ship is permitted.

(C) Drones must be kept away from railways, airports, highways, and elevated mass transit systems.

(D) It is permitted to fly a drone over crowd gatherings for photographs.

(E) Flying a drone at night without a drone license is allowed.

Drones are used for a wide variety of tasks. However, there is also much debate over their advantages and **potential disadvantages**.

Drones are remote-controlled flying vehicles commonly used for doing aerial **photography** and exploring places that are hard to reach. News organizations can send out drones to capture images that would be difficult for photographers to obtain. Additionally, drones play a **crucial** role in modern warfare, **undertaking** missions that would

endanger the lives of pilots. Police departments and security companies also use drones to **conduct surveillance** to keep their **squad** members safe.

Drones also have the potential to change the way many industries operate. For example, some companies in Australia have **embraced** unmanned aerial vehicles (UAVs) for delivering goods such as, snacks and **beverages**. Other companies like Amazon also **utilize** drones instead of **conventional** truck **fleets** to deliver packages. Drone delivery can be much faster than other **transportation** methods, especially when there is heavy traffic on the roads. It can save both time and money.

On the other hand, drones are not **exempt** from challenges or **criticisms**. For instance, drones can be hacked or stolen if the owner or operator is not careful. There are also many doubts over how to deal with **mechanical** problems such as malfunctions or power failures. In military settings, errors in drone attacks may even result in the deaths of innocent **civilians**. In addition, some people have objected to drones because of **invasion** of **privacy** issues. Other possible problems include noise pollution and overcrowded skies.

However, despite the pros and cons, people continue to use drones, and the drone industry continues to grow. After all, it is the users' duty to ensure that technology is used for good and not evil.

混合題

_______ 1. Which of the following best describes the author's attitude toward the future development of drones? (單選) 文意判斷

(A) Reserved. (B) Hesitant. (C) Neutral. (D) Pessimistic.

_______ 2. 請從下列 (A) 到 (F) 中，選出符合作者於文章內提及無人機的正確敘述。(多選)

文意理解、掌握細節

(A) Drones can cause noise and air pollution.

(B) Weather conditions can affect drone flights.

(C) Drones may raise concerns over personal information leakage.

(D) Using drones for product packaging is more efficient than conventional means.

(E) Companies are willing to utilize drones because they're cost-effective.

(F) Drones are too expensive for average people to buy.

3. 請從文章第三段中找出最適當的單詞 (word) 填入下列句子空格中，並視語法需要做適當的字形變化，使句子語意完整、語法正確，且符合全文文意。(填充) 掌握脈絡、字形變化

Drones, also known as (A) ______________ aerial vehicles, require no pilots but are instead controlled by personnel on the ground.

Drones have enormous potential to (B) ______________ parcels because of their speed advantage over other forms of transportation.

Words for Production

1) **potential** *(n.)* 可能，潛力 ❹

- Parents should allow their children to develop their full **potential** instead of forcing them down a specific path.

  家長應該讓孩子充分發揮他們的潛能，而非強迫他們走特定的路。

2) **disadvantage** *(n.)* 缺點，劣勢 ❹

- Being unable to use computer software is considered a **disadvantage** nowadays.

  如今，不會使用電腦軟體被認為是種劣勢。

3) **photography** *(n.)* 攝影 ❹

- Fred's passion for **photography** led him to choose it as his major in college.

  Fred對攝影充滿熱誠，因此他決定大學選攝影當主修。

4) **crucial** *(adj.)* 至關重要的 ❺

- Time management skills are **crucial** for meeting deadlines and maintaining productivity.

  時間管理技能對於在期限內完成和維持生產力是至關重要的。

5) **undertake** *(v.)* 從事 (困難之事) ❺

- The heads of the company were reluctant to **undertake** the venture to advance overseas.

  公司的高層不太願意從事進軍海外的商業冒險。

6) **endanger** *(v.)* 危及 ❹

- Reckless drivers **endanger** the lives of others and themselves.

  魯莽的駕駛危及他人與自身的性命。

7) **conduct** *(v.)* 實施 ❺

- Protesters called on biomedical industries to stop **conducting** unethical experiments on animals.

  抗議者呼籲生醫產業停止實施不道德的動物實驗。

8) **surveillance** *(n.)* 監控 ❺

- The apartment building has been kept under **surveillance** by the police because of suspected illegal activities.

  該棟公寓建築因被懷疑進行非法活動而受到警方監控。

9) **squad** *(n.)* 小隊 ❺

- Sergeant Horvath's **squad** spotted a column of enemy tanks while on patrol; he then radioed fighters to strike them.

  Horvath 士官的小隊在巡邏時發現一隊敵方坦克；他隨後用無線電呼叫戰機來攻擊它們。

10) **embrace** *(v.)* 樂意採納 ❺

- The COVID pandemic has pushed more and more people to **embrace** mobile payments for the sake of hygiene.

  新冠疫情催使越來越多人願意採納行動支付，以策衛生。

11) **beverage** *(n.)* 飲料 ❻

- We provide snacks and **beverages** free of charge, so feel free to enjoy yourselves.

  我們提供免費的點心和飲料，所以你們可盡情享用。

12) **utilize** *(v.)* 利用 ❺

- Nuclear power was first **utilized** by human beings for weapons of mass destruction before electricity generation.

  核子能在被用於電力生產以前，起初是被人類用於發展大規模毀滅性武器。

13) **conventional** *(adj.)* 傳統的 ❹

- Herbal medicine may complement **conventional** medicine for better results.

  草藥可與傳統醫藥互補以達到更好的療效。

14) **fleet** *(n.)* 車隊 ❺

- A **fleet** of fire trucks rushed to the fire site as fast as possible.

  一列消防車隊以最快的速度趕赴火災現場。

15) **transportation** *(n.)* 交通運輸 ❹

- The city's efficient public **transportation** system makes commuting convenient for residents. 這座城市高效的大眾運輸系統為居民的通勤帶來便利。

16) **exempt** *(adj.)* 被免除的 ❻

- Robert was **exempt** from mandatory military service because of his eyesight disorder.
  Robert因為眼疾而免服義務兵役。

17) **criticism** *(n.)* 反對 ❹

- The government's transportation reform was met with **criticism** from the opposition party.
  政府的交通改革受到反對黨的反對。

18) **mechanical** *(adj.)* 機械的 ❹

- Investigators concluded that the plane crash was caused by **mechanical** problems, not human errors.
  調查員裁決這起墜機事故是由機械問題所造成的，而非人為錯誤。

19) **civilian** *(n.)* 平民 ❹

- When soldiers finally took back the city, they found that the streets were littered with bodies of **civilians**.
  當士兵終於奪回了城市，他們發現街道上散布著平民的屍體。

20) **invasion** *(n.)* 侵犯 ❹

- There have been several **invasions** of our air defense identification zone by foreign warplanes in the past few days.
  過去幾天已發生數起外國軍機侵犯我國防空識別區的事件。

21) **privacy** *(n.)* 隱私 ❹

- Pompeo's mom has no respect for his **privacy** and insists on reading his diary.
  Pompeo的母親不尊重他的隱私，堅持看他的日記。

Words for Recognition

1) **drone** *(n.)* 無人機

2) **remote-controlled** *(adj.)* 遙控的

3) **aerial** *(adj.)* 空中的

4) **warfare** *(n.)* 戰爭

5) **unmanned** *(adj.)* 無人駕駛的

6) **hack** *(v.)* 駭入

7) **malfunction** *(n.)* 失靈，故障

8) **overcrowded** *(adj.)* 過度擁擠的

Idioms and Phrases

1) **the pros and cons** 優缺點

   • We invited some columnists to comment on **the pros and cons** of the new policy in our newspaper.

   我們邀請了幾位專欄作家在我們的報紙上針對新政策的優缺點寫評論。

2) **send out** 發出⋯

   • Crew members of the fishing boat **sent out** a distress signal when their boat lost power at sea.

   當漁船在海上失去動力時，船員們發出了求救訊號。

The Suffering of Refugees

Types of Refugees

asylum seekers 尋求庇護者

· people who have left their home country and are in the process of applying for asylum and seeking official recognition by the government they intend to stay

internally displaced persons (IDPs) 國內流離失所者

· people who have lost their homes because of conflict, violence, natural disasters, or human rights abuses and are forced to go to another safer place within their country

stateless persons 無國籍人士

· people who are not considered nationals by any country and thus lack legal protection and basic rights such as education and healthcare

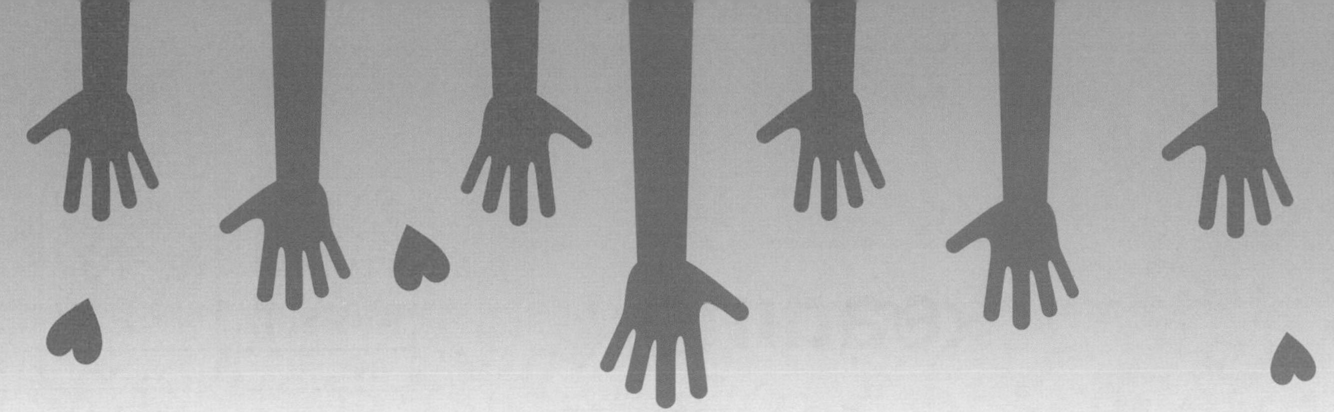

religious or political refugees 宗教或政治難民

- people who flee their homes because of persecution based on their nationality, race, religion, or political affiliation

hunger refugees 飢餓難民

- people who are forced to leave their homes because of unpredictable and changing climates, searching for reliable food sources

war refugees 戰爭難民

- people who escape their homes to seek safety and protection in another country because of armed conflicts or wars
  - * This type of refugee is the most common among all refugee categories.

Fun Facts

#TheUNRefugeeAgency

1. By the end of 2022, which of the following countries had produced the most refugees?
   (A) South Sudan. (B) Afghanistan. (C) Ukraine. (D) Syria.
2. By the end of 2022, which of the following countries hosted the largest number of refugees?
   (A) Colombia. (B) Turkey.
   (C) Germany. (D) United Kingdom.

The presence of refugees, or displaced persons, is not a rare **occurrence**. Throughout history, regular people have borne the brunt of conflicts and wars. Many have thus been **compelled** to **flee** their **homelands**, driven by violence or persecution, in search of safety and sanctuary in foreign countries. Unfortunately, now there are even more refugees in the world.

The growing global refugee crisis can be traced back to the events of 2011 and 2012 in the Middle East and Africa. The "Arab Spring" began as a peaceful pro-democracy movement but eventually **transformed** into terrible wars in Syria and Libya. Additionally, civil

wars have frequently **erupted** in various Islamic countries in the region. These conflicts have resulted in millions of Syrians, Iraqis, and Somalis being uprooted from their homes and becoming refugees.

Many refugees **aspire** to start new lives in Europe or North America. However, traveling to unfamiliar countries is difficult and often dangerous. Some refugees pay large sums of money for transportation that never arrives. Others die in accidents in **transit**. Photos of a little Syrian boy who drowned in the Mediterranean Sea when his family attempted to reach Greece from Turkey shocked and saddened the world. Nevertheless, this **tragedy** also raised greater awareness of the escalating refugee crisis.

▲ Mural of Alan Kurdi, the boy who drowned when seeking shelter, in Frankfurt am Main

Sadly, not all countries welcome refugees with open arms. Anti-immigrant **sentiments** have led some governments to restrict the

政治財經

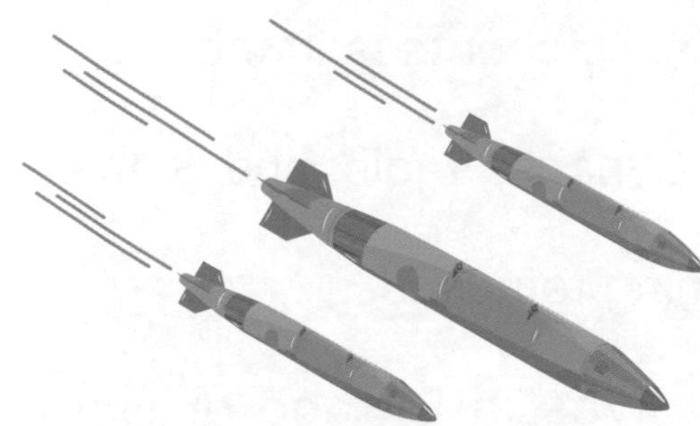

admission of refugees. Some refugees may fall victim to human trafficking. Even countries that welcome refugees often struggle to handle such a **substantial** influx of non-citizens. Many refugees are **confined** to **isolated** refugee camps and have limited contact with the local community. Under these **circumstances**, the **hardships** refugees face often **persist** even after they've resettled in a new country. They may have a hard time adjusting to life in a new location.

Being a refugee is never easy. However, as long as there are wars some people will be forced to leave home in search of peace and safety. That's one reason why the global refugee crisis is growing. Additionally, the refugee crisis also serves as a reminder that the struggle for human rights is an ongoing journey.

混合題

______ 1. What is the author's attitude toward the refugee crisis in the passage? (單選)

文意判斷

(A) Optimistic. (B) Concerned. (C) Delighted. (D) Indifferent.

2. Fill in the blanks with the information contained in the passage about the challenges refugees may face. (填表) 掌握細節、整合資訊

Difficulties After Arrival in a Foreign Country	➔	• Being restricted from entering the country. • Falling prey to (A) ________________________. • Being caged in remote refugee camps.
Difficulties After Settlement		• Having trouble (B) ______________________________________.

______ 3. 請從下列 (A) 到 (F) 中，選出以下圖片可正確對應本文文意的選項。(多選)

文意理解、圖文配對

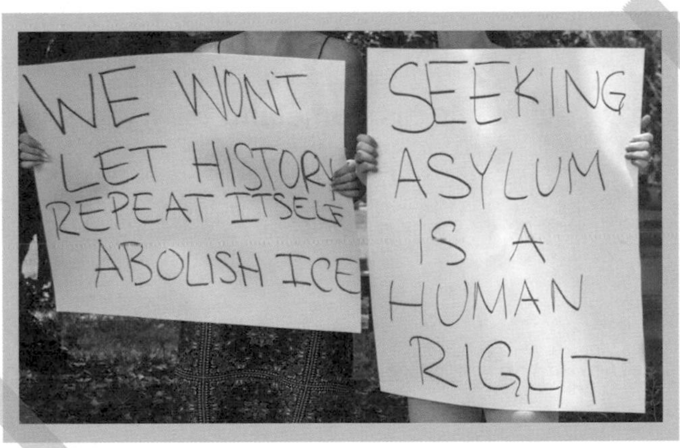

*ICE = (U.S.) Immigration and Customs Enforcement

(A) All refugees should be banned to maintain civic literacy.

(B) Wars worldwide must be stopped to reduce the number of refugees.

(C) It is difficult for a country to handle such an invasion of refugees.

(D) Pro-democracy movements in history were led by the right wing.

(E) Refugees deserve the basic human right to be resettled.

(F) The government should take people's anti-immigrant sentiments seriously.

Words for Production

1) **refugee** *(n.)* 難民 ❹
   - The **refugees** in the camp lack food and clean water.
   營區裡的難民缺乏食物與乾淨的水。

2) **occurrence** *(n.)* 存在 ❻
   - Although the principal insists that bullying isn't a common **occurrence** on campus, there have still been regular reports about it.
   儘管校長堅稱在校園內霸凌不常見，但仍時常有關此事的報導。

3) **compel** *(v.)* 迫使 ❺
   - The couple's constant arguing eventually **compelled** them to seek professional help.
   這對夫婦的不斷爭吵最終迫使他們去尋求專業幫助。

4) **flee** *(v.)* 逃跑 ❹
   - The thief **fled** the scene as soon as the police arrived.
   這名嫌犯在警方抵達現場後就馬上逃跑了。

5) **homeland** *(n.)* 祖國 ❹
   - When the old soldier returned to his **homeland** forty years later, nobody knew who he was.
   當這名老兵四十年後回到故鄉時，沒有人知道他是誰。

6) **transform** *(v.)* 演變 ❹
   - After drinking the Sea Witch's potion, the little mermaid **transformed** into a human.
   在喝下海巫的藥水後，小美人魚變成了人類。

7) **erupt** *(v.)* 爆發 ❹
   - Violence **erupted** after John was insulted by his neighbor.
   John受到他的鄰居侮辱後，爆發了暴力事件。

8) **aspire** *(v.)* 渴望 ❻
   - Many people nowadays **aspire** to fame by posting interesting videos on social media.
   現今許多人渴望透過在社群媒體上發布有趣的影片來成名。

9) **transit** *(n.)* 運輸 ❺

- Rebecca's luggage was damaged during **transit**.
  Rebecca的行李在運輸過程中毀損了。

10) **tragedy** *(n.)* 悲劇 ❹

- The sudden loss of Jack's daughter was an unexpected **tragedy** that left him heartbroken. Jack女兒突然逝世是場意想不到的悲劇，使他心碎不已。

11) **sentiment** *(n.)* 情緒 ❺

- A good ruling party can understand public **sentiment**.
  一個好的執政黨可以理解公眾的情緒。

12) **admission** *(n.)* 准許進入 ❹

- Timmy pretended to be an adult to enter the bar but was still denied **admission**.
  Timmy假裝成大人進入酒吧，但仍被拒絕進入。

13) **substantial** *(adj.)* 大量的 ❺

- Chris was an exceptional real estate agent, and he quickly earned a **substantial** amount of money. Chris是名優秀的房地產經紀人，他快速地賺進了大量的錢財。

14) **confine** *(v.)* 禁閉 ❺

- The kidnapper **confined** the children to the basement.
  這名綁匪將孩子們禁閉在地下室。

15) **isolated** *(adj.)* 偏遠的 ❹

- After retiring, Wesley wants to relocate to an **isolated** area.
  退休後，Wesley想搬到偏僻的地區。

16) **circumstance** *(n.)* 情況 ❹

- Under ordinary **circumstances**, this task should be completed within a week.
  一般情況下，這項任務應該在一週內完成。

17) **hardship** *(n.)* 困難 ❹

- The business failure has brought about financial **hardship** for the store owner.
  生意失敗給店主帶來財務困難。

18) **persist** *(v.)* 持續 ❺

- As long as justice remains unattained, the pain in the mother's heart will **persist**.
  只要正義未得到伸張，這位母親心中的痛將持續存在。

Words for Recognition

1) **displaced** *(adj.)* 流離失所的
2) **persecution** *(n.)* 迫害
3) **sanctuary** *(n.)* 庇護
4) **Syria** *(n.)* 敘利亞 補 官方作the Syrian Arab Republic 敘利亞阿拉伯共和國
5) **Libya** *(n.)* 利比亞
6) **Syrian** *(n.)* 敘利亞人
7) **Iraqi** *(n.)* 伊拉克人
8) **Somali** *(n.)* 索馬利亞人 補 也作Somalian
9) **uproot** *(v.)* 使離開家園
10) **sadden** *(v.)* 使悲傷
11) **escalate** *(v.)* 惡化
12) **anti-immigrant** *(adj.)* 反移民的
13) **influx** *(n.)* 湧入

Idioms and Phrases

1) **bear the brunt of sth** 承受…的衝擊 補 也作take/suffer the brunt of sth

• The tall tree in the forest had **borne the** full **brunt of** the lightning.

森林裡這棵高大的樹承受了閃電的所有衝擊。

2) **welcome sb with open arms** 熱烈地歡迎… 補 也作greet sb with open arms

• The host family **welcomed** the Japanese exchange student **with open arms**.

寄宿家庭熱情地歡迎這名日本籍交換學生。

3) **fall victim to sb/sth** 深受…之害 補 也作fall prey to sb/sth

• The young boy **fell victim to** a rare heart disease and passed away at the age of six.

這個年輕的男孩患上一種罕見的心臟疾病，在六歲時離世了。

4) **have a hard time** 艱難

• Melody **had a hard time** getting over the loss of her beloved pet.

Melody很難從失去心愛寵物的悲傷中走出來。

Is "Cold Hard Cash" Still King?

Cashless Payment Methods

credit card 信用卡

· It refers to a plastic chip card that applies near field communication (NFC) to pay without cold cash. The money spent will have to be paid monthly after purchase.

debit card 簽帳金融卡

· The working process is similar to that of credit cards. However, the debit cards will not work if there are not enough deposits in the user's accounts.

electronic payment 電子支付

· It can include any form of payment that is made electronically, but it mainly refers to paying through specific third-party payment applications with bank accounts.

mobile payment 行動支付

· It refers to a financial transaction conducted through electronic devices. Mobile payment uses NFC, QR codes, or bar codes to pay in a contactless way.

electronic ticket 電子票證

· It is a plastic chip card that can be mainly used as a commuting ticket or membership card.

mobile money transfer 行動銀行轉帳

· It refers to electronic payments made between bank accounts through mobile banking applications.

cryptocurrency wallet 加密貨幣錢包

· It is a kind of digital wallet that allows users to store, send, and receive cryptocurrencies and make digital transactions.

Buy Now, Pay Later (BNPL) 先買後付

· It refers to letting customers pay for the products in installments without using credit cards or having their credit score checked.

Fun Facts *#ForeignCurrency*

Match the correct currency symbol to the country of use.

EUR €	INR ₹	JPY ¥
(1) ________	(2) ________	(3) ________
GBP £	THB ฿	KRW ₩
(4) ________	(5) ________	(6) ________

(A) 

(B) 

(C) 

(D) 

(E) 

(F) 

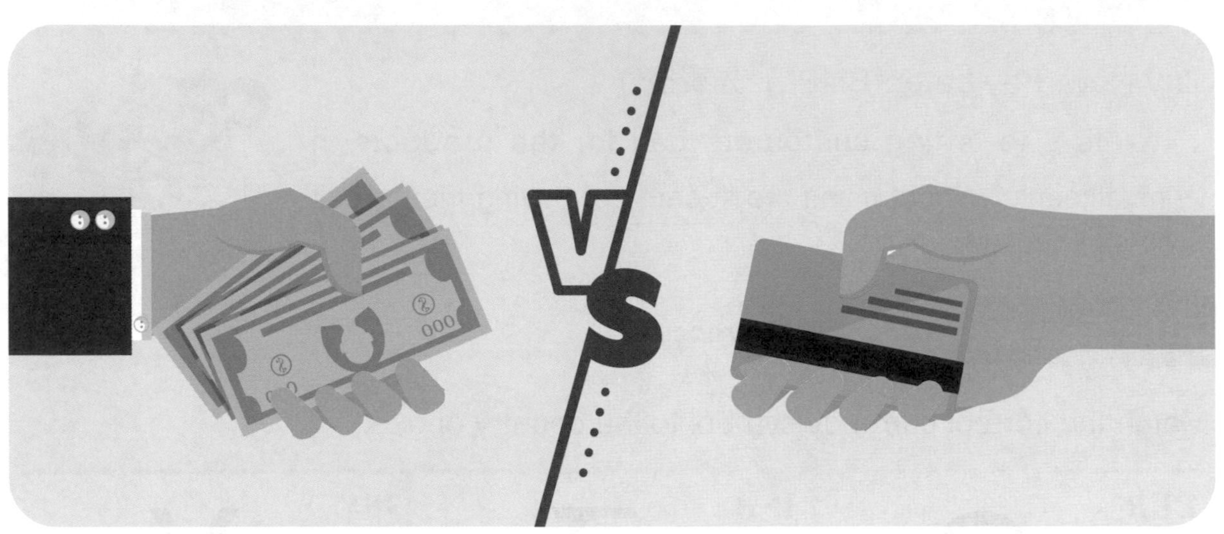

Have you ever heard the term "cold hard cash"? In contrast to checks and credit cards, it means **physical currency** in the form of coins or bills. Many people prefer to receive cash, also known as legal tender, rather than non-cash forms of payment. What's more, during crises or **catastrophes**, credit cards or other **digital** payment methods would likely prove ineffective. **Hence**, as the saying goes, "Cash is king." In fact, some people even hoard cash in their homes because they mistrust banks, and it gives them a sense of security.

Does this **imply** that cashless payment cannot withstand a crisis? Not necessarily. For example, the COVID-19 pandemic inadvertently **accelerated** the adoption of cashless payment methods. This is because physical bills and coins frequently change hands, **potentially facilitating** the **transmission** of disease. As a result, many stores around the world began to embrace credit cards or mobile payment apps. In extreme cases, some businesses **ceased** accepting physical currency. Instead, they went fully cashless, requiring customers to pay with debit cards, credit cards, or online or mobile payment systems.

While the vision of a cashless society is gradually gaining public **acceptance**, cash is here to stay for good reasons. First, cash payments are best for those who value privacy. Besides, there will always be people who have more trust in cash or simply appreciate its convenience. When using cash, people don't have to worry about unpaid bills or **loans** because the **transaction** is done on the spot.

Additionally, some people lack access to the Internet and have difficulty in **adopting** online or mobile payment systems.

Perhaps the **logical** conclusion is that although cash will never again be as **dominant** as before, it will still **retain significance**. After all, having cash on hand in unstable situations is useful.

混合題

______ 1. In which paragraph do the following sentences best belong? (單選) 文意理解、掌握脈絡

"Besides, the COVID-19 lockdown restrictions make people who are stuck at home switch to buying things online. The expansion of e-commerce also drives consumers to digital channels."

(A) Paragraph 1. (B) Paragraph 2. (C) Paragraph 3. (D) Paragraph 4.

2. 請從文章中找出最適當的單詞(word)填入下列句子空格中，並視語法需要做適當的字形變化，使句子語意完整、語法正確，且符合全文文意。(填充) 掌握脈絡、字形變化

Some people encounter challenges in embracing mobile payment systems because they either have no certain device to apply or cannot __________ the Net.

______ 3. 請從下列(A)到(E)中，選出符合本文對people who would prefer using cold hard cash的論述。(多選) 文意理解、掌握細節

(A) John says, "I love it because the process of making payments doesn't involve personal information or details."

(B) Mary states, "I prefer it because this type of payment helps prevent people from overspending or running up debts."

(C) Jane argues, "I favor it because it reduces the risk of crimes when every transaction is digitally tracked."

(D) Jerry says, "Currency in circulation, handled by numerous people over its lifespan, could serve as a medium of transmitting germs and viruses."

(E) Joan states, "Having some cash on hand at any given time gives users a sense of security."

Words for Production

1) **physical** *(adj.)* 實體的 ❹
   - Without **physical** evidence, convicting the murder suspect is very challenging.

     沒有實體證據的話，要將那名謀殺嫌犯定罪是很有挑戰性的。

2) **currency** *(n.)* 貨幣 ❺
   - Mrs. Chen made a fortune by investing in foreign **currencies**.

     陳太太靠著投資外國貨幣賺了一大筆錢。

3) **catastrophe** *(n.)* 災難 ❻
   - If the wildfire had not been controlled in time, it could have become a major environmental **catastrophe**.

     要是那場森林大火沒有及時受到控制，就會變成一場重大的環境災難。

4) **digital** *(adj.)* 數位的 ❹
   - **Digital** technology has changed many aspects of our daily lives, and our dependence on it continues to grow.

     數位科技已改變了我們日常生活的許多面向，而且我們對它的依賴也持續增強。

5) **hence** *(adv.)* 因此 ❺
   - The government imposed tariffs on imported cars. **Hence**, their prices went up.

     政府對進口車輛施加關稅。它們的價格因此上漲。

6) **imply** *(v.)* 暗示 ❹
   - The shell fossils found on the mountaintop **imply** that it was once under the sea.

     在山頂發現的貝類化石暗示該處曾經位於海底。

7) **accelerate** *(v.)* 加快 ❺
   - Local residents believe that this herbal medicine can **accelerate** wound healing.

     當地居民相信這種草藥可以加快傷口癒合。

8) **potentially** *(adv.)* 可能地 ❹

- After the earthquake, the village was declared a **potentially** dangerous zone, and most villagers were evacuated.
  地震之後，該村落被宣告為可能有危險的地區，多數村民也都疏散處置。

9) **facilitate** *(v.)* 促進 ❺

- The new highway system is expected to **facilitate** the growth of the rural economy.
  新建的公路系統可望促進鄉村經濟的成長。

10) **transmission** *(n.)* 傳播 ❺

- Improvement in public hygiene helps prevent disease **transmission**.
  公共衛生的改善有助於防止疾病傳播。

11) **cease** *(v.)* 停止 ❹

- Fast-food restaurants **ceased** providing plastic straws last year.
  速食餐廳去年就停止提供塑膠吸管了。

12) **acceptance** *(n.)* 認可，接納 ❹

- The study shows that the idea of animal rights has gained widespread **acceptance** in developed countries.
  該份研究顯示，動物權的概念在已開發國家受到廣泛認可。

13) **loan** *(n.)* 貸款 ❹

- Cindy took out a **loan** to renovate her house, but now she cannot repay it.
  Cindy辦了一筆貸款來整修房屋，但現在她卻無法償還。

14) **transaction** *(n.)* 交易 ❺

- Thanks to the new trade agreement, commercial **transactions** between the two countries have doubled in the first quarter.
  多虧了新的貿易協定，兩國間的商業交易在第一季就成長了一倍。

15) **adopt** *(v.)* 採用 ❹

- The management has **adopted** a stricter approach to address the problem of low efficiency. 管理階層採用了更嚴格的方式來處理效率低落的問題。

16) **logical** *(adj.)* 合乎邏輯的 ❹

- Since David is a devout Muslim, it is **logical** to assume that he does not drink.
  既然David是一位虔誠的穆斯林，假定他不喝酒是很合理的。

17) **dominant** *(adj.)* 主導的 ❹

- Because of historical reasons, the church plays a **dominant** role in the tribe.
  基於歷史因素，該教會在部落裡具有主導地位。

18) **retain** *(v.)* 保持 ❹

- After a power struggle, Jessica successfully **retained** her position as general manager.
  經過一番權力鬥爭後，Jessica成功保住了總經理的職位。

19) **significance** *(n.)* 重要意義 ❹

- These findings hold great **significance** for the development of artificial intelligence.
  這些發現對於人工智慧的研發具有重大意義。

Words for Recognition

1) **legal tender** *(n.)* 法定貨幣

2) **ineffective** *(adj.)* 無效的

3) **hoard** *(v.)* 囤積

4) **mistrust** *(v.)* 不信任

5) **withstand** *(v.)* 承受

6) **inadvertently** *(adv.)* 無意地

7) **adoption** *(n.)* 採用

8) **debit card** *(n.)* 簽帳金融卡

9) **unpaid** *(adj.)* 未支付的

Idioms and Phrases

1) **change hands** 轉手

• The haunted mansion has **changed hands** many times and is now owned by a retired doctor.

那座鬧鬼的豪宅經過多次轉手，現在的屋主是一位退休醫師。

2) **on the spot** 當場，立即

• After an interview with the managing team, Lisa got the job offer **on the spot**.

在與管理團隊面談後，Lisa當場就錄取了。

3) **after all** 畢竟

• I think you should take a break. **After all**, nothing is more important than your health.

我想你應該休息一下。畢竟，沒有什麼是比健康更重要的。

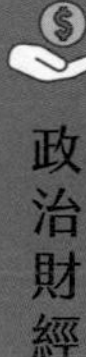

Will Taiwan Benefit from the U.S.-China Trade War?

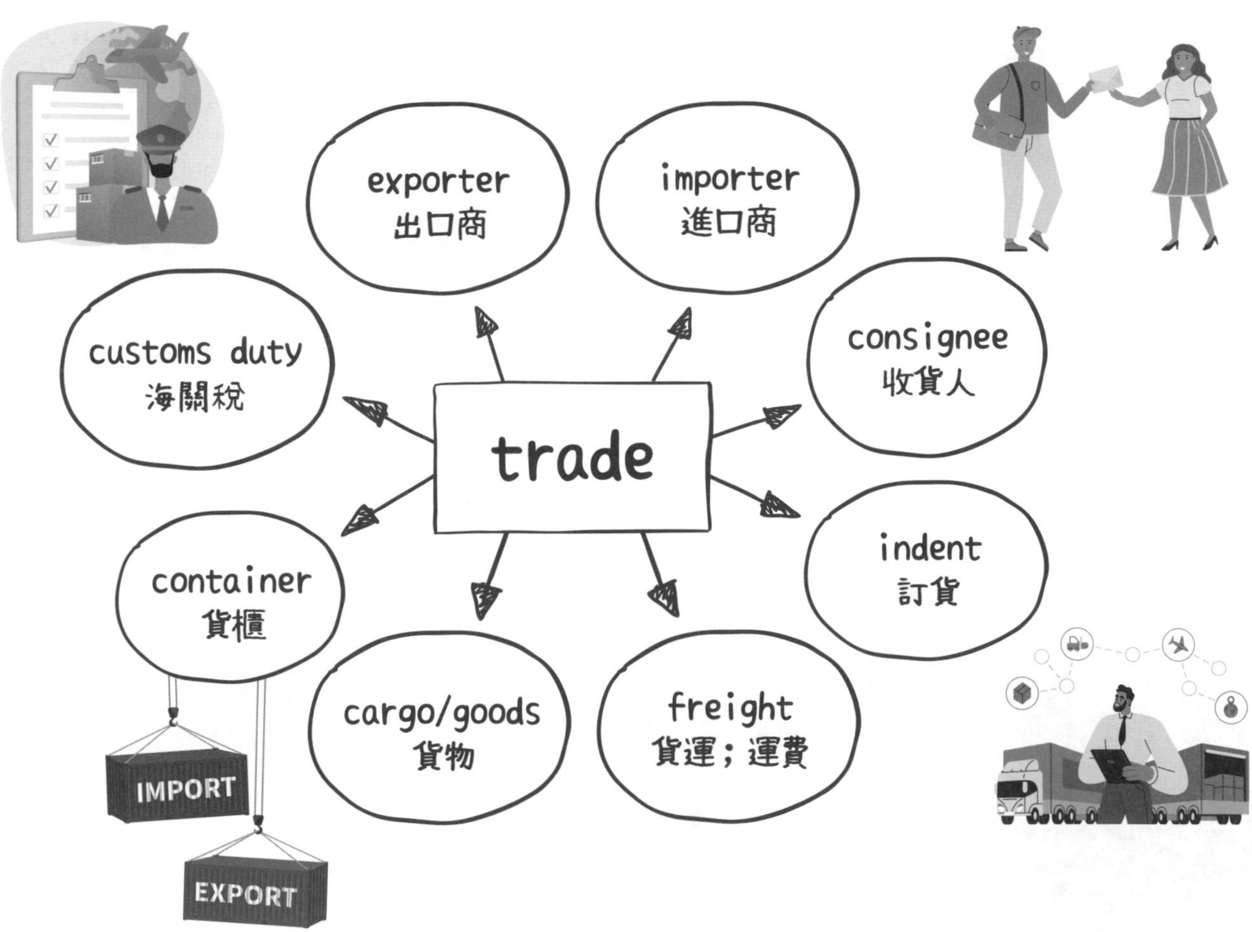

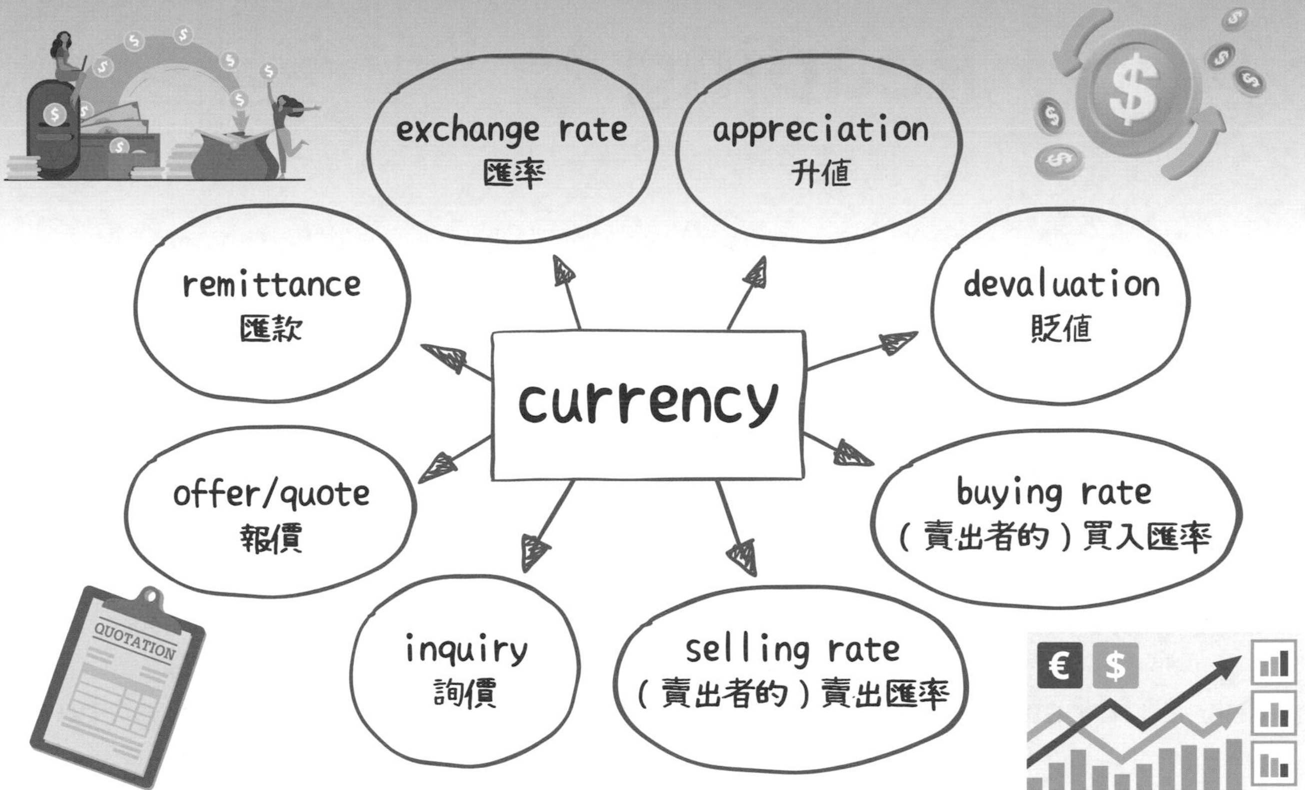

Fun Facts

#StockMarket

Match the animals to their commonly represented market conditions.

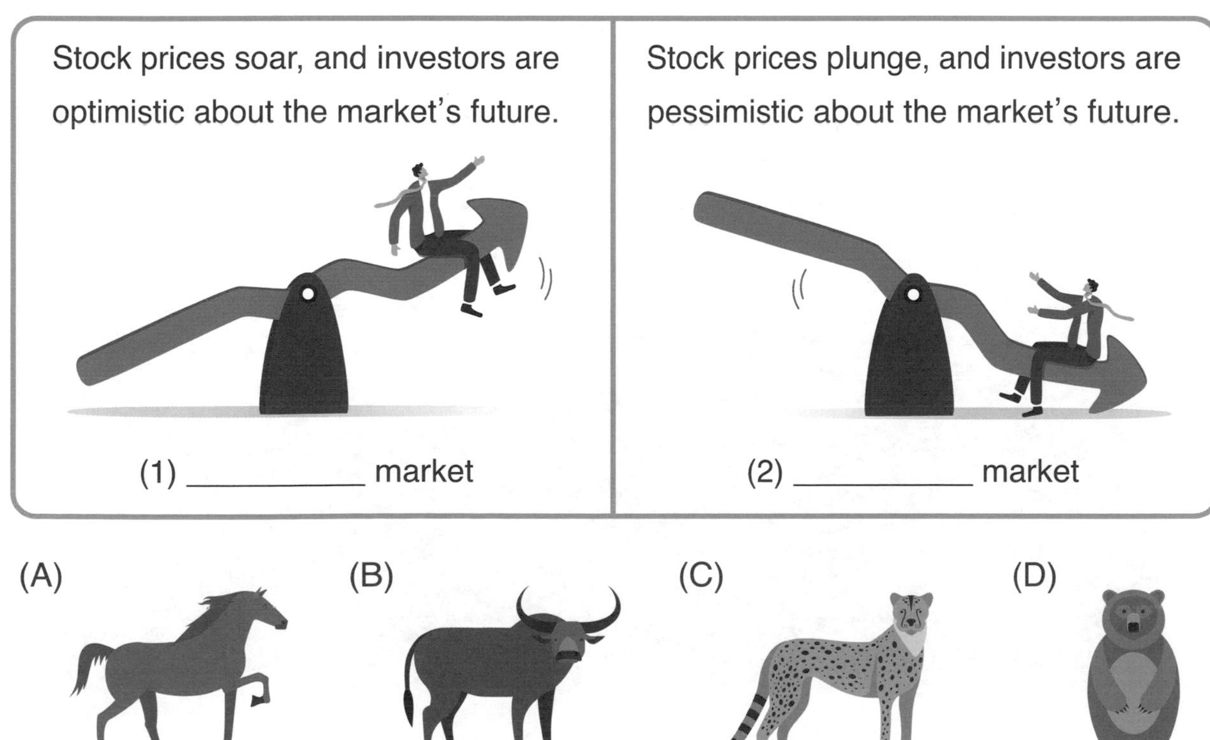

Stock prices soar, and investors are optimistic about the market's future.
(1) ____________ market
Stock prices plunge, and investors are pessimistic about the market's future.
(2) ____________ market
(A)
(B)
(C)
(D)

The United States and China **boast** the world's most **formidable economies**. Whatever happens between these two superpowers **inevitably** impacts the rest of the world. The trade war which began in July 2018 between these two countries could be called a "**clash** of the titans."

Taiwan, a small island country, has been caught between these two fighting giants. The country has been a close trading partner of the U.S. and China for many years and has **prospered** by engaging in manufacturing and exporting products to both countries. Some people

say that Taiwan will be **crushed** in this trade war while others claim that Taiwan could actually end up **reaping** some benefits.

In the 1990s, many Taiwanese companies moved their manufacturing to China to capitalize on its cheaper labor costs. However, with the rise in Chinese labor costs and higher U.S. tariffs on goods imported from China because of the trade war, manufacturing in China has become **progressively** more expensive. As a result, a number of Taiwanese companies have **opted** to move their factories back to Taiwan, creating potential **economic** growth and job opportunities in the country. Also, a "Welcome Back Action Plan" **initiated** by Taiwan's Ministry of Economic Affairs has **rewarded** returning companies with **incentives** such as grants-in-aid, low-interest bank loans, and tax **consultations**.

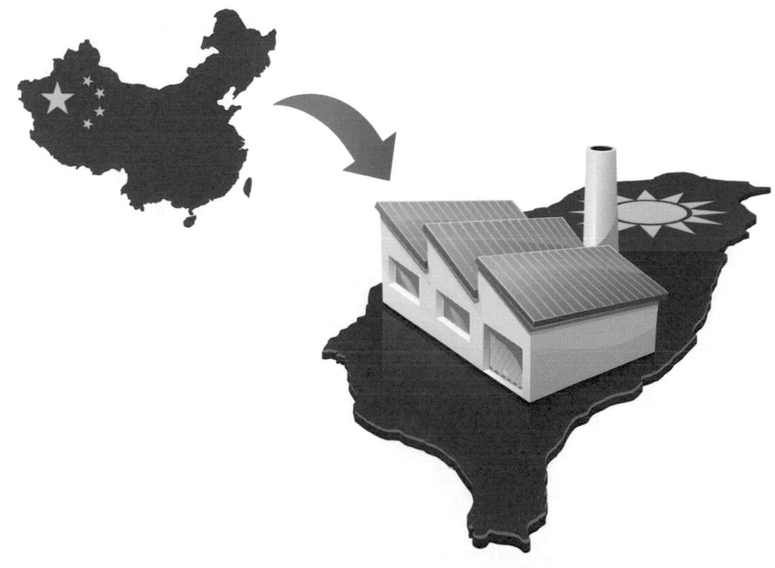

Moreover, some multinational companies have also chosen to **invest** in Taiwan because of its more **robust** protection of **intellectual** property rights. Google, for instance, has built Asia's largest R & D center in Taiwan. Other major foreign companies, such as Microsoft, Amazon, Apple, and IBM, plan to expand their activities in Taiwan as it offers greater freedom from worries over the security of their data centers.

It's hoped that the trade war between the U.S. and China can be **resolved** quickly and satisfactorily. In the meantime, **regardless** of how the situation develops, Taiwan should **endeavor** to benefit from this "dangerous opportunity."

混合題

______ 1. According to the passage, which of the following graphs best describes the changes in the number of Taiwanese factories operating in China over the years? (單選) 圖表判讀

(A)

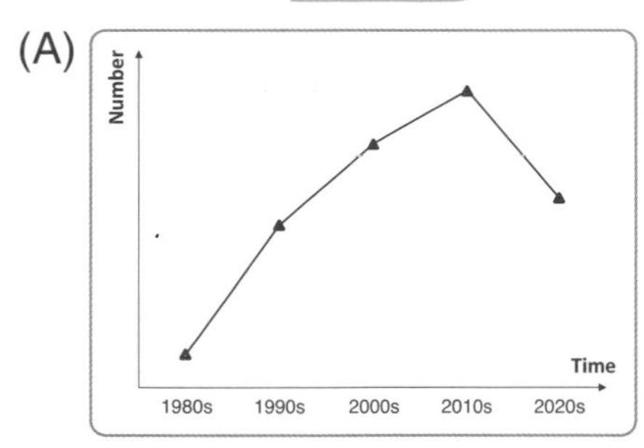

(B)

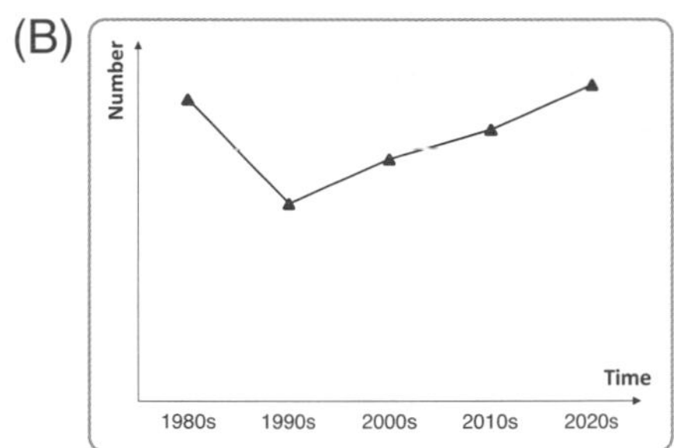

(C)

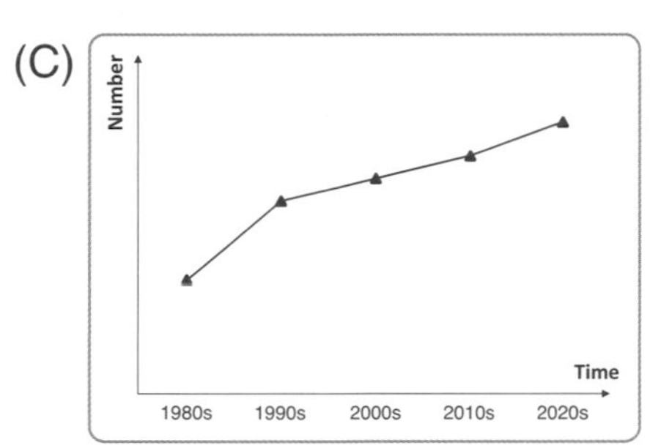

(D)

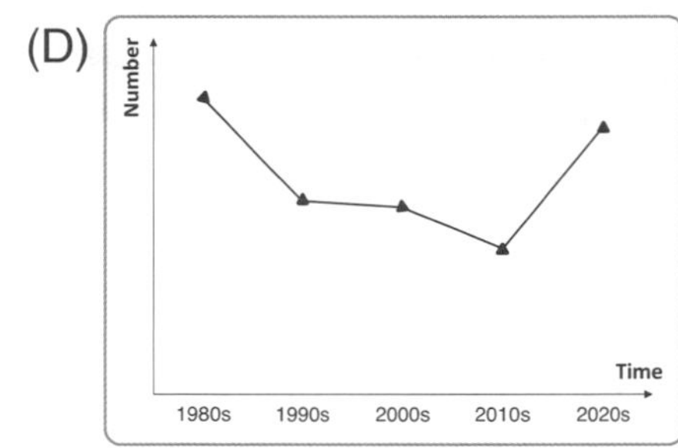

______ 2. 請從下列(A)到(E)中，選出本文中為「意見」，而非「事實」的選項。(多選) 文意理解、掌握細節

(A) The manufacturing expenses in China have increased recently.

(B) Taiwan could end up benefiting from the clash between the two titans.

(C) Google has built its largest research and development center in Asia in Taiwan.

(D) Taiwan's government launched a "Welcome Back Action Plan" to attract businesses back home.

(E) Some individuals claimed that Taiwan would be crushed in the trade dispute.

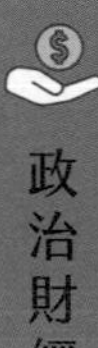

3. Fill in the blanks with the information contained in the passage about why Taiwanese and multinational companies move to Taiwan. (填表) 掌握細節、整合資訊

Why are Taiwanese companies sailing home?
➔ because of the increased (1) ________ costs in China
➔ because the U.S. set high (2) ________ on goods imported from China
Why do multinational companies come to invest in Taiwan?
➔ because of the stronger (3) ________ of intellectual property rights in Taiwan
➔ because the data (4) ________ in Taiwan is higher than in China

Words for Production

1) **boast** *(v.)* 擁有 (值得自豪的東西) ❹

• The township **boasts** the country's best natural resources.

這小鎮擁有全國最佳的自然資源。

2) **formidable** *(adj.)* 令人敬畏的 ❻

• In the movie, Sabrina was a **formidable** figure who controlled the entire magic world.

在電影中，掌管整個魔法世界的Sabrina是個令人敬畏的人物。

3) **economy** *(n.)* 經濟 ❹

• The French **economy** mainly relies on tourism and luxury goods.

法國經濟主要依賴旅遊業和奢侈品。

4) **inevitably** *(adv.)* 不可避免地，必然地 ❺

• Candidates who don't understand the needs of voters will **inevitably** lose the election. 不了解選民需求的候選人必然會輸掉選舉。

5) **clash** *(n.)* 鬥爭，衝突 ❹

• The **clash** of thunder and lightning signaled the onset of a powerful storm.

雷聲與閃電交響，示意著一場強大風暴的來臨。

6) **prosper** *(v.)* 繁榮 ❹

• The village began to **prosper** as people started visiting its stunning waterfalls.

這村落因為人們開始造訪它美麗的瀑布而開始繁榮起來。

7) **crush** *(v.)* 徹底擊垮 ❹

• The fleet admiral commanded the naval forces to **crush** the enemy troops.

這名海軍元帥指揮海軍部隊要徹底擊垮敵軍。

8) **reap** *(v.)* 收獲 ❻

• With the prevalence of the #MeToo movement, more and more sexual offenders are now **reaping** what they have sown.

隨著#MeToo運動的盛行，越來越多的性犯罪者正在自食其果。

9) **progressively** *(adv.)* 逐漸地 ❺

• Liam's heart condition has **progressively** worsened day by day.

Liam的心臟狀況每天逐漸惡化。

10) **opt** *(v.)* 選擇 ❺

• Penelope **opted** to go fishing rather than go shopping last weekend.

Penelope上週末選擇去釣魚，而不是去購物。

11) **economic** *(adj.)* 經濟的 ❹

• From an **economic** perspective, the proposal lacks profitability.

從經濟角度來看，這項提案缺乏獲利能力。

12) **initiate** *(v.)* 開始 ❺

• The company **initiated** a new project to develop potential customers.

這間公司開始一項新專案以開發潛在客戶。

13) **reward** *(v.)* 獎賞 ❹

• Hannah **rewarded** her dog with a treat for its good behavior.

Hannah用零食獎勵她狗狗的好表現。

14) **incentive** *(n.)* 激勵措施 ❺

- Generous year-end bonuses give employees **incentives** to improve their work performance. 豐厚的年終獎金能夠做為員工提高績效的激勵措施。

15) **consultation** *(n.)* 諮詢 ❺

- Austin offers medical **consultations** for women experiencing prenatal depression in the hospital. Austin在醫院為患有產前憂鬱症的女性提供醫療諮詢。

16) **invest** *(v.)* 投資 ❹

- The mayor has **invested** a substantial amount of money in the aquarium.
市長為水族館投資了大量資金。

17) **robust** *(adj.)* 穩固的 ❻

- The **robust** antivirus software effectively safeguards your computer against malware. 這款強大的防毒軟體有效地保護你的電腦免受惡意軟體的侵害。

18) **intellectual** *(adj.)* 智力的 ❹

- The book focuses on the **intellectual** development of infants.
這本書著重在嬰兒的智力發展。

19) **resolve** *(v.)* 解決 ❹

- The government is striving to **resolve** the ongoing political crisis.
該政府正在努力解決當前的政治危機。

20) **regardless** *(adv.)* 無論如何，不顧⋯ ❺

- Many people were fooled into taking illegal jobs in Southeast Asia **regardless** of the warning from the police.
許多人不顧警方的警告，還是被騙去東南亞從事違法工作。

21) **endeavor** *(v.)* 努力 ❻

- Since my youth, my parents have **endeavored** to teach me to be an upright person.
我的父母從我小時就努力教導我成為一個正直的人。

Words for Recognition

1) **superpower** *(n.)* 超級強權

2) **titan** *(n.)* 強者，巨人

3) **Taiwanese** *(adj.)* 臺灣的

4) **tariff** *(n.)* 關稅

5) **grant-in-aid** *(n.)* 補助金

6) **multinational** *(adj.)* 跨國的

7) **R & D** *(n.)* 研究與開發　補 為research and development的縮寫

Idioms and Phrases

1) **end up** 最終(成為…)

- If Robert continues to ignore his doctor's advice, he'll **end up** in the hospital.

  如果Robert繼續忽視他醫生的建議，他最終會進醫院的。

2) **capitalize on** 從…中獲利

- The influencer **capitalized on** his fame by promoting products to his fans.

  該網紅利用自己的名氣向粉絲推銷產品。

3) **in the meantime** 在此期間，與此同時

- Olivia was attending an online meeting. **In the meantime**, Benjamin was taking a nap.

  Olivia正在參加線上會議。在此期間，Benjamin正在小睡。

國家圖書館出版品預行編目資料

讀力報導：看新聞學英文／朱嬿婷,李秀玲,巫沂璇編著.——初版一刷.——臺北市：三民，2023
面； 公分

ISBN 978-957-14-7700-8（平裝）
1. 新聞英文 2. 讀本

805.18 112014614

讀力報導：看新聞學英文

編 著 者	朱嬿婷 李秀玲 巫沂璇
審 閱 者	Graeme Todd 蘇文賢 葉秋菊
責任編輯	陳妍妍
美術編輯	陳欣妤
發 行 人	劉振強
出 版 者	三民書局股份有限公司
地 址	臺北市復興北路 386 號 (復北門市) 臺北市重慶南路一段 61 號 (重南門市)
電 話	(02)25006600
網 址	三民網路書店 https://www.sanmin.com.tw
出版日期	初版一刷 2023 年 11 月
書籍編號	S872360
I S B N	978-957-14-7700-8

三民書局

Learn ENGLISH with NEWS

讀力報導：看新聞學英文

朱嫵婷、李秀玲、巫沂璇　編著
Graeme Todd、蘇文賢、葉秋菊　審訂

解析本

Global News,
Global Views.

三民書局

Contents

Japanese Collectors of Cambodian Art Do the Right Thing
日本的柬埔寨藝術品收藏家做了正確的事

Fun Facts

▶ 解答

A、C、E

▶ 小故事

下列哪三項關於柬埔寨的敘述是正確的？

(A) 柬埔寨是世界上擁有最多勞斯萊斯汽車的國家。

(B) 在柬埔寨最多人信奉的宗教是伊斯蘭教。

(C) 參觀吳哥窟的遊客需著有袖上衣及過膝長裙或長褲。

(D) 柬埔寨的麥當勞是世界上提供最便宜食物的麥當勞。

(E) 柬埔寨人認為左手不潔，右手才乾淨。

✎ 正確：

(A) 柬埔寨雖目前屬低開發國家，卻是世界上擁有最多勞斯萊斯的地方。據說首都金邊 (Phnom Penh) 每年買進的勞斯萊斯的比例高達該品牌全球銷量的 30%！

(C) 根據當地管理局規定，為了保護文化古蹟的莊嚴，進入吳哥窟必須穿著有袖上衣、過膝的長褲或長裙，不符規定者將無法進入吳哥窟。

(E) 柬埔寨人認為左手是不潔的，因此在當地用左手拿東西或食物可能會被視為是不禮貌的表現。另外，他們也認為頭部是人最神聖的部位，因此不應隨意撫摸小孩的頭部。

錯誤：

(B) 在柬埔寨最多人信仰的是佛教。

(D) 由於當地飲食習慣更傾向於米飯和湯，加上需花費相當高額才能取得美國速食品牌的經營權，因此麥當勞截至 2023 年為止，尚未進駐過柬埔寨。

Reading

柬埔寨在 1970 年代經歷了血腥內戰，使國家陷入混亂之中。紅色高棉最終奪取政權並處決了國內許多菁英分子。還有許多人被送進戰俘集中營接受再教育。剩下的人則是被迫參加鄉村的大規模公共勞動工程。

在這段黑暗時期，數不盡的柬埔寨文物下落不明。佛像以及其他雕刻品和藝術品從廟裡被偷走並出售以謀取利潤。這些被盜取的文化瑰寶大多被走私出國，落入像是高桑富美子和她丈夫的私人藝術收藏家手中。這些年來，這對日本夫婦購入近百件柬埔寨文物並將它們陳列在家中。他們雖然很欣賞這些物品，但也感到愧疚。他們知道這些藝術品極有可能是被偷來的，而也就是為何他們決定在 2019 年把這些物品歸還給柬埔寨國家博物館的原因。

該博物館對自願做出正確之事並歸還他們所擁有的雕像、瓶罐和珠寶的高桑夫婦表示感謝。這些古物可以追溯回 8 至 14 世紀且對柬埔寨人來說無疑是無價之寶。柬埔寨已重獲和平與繁榮，其政府非常想要恢復其遺落的文化遺產。除了表達感謝，該國的文化藝術部希望其他收藏家能遵循柬埔寨法律、國際協議與高桑家族樹立的榜樣，歸還他們買走的瑰寶。如此一來，這些瑰寶或許得以受到大家重視與欣賞。

混合題

▶ 解答

1. (A) execution；(B) possess
2. (A) ③；(B) ②　3. A

▶ 解析

1. 紅色高棉奪權之後，該國的菁英分子面臨 **(A) 處決 (execution)**，還有許多人被送進戰俘集中營接受再教育。
東埔寨政府希望會有更多像高桑家族的收藏家願意放棄他們 **(B) 持有 (possess)** 瑰寶的權利，並將它們歸還給柬埔寨。
✎ 本題測驗能否依據上下文脈絡，從指定的段落中選出一個單詞，並運用語法知識做適當字形變化。根據第一段第二句提及紅色高棉奪權後，許多菁英分子被「處決」，可知 (A) 應選擇該句的動詞 execute (處決)，並根據本題空格在動詞 faced 後，將之變化成名詞 execution；根據第三段第一句提及高桑夫婦將他們「擁有」的瑰寶歸還給柬埔寨政府，可知 (B) 應選擇該句的名詞 possession (持有)，並根據本題空格在介系詞 to 後，將之變化成動詞 possess。

2. 根據本文配對正確的背景與結果。

背景	結果
柬埔寨因內戰而陷入混亂。	許多柬埔寨國民被送進戰俘集中營。
竊賊從許多柬埔寨寺廟中偷走了文化瑰寶。	(A) ③
(B) ②	他們將柬埔寨丟失的寶藏歸還給該國博物館。

① 柬埔寨國民被迫販賣文化瑰寶給其他國家以牟利。
② 日本藝術收藏家因知道他們的收藏品是從柬埔寨偷來的而感到愧疚。
③ 大部分的文物被走私出國並被藝術收藏家收購。
✎ 本題測驗能否掌握文章細節並依據上下文分析句子間正確的背景與結果。空格 (A) 可從第二段第三句找到作答線索「被竊取的文物大多被走私出國並落入私人藝術收藏家手中」，故選③。空格 (B) 可從第二段最後兩句找到作答線索「日本收藏家因為知道大部分的文物是從物主那被偷來的而感到愧疚，最終決定將文物歸還給柬埔寨國家博物館」，故選②。

3. 根據本文，下列何者最能表達柬埔寨政府對日本藝術品收藏家的態度？
(A) 感激的。　(B) 不認同的。
(C) 中立的。　(D) 不感興趣的。
✎ 本題測驗引申推論，依據文意推論指定對象態度。由文章最後兩句可看出柬埔寨政府表達感謝，並希望日本藝術收藏家的模範能帶來正面效應，故選 (A)。

The Olympic Games 奧運

Fun Facts

▶ 解答

1. C　2. B

▶ 小故事

1. 奧林匹克五環的五個顏色代表的是什麼？
   (A) 五行理論。　(B) 五大洋。
   (C) 五大洲。　(D) 一週五天。
   ✎ 奧林匹克五環是五個互扣的環圈，代表著世界五大洲：亞洲、非洲、歐洲、美洲和大洋洲，象徵全世界的運動員以公正、坦率的比賽和友好的精神在奧運上相見，即「五大洲的團結」。顏色自左至右為藍、黃、黑、綠、紅，底色為象徵和平的白色。
2. 目前夏季奧運跟冬季奧運的舉辦區間是多久呢？
   (A) 1 年。　**(B) 2 年。**
   (C) 3 年。　(D) 4 年。
   ✎ 目前夏季奧運與冬季奧運會以 2 年為相隔，並在不同國家舉行。

夏季奧運與冬季奧運舉辦的演變史▼

最早期	皆 4 年一次、同年、同一國家
1928 年起	皆 4 年一次、同年、不同國家
1994 年起	夏奧 (4 年一次)、 冬奧 (2 年一次)、不同國家

Reading

奧運是世上最重要的體育賽事之一。它們將來自不同國家的最優秀運動員齊聚一堂參賽，希望能贏得獎牌。各國也爭取主辦奧運的榮耀，因為這場賽事能吸引全球目光。國際奧林匹克委員會對奧運主辦城市擁有最終決定權。

主辦城市以激勵人心的儀式開幕奧運。接著，體育競賽就開始了。運動員參加各個項目，包括短跑、接力賽、馬拉松、跳遠、角力。

觀眾們迫不及待地想看運動員們表演。奧運傳奇選手能再多拿幾面獎牌，還是被他們的年輕對手擊敗呢？一些運動員在每次得勝後都會擺出招牌動作。其他人可能一開始較慢進入狀態，但最終以奪得金牌、銀牌或銅牌收場。還有些人表現出色，在團體和個人賽都取得了勝利，為奧運創造了更多亮點。另一個關注焦點是各國獎牌總數爭霸戰。人們很有興趣哪一個國家贏得最多獎牌。

最後，在閉幕式上，奧運聖火被熄滅。緊接著，下屆奧運的主辦國家正緊鑼密鼓地做好準備，目的是為了追上今年才剛剛正式落幕的奧運的妙趣橫生和緊張刺激。通常，奧運每四年辦一次，只有世界大戰和新冠肺炎疫情造成少數例外。

總而言之，奧運促進國與國之間和平友好的競爭精神。最重要的不是獲勝，而是參與。

混合題

▶ 解答

1. A　2. A、D
3. (A) four years；(B) individual

▶ 解析

1. 根據本文，下列哪一個選項最能表達第三段中「其他人可能一開始比較慢進入狀態，但最終以奪得金牌、銀牌或銅牌收場」？
   (A) 大橡樹都由小橡果長成。
   (B) 黑暗中總有一線光明。
   (C) 江山易改，本性難移。
   (D) 遲做總比不做好。
   本題測驗引申推論，依據文意推論符合情境敘述之選項。「大橡樹都由小橡果長成」這句諺語其實就是「萬丈高樓平地起」之意，比喻萬事都是從基礎做起，然後逐漸發展而成，最適合用來呼應文意「一開始發展得比較慢，但最終奪得獎牌」，故選 (A)。

2. 請從下列 (A) 到 (F) 中，根據文章內容選出 對 countries all over the world 和 the audience of the Olympics 都正確的選項。
   (A) 希望贏得獎牌。
   (B) 相爭舉辦奧運。
   (C) 贊助運動員的個人特色。
   (D) 參與以實現和平精神。
   (E) 打敗競爭國家的觀眾。
   (F) 決定哪一個城市可以舉辦奧運。
   本題測驗能否掌握文章細節與關係，作答線索在全文內容。(A) 可從第一段第一句與第三段第一句得知，各國與其觀眾都希望代表自己國家的運動員能贏得獎牌，而 (D) 可從最後一段得知，故選 (A)、(D)。

3. 將文章內提及有關奧運的資訊填入空格中。

與奧運有關的事實

- 世界上的城市彼此競爭主辦奧運的權利。
- 奧運於每 **(A)** **四年 (four years)** 舉辦。
- 運動員可以參與團隊與 **(B)** **個人 (individual)** 競賽。
- 奧運聖火的熄滅代表著奧運的閉幕。

本題測驗能否掌握並歸納文章細節訊息。(A) 可從第四段第三句找到作答線索「奧運每四年舉辦」，故 (A) 答案為 four years。(B) 可從第三段倒數第三句找到作答線索「運動員可在團隊與個人競賽皆贏得獎牌」，故 (B) 答案為 individual。

Learn to Identify Facts and Fake News 學會辨別事實與假新聞

Fun Facts

▶ 解答

B

▶ 小故事

「媒體素養」是現代人一項重要的技能。根據歐盟的報告，下列哪些能力被認為是媒體素養的重要組成部分？

① 行動 / 能動	⑤ 宣傳
② 檢查和認證	⑥ 近用
③ 反思	⑦ 挑戰
④ 創造	⑧ 分析和評估

(A) ①，②，③，④，⑤

(B) ①，③，④，⑥，⑧

(C) ①，④，⑤，⑦，⑧

媒體素養又稱媒體識讀，是指人們對媒體的理解和辨別能力，讓人們能夠有效地且聰明地解讀其所傳達的訊息。

根據歐盟 2018 年公布的《歐洲的媒體素養教學：中小學教育有效實踐的證據》報告，提出以下 5 種媒體素養基本能力框架。

(1) 近用 (access)：熟練地瀏覽、搜尋、過濾與使用媒體和資訊，並與他人共享適當且有用的資訊。

(2) 分析和評估 (analysis and evaluation)：用批判思維分析訊息，以辨別事實與意見，同時評估訊息潛在的影響或後果。

(3) 創造 (creation)：認識傳播目標、對象及技巧，並創作媒體內容以表達個人觀點。

(4) 反思 (reflection)：落實社會責任和倫理原則，認識並管理自己的媒體生活。

(5) 行動 / 能動 (action/agency)：透過媒體來參與社會，行使發言權，成為具備民主價值和態度的積極公民。

即是⑥、⑧、④、③、①，故選 (B)。

Reading

現今，新聞使用越來越多聳動的頭條來引誘人們前往閱讀。然而，它們很多都是「假新聞」，引人注目卻不真實的報導。這些假新聞在報刊、電視、社群媒體，甚至在聊天應用程式上都可以找到。

由於網路使用的便利，人們每天都接收到大量資訊。假消息和謠言如野火般地蔓延開來，影響人們的看法並引起誤解。前英國廣播公司新聞部總監 James Harding 說：「現在的訊息比以往都多，有些是舊聞。有些真假參半。有些則是徹頭徹尾的謊言。當你檢視那些訊息來源時，要辨識何者為真、何者為假比過去更困難了。」因此，過濾假訊息和捏造出來的新聞是有必要的，以避免受到矇騙。

許多人已經意識到處理假新聞的重要性，並開始採取行動。例如，臺灣政府設立了一間查核事實的辦公室來辨認虛假的新聞報導，並加以阻絕。英國廣播公司 (BBC) 也發起了一項教育計畫，目標是教導學生如何分辨新聞報導的真假。

其實，人們可以利用某些技能來辨認假新聞。首先，確認消息來源。名譽良好的來源比較可靠。接下來，評估調性。一個誇大其詞或使用粗鄙文字批判某事的報導，很可能就不是真實的。

假新聞也會利用人們的無知。因此，人們應該要讓自己具備更好的新聞過濾能力，並明智選擇他們吸取的資訊。這麼一來，他們就能更輕易地區分真相與謊言！

混合題

▶ 解答

1. C　2. (A) fact-checking office；(B) educational program
3. (A) rely；(B) equipped/able

▶ 解析

1. 根據本文，下列敘述何者正確？
   (A) 英國廣播公司新聞部不相信報紙上的新聞。
   (B) 誇大的內容是好新聞報導的必要條件。
   (C) 有引人注目和令人吃驚標題的新聞很有可能會被辨認為假新聞。
   (D) 新聞媒體不會在社群媒體或電視中發布假新聞。

   本題測驗能否掌握文章細節，可從第一段前兩句得知「有著聳動頭條的報導很多都是假新聞」，故選 (C)。(A) 文中並未提及報紙以及英國廣播公司新聞部不相信報紙；(B) 可從全文對假新聞的描述判斷，誇大的敘述可能有假新聞之嫌，而非構成好報導的必要條件；(D) 可從第一段最後一句「假新聞在報刊、電視、社群媒體，甚至在聊天應用程式上都可以找到」得知，故 (A)、(B)、(D) 不可選。

2. 根據本文資訊，分別將臺灣與英國對假新聞所做的反應填入下表。

國家	對假新聞所做的反應
臺灣	設立 **(A) 查核事實的辦公室 (fact-checking office)**
英國	發起 **(B) 教育計畫 (educational program)**

   本題測驗能否掌握文章細節，作答線索在第三段。(A) 可從第二句得知「臺灣政府設立了一間查核事實的辦公室來辨認虛假的新聞報導」，故 (A) 答案為 fact-checking office。(B) 可從第三句得知「英國廣播公司決定發起一項教育計畫，目標是教導學生如何分辨新聞的真假」，故 (B) 答案為 educational program。

3. 對人們來說 **(A) 依賴 (rely)** 來源可信的資訊是很重要的。
   人們應該要 **(B) 能夠 (equipped/able)** 分辨他們所獲得的資訊是否真實。

   本題測驗能否依據上下文脈絡，從指定的段落中選出一個單詞，並運用語法知識做適當字形變化。(A) 可選擇第四段第二句的形容詞 reliable (可靠的)，並根據本題空格在不定詞 to 後與介系詞 on 前，將之變化成動詞 rely。(B) 可選擇第五段第二句的動詞 equip (具備…)，而此處做「使能夠」之意，並根據本題被動式時態，改為過去分詞 equipped；也可選擇第五段第二句的名詞 ability (能力)，並根據本題空格在 be 動詞之後，變化成形容詞 able。

The Rise of Phubbing—How Are Smartphones Affecting People? 低頭滑手機越見普遍——智慧型手機如何影響人們？

Fun Facts

▶解答

1. B　2. A

▶　小故事

1. 哪間公司發明了世界上第一支手機？
   (A) Nokia.　　　　**(B) Motorola.**
   (C) Sony Ericsson. (D) BlackBerry.
   ✎世界上第一支手機是由 Motorola 公司於 1973 年發表的 DynaTAC 8000X，發明人 Martin Cooper 僅用短短三個月就完成開發，也因此被稱為手機之父。Martin Cooper 在發表會現場撥出電話打給競爭對手，完成了該發明第一次的無線通話。此外，世界上第一支掀蓋手機也是由 Motorola 公司所發行的。

◀手機之父 Martin Cooper 手裡拿著由他發明的世界第一支手機——DynaTAC 8000X

2. 3C 產品的 3C 不包含下列何者？
   (A) 行動電話。
   (B) 通訊。
   (C) 消費性電子產品。
   (D) 電腦。
   ✎3C 是對電腦與其週邊商品、通訊以及消費性電子產品這三種家用電器的代稱，不包含行動電話，故選 (A)。

Reading

在這個現代世界，「低頭滑手機」(phubbing) 隨時都在發生。phubbing 這個詞結合了「手機」(phone) 和「不理睬人」(snubbing)，意思是只顧盯著自己的智慧型手機而無視他人。做這行為的人就是所謂的「低頭族」(phubbers)。我們現在越來越常在各處看到低頭族，甚至在餐廳和咖啡廳等地方也是如此。現今，親朋好友經常寂靜地坐在一起，因為大家都不自覺地盯著自己的手機。

❶許多人已經太習慣低頭滑手機，以至於他們認為這是正常現象，而不認為這是有問題的。❷然而，一些觀察家認為低頭滑手機是反社會行為，並相信它可能代表我們所知的禮貌與文明就此告終。❸全球各地的教師也都注意到學生行為的變化。❹過去，大多數學生上課和聽講時會集中注意力。❺但現在，即使是勤奮的學生也會時不時想偷瞄一眼智慧型手機。❻這不僅導致學習成績不佳，也顯得很不尊重老師。

除此之外，低頭滑手機可能會對人際關係產生負面影響。雖然智慧型手機是與他人保持聯繫的絕佳方法，但低頭族會因此容易忽視身邊的人，並逐漸與他們疏遠。

目不轉睛地盯著螢幕數個小時也會導致健康問題，例如肩頸和上背部僵硬和疼痛。頭痛、視力模糊和眼睛乾澀也是與長時間盯著螢幕相關的常見問題。此外，手指和拇指可能會發炎甚至抽筋，這會帶來疼痛並使低頭族無法輕易移動。

低頭滑手機已成為要仔細思考的問題。與其讓智慧型手機對我們施加控制，與其讓智慧型手機控制我們，對智慧型手機的使用量施加控制才是至關重要的。藉由減少螢幕使用時間，我們能更關心周圍的人並享受更好的生活。

混合題

▶ 解答

1. cramp/Cramp.　2. ❶
3. (A) behavior；(B) alienated；(C) vision

▶ 解析

1. 本文中的哪一個字為「一種會限制身體行動且疼痛的肌肉緊繃感」之意？

   cramp/Cramp. (抽筋)

   本題測驗能否根據文意理解文章中的生字。作答線索在第四段最後一句「手指和拇指可能會發炎甚至抽筋，這會帶來疼痛並使低頭族無法輕易移動該部位。」，符合本題的單字定義，故選擇填入 cramp 或 Cramp. (抽筋)。

2. 第二段中的句子已標示為❶到❻。其中哪一句說明了為何有些人並不認為低頭滑手機值得大眾關注？寫下該句的**編號**。

   ❶

   本題測驗能否理解文意後加以舉證以及因果分析的能力。由第二段句子❶可知，許多人已習慣低頭滑手機，並認為低頭滑手機不過是日常生活中的一個正常現象，因此認為並不值得關注，故選句子❶。

3. 本文中提及了許多低頭滑手機的影響層面。使用本文中的單字填空下表。每格限一字。

影響層面	可能後果
學生 **(A) 行為 (behavior)**	・學習成績差 ・缺乏對老師的尊敬
人際關係	・容易忽視他人 ・**(B) 疏遠 (alienated)** 他人
健康	・上半身身體疼痛 ・**(C) 視力 (vision)** 模糊，眼睛缺乏水分 ・被感染或難以移動身體部位

本題測驗能否掌握並歸納文章細節訊息，將本文低頭滑手機可能影響的層面及後果歸納出來。(A) 可從第二段第三句找到作答線索，從可能的後果可知影響的是學生的行為層面，故 (A) 答案為 behavior。(B) 可從第三段第二句找到作答線索，低頭滑手機可能會漸漸地使自己疏遠他人，故 (B) 答案為 alienated。(C) 可從第四段第二句找到作答線索，低頭滑手機常造成頭痛、視力模糊和眼睛乾澀等問題，故 (C) 答案為 vision。

Help Sufferers Battle Depression
幫助患者對抗憂鬱症

Fun Facts

▶ 解答

C

▶ 小故事

我們應如何正確陪伴憂鬱症患者？

(A) 鼓勵他們著重在好的方面，不要想太多。

(B) 感同身受他們的情緒，並與他們同擔低潮時刻。

(C) 靜靜傾聽他們訴說，不帶批判的態度。

(D) 建議他們想想世界上更不幸的人們。

面對憂鬱症患者，身邊親友應要以 (C) 不帶批判的態度來陪伴，並靜靜聆聽憂鬱症患者的情緒。而像是 (A) 這種正向的鼓勵反而會適得其反，容易加重患者的憂鬱傾向；也切勿像 (B) 一樣被患者的情緒帶著走，沒有安慰到患者，反而自己被憂鬱症患者的情緒吞噬，最終自己也容易罹患憂鬱症。(D) 的方法則過於激進，會讓憂鬱症患者認為自己受到譴責，開始懷疑自己是否不夠知足，進而加重病情。

Reading

憂鬱症是一種普遍的心理健康問題，全球正經歷著病例急遽上升的情況。當提到亞洲憂鬱症患者，其自殺率遠遠高於西方觀測到的比率。遺憾的是，臺灣也有可觀的人數正在與這個令人脆弱的疾病對抗。

根據「社團法人臺灣憂鬱症防治協會」(TAAD)，臺灣受憂鬱症所擾的人只有大約五分之一實際上有尋求專業協助。而且，在那些確實有尋求協助的人裡，將近三分之一的人在看過醫生或心理健康專業人士一次後，就沒有繼續接受治療。

為何臺灣許多的憂鬱症患者，似乎不願意得到他們迫切需要的幫助呢？專家說，有些人可能不相信自己患病。其他人可能會因為害怕表達而受限，覺得很難清楚說明他們的掙扎。還有一些人可能對現行已廣泛使用的可用資源和治療方案不了解。

社團法人臺灣憂鬱症防治協會也認為，臺灣有相當多的憂鬱症患者是因為對某些治療的潛在副作用的擔憂，而停止尋求治療。因此，它決定採取措施，提高大眾對憂鬱症的認知，尤其是那些目前苦於此症的人。例如，該組織已經在高人氣社群通訊應用程式——LINE 上建立了一個頁面。透過私訊，社團法人臺灣憂鬱症防治協會的輔導員可以直接與憂鬱症患者溝通。他們還可以在 LINE 聊天室裡分享有關憂鬱症及其治療方案的有用資訊。

但願像是社團法人臺灣憂鬱症防治協會 LINE 聊天室這些措施的實行，能夠提供憂鬱症患者重拾幸福的一線希望。

混合題

▶ 解答

1. C　2. 6/six/Six (people).
3. accessible/Accessible.　4. A、D

▶ 解析

1. 根據本文，作者對財團法人臺灣憂鬱症防治協會能為憂鬱症患者帶來的改變抱持什麼樣的態度？

   (A) 不關心的。　(B) 懷疑的。
   (C) 樂觀的。　(D) 批評的。

   ✎ 本題測驗能否理解文意並判斷作者的態度。作答線索在最後一段，由作者使用 hopefully (但願) 以及 a ray of hope (一絲希望) 可知，作者對於該組織實行的措施抱持樂觀態度，故選 (C)。

2. 根據本文，在臺灣一組 30 位憂鬱症患者的團體中，其中會有多少人找專業人士求助？

   6/six/Six (people). (6 個人)

   ✎ 本題測驗能否掌握文章細節。作答線索在第二段，可知根據統計在臺灣約只有五分之一的憂鬱症患者中會尋求協助，計算式為 30 人 ×1/5 = 6 人，故答案為 6 或 six 或 Six (people).。

3. 本文中的哪一個字為「能夠被使用、得到、或取得」之意？

   accessible/Accessible. (可用的、可得到的)

   ✎ 本題測驗能否利用上下文理解文章中的生字。作答線索在第三段最後一句提到「許多臺灣的憂鬱症患者因為不了解或不認識現行廣泛使用的可用資源和可得到的治療方案而停止尋求治療」，故選擇填入 accessible (可用的、可得到的)。

4. 請從下列 (A) 到 (E) 中，選出對本文提及 the reasons why people burdened by depression in Taiwan seem to be negative about seeking assistance (臺灣受憂鬱症所苦的人不願尋求援助的原因) 正確的選項。

   (A) 他們不相信自己有心理疾病。
   (B) 他們害怕在去診所的路上迷路。
   (C) 他們因太害羞而不敢靠近其他病患。
   (D) 他們缺乏常用治療方案的了解。
   (E) 他們擔心高額的治療費用。

   ✎ 本段測驗能否掌握文章細節。作答線索在第三段，(A) 可從第二句得知「有些人可能拒絕相信自己的疾病」，而 (D) 可從第四句得知「還有一些人可能對現行廣泛使用的可用資源和治療方案不了解」，故選 (A)、(D)。其餘選項均未被提及。

The Dangers of Smoking: What You May Not Know About Smoking
吸菸的危害：關於吸菸你可能不知道的事

Fun Facts

▶ 解答

1. third-hand smoke > second-hand smoke > first-hand smoke　2. B

▶ 小故事

1. 請按照對人體的毒性順序排列一手菸、二手菸與三手菸。

   三手菸 > 二手菸 > 一手菸

   ✎根據醫學報告，二手菸的有毒物質是一手菸的 3 到 5 倍，而三手菸因為附著在物品、身體或食物上，其毒性會隨著時間越來越強，且幾乎很難完全消除，因此是三種裡面能傷害人體最深的，故對人體毒性由強至弱排列為三手菸、二手菸、一手菸。嘉義縣衛生所網站也以「一手菸害已、二手菸害人、三手菸遺毒人間」的標語提醒人民吸菸有害健康。

2. 下列哪項菸草製品中的成分會使人容易染上菸癮？

   (A) 一氧化碳。　**(B) 尼古丁。**
   (C) 焦油。　(D) 砒霜。

   ✎尼古丁是造成人們對香菸成癮的最大元兇，根據調查，尼古丁只要 10 秒鐘就能由肺部傳到腦部，讓人產生與吸毒類似的「舒爽感」，在當下可以提高注意力與穩定情緒，然而尼古丁作用時間一過就會使焦慮感再度出現，導致吸菸者產生菸癮。尼古丁讓吸菸者持續吸菸約半年至一年就能產生依賴，故選 (B)。

Reading

現今，人們都意識到吸菸有害健康。他們也知道，吸菸不僅損害吸菸成癮者的健康。從未吸過菸的人也會受到影響。

香菸的煙霧含有上千種化學物質，包含超過 65 種已知會致癌的物質。當人們吸菸時，很大一部份的有害物質會直接進入肺部，而其餘物質會隨著吸菸者呼氣時釋放到空氣中。值得注意的是，研究顯示，香菸的煙霧及其有毒的化學物質能在空氣中停留數小時，在氣味和顏色消失很久後仍然構成風險。這也解釋了為何不吸菸者也會患有與吸菸相關的疾病。

此外，一些報告指出，吸菸對不同性別的人有不同影響。例如，人們經常將吸菸和肺癌與男性聯結在一起，但研究卻提供了不同的觀點。根據研究，和男性相比，吸菸的女性確實更容易在年輕時患上肺癌。此外，女性也更容易罹患擴散迅速的小細胞肺癌。研究已發現，男性與女性之間的生理差異可能導致女性罹患肺癌的可能性更高。

儘管人們認知吸菸是個嚴重的問題，但有些人發現要擺脫它的控制是有挑戰性的。為了減少吸菸造成的危害，世界各國政府已通過法律禁止在公共場所吸菸。這些政策不僅確保非吸菸者的安全，也培養吸菸者自身的意識。終究不可否認的是，香菸中發現的化學物質可能致命。戒菸仍是個好主意，或者從一開始就別開始吸菸更好。

混合題

▶ 解答

1. exhale　2. (A) spreads；(B) Women
3. B、E

▶ 解析

1. 吸菸者不僅吸入了有害的物質進入了他們的肺中，也**呼出 (exhale)** 了有毒的化學物質到空氣中。

   ✎ 本題測驗能否掌握段落脈絡，從指定的段落中選出一個單詞，並運用語法知識做適當字形變化。根據第二段第二句提及吸菸時有害物質會隨著吸菸者「呼氣」時釋放至空氣中，可知本題空格應選擇該句的動詞 exhale (吐氣)，並根據本題句型為現在簡單式，將之變化成 exhale 填入。

2. 根據本文提及資訊，將小細胞肺癌的相關資訊填入空格中。

小細胞肺癌	
主因	暴露於來自香菸煙霧的有害化學物質中。
特徵	· 小細胞肺癌 **(A) 傳播 (spreads)** 快速。 · **(B) 女性 (Women)** 較容易罹患小細胞肺癌。

   ✎ 本題測驗能否掌握文章細節，作答線索在第三段。(A) 和 (B) 皆可從第四句得知「女性也更容易罹患擴散迅速的小細胞肺癌」，故 (A) 答案為 spreads；(B) 答案為 Women。

3. 請從下列 (A) 到 (E) 中，選出作者於文章中有提及的選項。
   (A) 為何許多人認為戒菸很難的原因。
   (B) 香菸含有危及生命的物質之事實。
   (C) 吸菸對不同年齡層的負面影響。
   (D) 對診斷出罹癌的人最有效的治療方法。
   (E) 全世界的政府都在努力阻止在公共場所吸菸。

   ✎ 本題測驗能否理解文意並掌握文章細節，作答線索在於全文內容。(B) 可從第二段第一句與第四段最後一句得知「香菸內含有數千種致命的化學物質」；(E) 可從第四段第二段得知「世界各國政府已通過法律禁止在公共場所吸菸」，故選 (B)、(E)。其餘選項均未被提及。

Taking Action: Standing Up for Others
採取行動：為他人挺身而出

Fun Facts

▶ 解答

D

▶ 小故事

下列哪項是「反霸凌日」的別稱？

(A) 閨蜜節。 (B) 世界棉花日。

(C) 全球愛心日。 **(D) 粉紅 T 恤日。**

反霸凌日又稱為「粉紅 T 恤日」，臺灣普遍於每年 4 月的第 2 個星期三響應反霸凌日，而響應日會隨著地區不同有差異。粉紅 T 恤日的由來，是因發起人當時看見同校男同學因穿著粉紅色衣服而遭受到霸凌，為了表達對被霸凌者的支持，發起人號召全部的人，不分性別，一起穿上粉紅色衣服，以推廣「任何性別都擁有喜歡任何一種顏色的權利」，一起響應反霸凌，故選 (D)。

另外，其實還有另一個國際粉紅日是在 6 月 23 日，單純為了慶祝粉紅色這個顏色，散播其甜蜜、浪漫以及夢幻等意義。

Reading

當目睹意外事故時，大多數人會先評估涉事者是否受傷，然後可能會報警。但如果在目擊某人在公共場合遭到言語攻擊時呢？雖然這可能不致於對受害者造成肢體傷害，但可能是一樣令人痛苦的。你會做任何事嗎？對於一般人來說，答案可能是否定的。

當目擊不公不義的事時，常見的反應是忽略它。它似乎與我們無關。然而，什麼都不做，基本上就是縱容攻擊者。這並不表示我們是壞人，但我們確實必須設身處地為受害者著想。如果我們受到言語或肢體攻擊，我們會希望有人介入嗎？答案絕對是肯定的。

如果我們遇見有人蒙受不公待遇，我們應該接近那個人，而非視若無睹。通常，霸凌者的目的是嚇唬或激怒受害者，且如果他們覺得沒有擁護受害者的朋友，他們還很有可能會繼續。透過向前援助，我們明確傳達霸凌者的行為是不可接受的這件事。我們必須直接正視不公不義。當看到有人被霸凌時，我們可以幫助他們逃離該情況。如果我們從不為有需要的人挺身而出，那麼當我們需要幫助時，還會有誰留下來為我們挺身而出呢？

為了創造更好的社會，當我們見到不當之事時，我們必須採取行動，而非袖手旁觀。如果角色互換，我們會期望有人來幫助我們，所以，讓我們以自己希望被對待的方式對待他人吧。

混合題

▶ 解答

1. injustice/Injustice.　2. A　3. C
4. B、D、F

▶ 解析

1. 第二段中哪一字為「不公平的對待或欠缺公平性」之意？

   injustice/Injustice. (不公不義的事)

   本題測驗能否利用上下文理解文章中的生字。此字其實在第二段至第三段皆有出現，作答線索在第二段第一、二句，「如果看到不公不義的事發生，我們常見的反應是不理會」，又第三段第一句和第四句也提到「如果我們遇見有人蒙受不公待遇，我們應該接近那個人，而非視若無睹，且必須直接正視不公不義」，不斷使用 injustice 來指稱霸凌行為，故選擇填入 injustice 或 Iinjustice. (不公不義的事)。另外，最後一段第一句的 wrongdoing 其實也與 injustice 意思相近，若本題無限制在第二段中選字，wrongdoing 就也是可能解答之一。

2. 根據本文，最後一段中的 "**reversed**" 一字最有可能是什麼意思？

   (A) 改變。　(B) 接受。
   (C) 忽略。　(D) 霸凌。

   本題測驗能否理解文意並依據上下文推論出字義。作答線索在第四段第一句提到「如果看到不當之事，我們必須採取行動」，可推論出下一句應是呼籲讀者換位思考，「假設角色互換，我們也會期望有人前來協助我們」，故選 (A)。

3. 根據本文，為何人們在目擊霸凌時採取行動很重要？

   (A) 避免捲入衝突。
   (B) 保護自己免受潛在傷害。
   (C) 防止不當之事繼續。
   (D) 獲得他人的認可和支持

   本題測驗能否理解文意。作答線索在第二段，第二句提到「如果什麼都不做就是縱容攻擊者繼續進行」，代表如果我們採取行動，就是在防止不公不易的事 (injustice) 或不當之事 (wrongdoing) 繼續發生，故選 (C)。

4. 根據本文，選出當看到小男孩被霸凌時，應該如何幫助他的正確敘述。

   (A) 視而不見。
   (B) 介入以救援他。
   (C) 激怒或嚇唬他。
   (D) 成為他的支持群眾。
   (E) 讓自己遠離這情況。
   (F) 協助他。

   本題測驗能否掌握文章細節與歸納重點。作答線索主要在第三段，(A) 和 (B) 解釋可從第一句找到「應該接近受害者並給予救援，而非視而不見」；(C) 和 (D) 可從第二句至第三句找到「霸凌者的目的在嚇唬或激怒受害者，所以我們應該要變成支持受害者的群眾，讓霸凌者不敢輕舉妄動」；(E) 可從第五句找到「我們應該幫受害者擺脫那種情況」；而 (F) 則可在最後一段第二句找到「應換位思考，前去協助受害者」，故選 (B)、(D)、(F)。

Japanese Women Outraged at Discrimination by Tokyo Medical University
東京醫科大學的歧視激怒日本女性

Fun Facts

▶ 解答

(1) yours；(2) him；(3) hirs/zirs；(4) xemself；(5) them

▶ 小故事

「大家好，我是 Simon。我的代名詞是 they/them。」

你是否有聽過有人使用首選性別代名詞 (PGPs) 來介紹自己呢？ PGPs 是一種新趨勢，讓擁有自己性別認同的人們選擇他們想要被人們識別的代名詞。

讓我們填滿表格空白處來學習新的性別代名詞，並嘗試用你的首選性別代名詞來進行自我介紹吧！

主格代名詞	受格代名詞	所有格形容詞	所有格代名詞	反身代名詞
I	me	my	mine	myself
you	you	yours	(1) **yours**	yourself
he	(2) **him**	his	his	himself
she	her	her	hers	herself
it	it	its	its	itself
ze/zie/sie	hir/zir	hir/zir	(3) **hirs/zirs**	hirself/zirself
xe	xem	xir/xyr	xirs/xyrs	(4) **xemself**
they	(5) **them**	their	theirs	themselves

隨著性別意識抬頭，現代人們對自身性別都有著自己的認同，也出現不少跨性別者與非二元性別 (non-binary) 者，而常規的人稱代名詞 he (他) 或 she (她) 明確地指出所代稱之人的性別為男生或女生，並不適合這些有自己性別認同的人。因此在許多英語系國家已經廣泛地接受新型態的性別代名詞，在一些學校或是職場上，人們常常會在自我介紹中加入自己的「首選性別代名詞」，以讓他們知道如何稱呼自己。

Reading

當某人因其性別而受到不同對待時，性別歧視就發生了。這通常是令人不快的，可能是一次性的舉動或某種形式的規則造成的。雖然性別歧視在世界各地都有發生，但幾年前在日本有個值得注意的案例。

2018 年，日本調查了其醫學大學內的性別歧視證據。東京醫科大學的校方人員已承認他們篡改了女性申請者的考試成績，降低了考試成績以阻止太多女性被錄取入學。這些校方人員設法將女性排除在醫療行業外，因為他們相信女性結婚後就會辭去工作去生孩子。這種全面性的歧視不公平地為男性保留了百分之 60 以上的醫學院培訓名額——即使是那些考試成績低於女性申請者的男性也得以被納入。不出所料，隨著醜聞最終浮上檯面，日本女性以及各地的女性主義者都非常憤怒。日本國內所有醫學院都因此受到了調查，並特別關注男女申請者的比率以及他們的入學考試成績。

現實情況是，和許多其他國家相同，日本社會上存有普遍的性別歧視。不只在教育上，在職場或甚至在家中也是如此。日本人普遍的態度是，男性應該成為一家之主，因為他是養家活口的人。相比之下，女性的角色主要是服從和支持丈夫。雖然這種思維方式已經無可救藥地落伍了，但日本女性仍然面臨著要順從丈夫意願的巨大壓力，即待在家裡養育孩子。

儘管越來越多人認可根據人們的性別而歧視任何人都是不公平的，而且通常其實是違法的，但這種傳統的態度仍舊根深蒂固。

混合題

▶ 解答

1. admitted　2. D
3. recognition/Recognition.　4. A、E

▶ 解析

1. 在被指控性別歧視後，東京醫科大學承認 **(admitted)** 它的錯誤，接著國內所有醫學院都被仔細審查。

   ✎ 本題測驗能否依據上下文脈絡，從指定的段落中選出一個單詞，並運用語法知識做適當字形變化。本題其實就是第二段的大意，可從第二句選出 admitted(承認) 來填入。本題亦為過去式時態，故答案為 admitted。

2. 第二段中的 “the scandal” 指的是什麼？
   (A) 日本社會中普遍存在性別歧視的事實。
   (B) 女性一旦結婚就會放棄行醫的想法。
   (C) 針對日本所有醫學院進行的調查。
   (D) 關於校方人員竄改女性申請者考試成績的事件。

   ✎ 本題測驗能否掌握文章脈絡並了解指代詞組的指涉對象。作答線索在第二句及第五句提到「東京醫科大學的校方人員承認竄改分數，而這樣的醜聞曝光後讓女性非常憤怒」，這裡的 the scandal 即指涉竄改分數一事，故選 (D)。

3. 本文中的哪一個字為「認可某件事是對的或重要的」之意？

recognition/Recognition. (認可)

本題測驗能否利用上下文理解文章中的生字。作答線索在最後一段 a growing recognition 後面引導的 that 名詞子句，說明「越來越多人認可根據性別去歧視任何人是不公平的且是違法的」，可推論出 recognition 的詞意，故選擇填入 recognition 或 Recognition. (認可)。

4. 請從下列 (A) 到 (E) 中，選出符合文意的選項。

(A) 本文中的 "counterparts (相對應者)" 一詞很可能是指 "applicants (申請者)"。

(B) 東京醫科大學因部分學生為了畢業竄改分數而被調查。

(C) 即使性別歧視在校園裡很普遍，但不存在於工作場所。

(D) 許多日本女性寧願在家養育孩子也不願追求自己的職涯，這就是為何她們得不到醫學培訓機會。

(E) 男性和女性申請者的人數和他們入學考試成績都會是本次調查的重點。

本題測驗能否理解文意並掌握文章細節。作答線索在於全文內容，(A) 可從第二段第二句及第四句得知「男性申請者對應的是與之競爭的女性申請者」，而 (E) 可從第二段最後一句得知「本次調查將特別關注男女申請者的比率以及他們的入學考試成績」，故選 (A)、(E)。其餘選項均不符合文意。

The Psychology of Panic Buying 恐慌性購買的心理

Fun Facts

▶ 解答

B

▶ 小故事

以下哪個因素**不會**觸發恐慌性購買？

(A) 價格上漲或產品短缺的聲明。

(B) 媒體廣泛報導某些農產品的盛產狀況。

(C) 幾個主要進口國之間爆發戰爭。

(D) 政府暗示可能實施鎖國政策。

農產品盛產的報導並不會引發人們產生恐慌的情緒，並因為害怕購買不到就大量囤貨該農產品，故選 (B)。而其他選項提到的：漲價、戰爭爆發與鎖國政策的啟動都會引發人民緊張且恐慌的情緒，進而為了買到未漲價或足夠的商品而同時大量購買各種用品，產生商品的短缺，也讓買不到商品的人更加恐慌，故其餘選項會觸發恐慌性購買。

Reading

恐慌性購買是在遭受危機或災難衝擊的社區中可能會發生的一種現象。新聞報導顯示出超市貨架空空如也，且人們大排長龍急切地大量囤積日常用品。購物者看起來愁眉苦臉，常要等上數小時才能買到日用品。當他們終於排到隊伍的最前面時，許多人會把搬得動的東西全都買回家，即便沒留任何一點給其他人。舉例來說，新冠肺炎疫情在全球許多國家引發口罩、消毒用酒精和衛生紙的恐慌性購買。

研究人類行為的研究員解釋了促成恐慌性購買的心理。第一個因素是焦慮。當面對戰爭、天災或是傳染性疾病爆發時，人們自然會感到擔心。恐慌性購買也可能源自於對生活必需品會漲價的憂慮。因此，第二個因素是經濟學家所謂的「損失迴避」。人們會因為一種認知偏見而認為避免損失比得到收益更加重要。第三個因素則是稱作「羊群效應」的一種傾向。這指的是對「隨波逐流」的渴望，且不經自我思考就做他人在做的事。

恐慌性購買不僅造成不便，也導致許多問題。需求的增加可能會使短缺變得更嚴重。而這很可能又因此抬升物價，因為有些供應商和零售商會趁機漲價。結果通常會變成有些人擁有的超過自身需求，而另一些人則什麼都沒有，這意味著弱勢者變得更難以生存。

為了避免恐慌性購買可能帶來的問題，我們應該保持冷靜、充分了解情況、不理會謠言並抗拒過量購買的衝動。

混合題

▶ 解答

1. Anxiety, loss aversion, and herd mentality. 2. C 3. (1) C；(2) D；(3) B

▶ 解析

1. 根據本文，造成恐慌性購買的 3 個原因為何？

   Anxiety, loss aversion, and herd mentality. (焦慮、損失迴避與羊群效應。)

   ✎ 本題測驗能否理解文意並整合相關資訊。作答線索在第二段第二句、第五句與七句，故答案為 Anxiety, loss aversion, and herd mentality.。

2. 第一段中的 "others" 指的是什麼？

   (A) 其他隊伍。 (B) 其他災難。

   (C) 其他購物者。 (D) 其他必需品。

   ✎ 本題測驗能否掌握文章脈絡並了解指代詞組的指涉對象。作答線索在第一段第三句與第四句，由第三句提到 shoppers 可知第四句的 they finally 的 they、many of them 的 them、they can carry 的 they 指的都是第三句的 shoppers。而第四句句尾的 others 指的是 many of shoppers 以外的沒有搶購到東西的 shoppers，故選 (C)。

3. 以下為有關恐慌性購買可能造成的問題之敘述。根據本文，將下方敘述 (A) 到 (D) 按時間先後的正確順序排列。

   (A) 颱風襲擊本島。

   (B) 蔬菜價格抬升。

   (C) 對蔬菜的需求增加。

   (D) 島上蔬菜的短缺問題惡化。

   A → (1) C → (2) D → (3) B

   ✎ 本題測驗能否理解文意以及因果分析的能力。作答線索在全文，尤其在第三段，由第二句可得知先有「需求量的增加」，才造成「產品短缺問題惡化」，再因此而造成「價格抬升」，故正確時間順序為 A → C → D → B。

Dengue Fever Spreads to Nepal's High Mountains
登革熱傳入尼泊爾高山區

Fun Facts

▶ 解答

1. C　2. B

▶ 小故事

1. 下列何者**不是**登革熱的症狀？
   (A) 關節疼痛。　(B) 嘔吐。
   (C) 失去味覺或嗅覺。　(D) 疹子。
   根據衛福部疾病管制署的資訊表示，登革熱的主要症狀為 (A) 關節疼痛、(B) 嘔吐以及出現 (D) 疹子，並無提及 (C) 失去味覺或嗅覺，故選 (C)，而 (C) 為新冠肺炎之常見症狀。
2. 下列何者**不是**由蚊子傳播的疾病？
   (A) 瘧疾。　**(B) 新冠肺炎。**
   (C) 西尼羅熱。　(D) 茲卡病毒感染症。
   根據衛福部疾病管制署的資訊表示，蚊媒傳染病包含登革熱、(A) 瘧疾、(C) 西尼羅熱、(D) 茲卡病毒感染症，並未提及 (B) 新冠肺炎，故選 (B)。另外還有一些傳染病：日本腦炎、黃熱病、屈公病、淋巴絲蟲病、裂谷熱，也屬蚊媒傳染病。

Reading

一個被譽為世上最冷、最偏遠的地方之一的南亞國家，卻正在與一種和溫暖熱帶氣候較密切相關的不速之客搏鬥：登革熱已經散播到了尼泊爾。

這個內陸國度位於西藏邊界以南和印度邊界以北。想探索尼泊爾自然美景和豐富文化內涵的遊客必須要適應將近 3,300 公尺的平均海拔，然而喜馬拉雅山脈著名的山峰高達這高度的兩倍多。即使是地勢低窪的首都——加德滿都，也座落在平均海拔約 1,350 公尺之處。稀薄的空氣可能會讓遊客喘不過氣。

然而儘管尼泊爾位於北緯，且平均氣溫相對較低，但由蚊子傳染的登革熱，已對該國構成威脅。公共衛生專家指責氣候變遷是罪魁禍首。近年來，尼泊爾經歷高於平均的氣溫。再加上大量降雨，這為蚊子的繁殖創造了完美條件。從前，高海拔地區的低溫成為一道天然屏障，阻止了蚊子的繁殖。然而，氣候暖化意味著這害蟲現在能在高達海拔 2,000 公尺之處生活了。透過汽車和卡車運送，牠們可以去到更高的地方，把病傳給喜馬拉雅山脈的人們，而那裡以前蚊子並不常見。

雖然發高燒、頭痛、眼後疼痛、肌肉和關節疼痛以及疹子等登革熱症狀是可治療的，但尼泊爾的醫療照護系統要跟上不斷增加的染病人數還是很吃力。全球各國的登革熱病例最近也有所增加。冬季變短而夏季變得更長更熱，使得蚊子大量孳生，並將疾病傳播到越來越廣泛的區域。

登革熱在尼泊爾登陸清楚提醒我們，地球上沒有任何一隅能夠免受氣候變遷波及廣泛的影響。需要立即採取措施以減輕它的影響並保護弱勢群體免受環境條件變化引起的健康風險。

混合題

▶ 解答

1. heavy、rainfall　2. point the finger at
3. A、C　4. B

▶ 解析

1. 溫暖的天氣和大量降雨 (heavy rainfall) 這兩個條件，使蚊子能夠在尼泊爾繁殖。

   ✎ 本題測驗能否理解文意，從指定的段落中選出一個單詞填入並使句意完整。作答線索在第三段第二句至第三句，可得知「除了高於平均的氣溫，大量降雨也使得環境適合蚊子在尼泊爾繁殖」，故選擇填入 heavy rainfall (大量降雨)。

2. 本文中哪個動詞片語為「責備或指責某人」之意？以現在簡單式時態寫出。

   point the finger at (指責…)

   ✎ 本題測驗能否利用上下文理解文章中的片語。作答線索在第三段，第一句敘述「儘管尼泊爾位於北緯且平均氣溫低，但蚊子卻造成威脅」，緊接著第二句說明「公共衛生專家點出蚊子造成威脅的原因是氣候變遷」，故可合理推測第二句中的動詞片語 point the finger at 有表達指責、咎責之意。故選擇填入 point the finger at (指責…)。

3. 請從下列 (A) 到 (E) 中，選出符合文意的選項。

   (A) 尼泊爾的醫療照護系統難以應付快速增長的登革熱案例。

   (B) 蚊子可以透過躲在遊客的衣服和行李中去到更高的地方。

   (C) 如果全球暖化繼續惡化，登革熱將傳播至更廣的範圍。

   (D) 登革熱爆發是因為我們的地球大部分都被熱帶氣候所覆蓋。

   (E) 最近爆發的登革熱是個例外，在尼泊爾以外地方很少見。

   ✎ 本題測驗能否理解文意並掌握文章細節，作答線索主要在第四段。第一句提到「登革熱症狀是可加以治療的，但不斷增加的案例對尼泊爾的醫療照護系統來說是超出負荷的」，故 (A) 正確；最後一句提到「全球暖化導致夏季變長變熱，使得蚊子大量孳生，登革熱將會越來越廣傳」，故 (C) 正確；(B) 可由第三段最後一句得知，本文只有提及蚊子是透過躲進汽車和卡車裡去到更高的地方，並非躲進遊客的衣物內；(D) 在本文中並無提及故不符合文意；(E) 則與文意相反，應是在尼泊爾以外很常見，目前也傳入了尼泊爾當地，故選 (A)、(C)。

4. 根據本文，下列哪個折線圖是正確的？

(A)

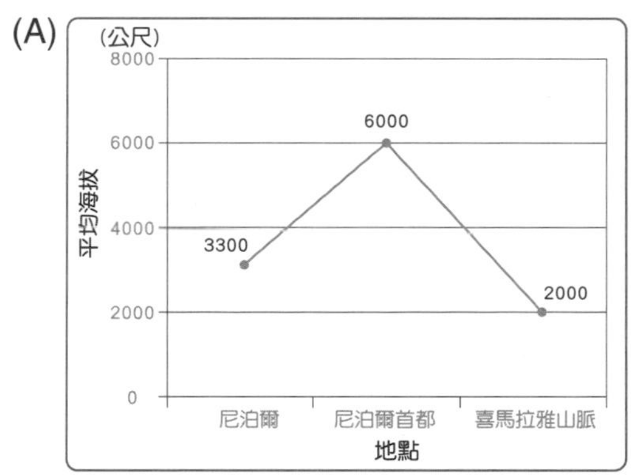

(B)

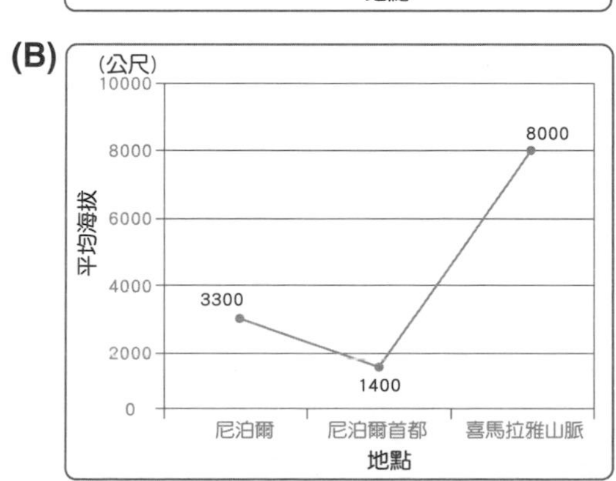

(C)

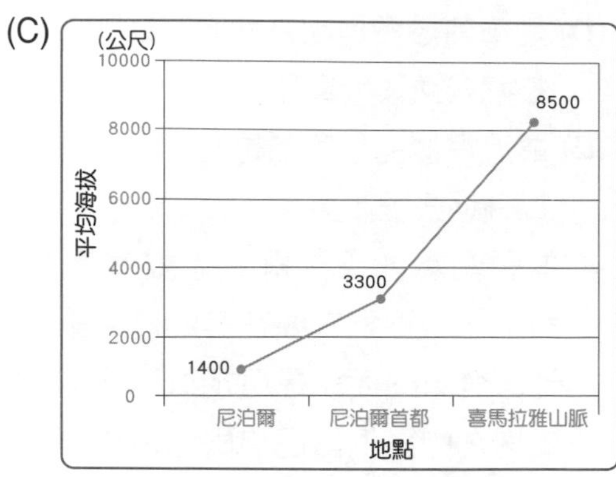

(D)

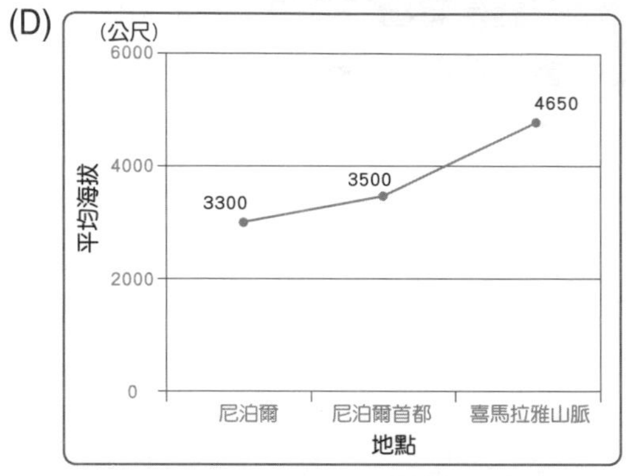

本題測驗能否理解文意並正確判讀圖表。作答線索在第二段第二句至第三句，可得知「尼泊爾平均海拔高度為 3,265 公尺，而喜馬拉雅山脈高度為 3,265 公尺的兩倍多，即海拔超過 6,530 公尺。地勢較低窪的尼泊爾首都位於海拔 1,400 公尺」，故選 (B)。

From San Francisco to Hualien: What Earthquakes Can Bring 從舊金山到花蓮：地震會帶來什麼

Fun Facts

▶ 解答

A、B、D

▶ 小故事

下列哪三項關於地震的敘述**不是**正確的？

(A) 躲避時應靠近窗戶及冰箱，以利逃生與生存。

(B) 人們可躲避在家具間高低差所形成的生命黃金三角內。

(C) 人們應將家具往牆壁固定，以防止地震時家具傾倒。

(D) 地震來襲時，應避免搭乘電梯，並迅速逃往戶外。

(E) 受困時，最好發出敲擊聲，而不要大聲呼救。

錯誤：

(A) 躲避時應遠離窗戶、玻璃、吊燈以及易倒塌的櫥櫃或冰箱，避免地震時造成玻璃破裂而刺傷，且雖然曾經有躲在冰箱旁最後獲救的案例，但一般家庭的冰箱或櫥櫃都未經固定，在地震劇烈搖晃時很可能因為傾倒而先被壓傷。

(B) 雖也曾經有躲在生命黃金三角內獲救的案例，但地震會為帶來家具帶來怎樣的位移是我們無法預測的，最保險的還是躲在堅固的桌子下方，避免躲在所謂的「生命黃金三角內」，可能因家具左右位移造成傷亡。

(D) 地震發生時很可能造成電力供應的不穩並影響電梯運作，故地震來襲時應避免搭乘電梯逃生是正確的。但地震發生時若人在室內，最重要的三步驟是① 趴下 (drop)、② 掩護 (cover)、③ 穩住 (hold on)，並非急著逃往戶外。

正確：

(C) 平時居家防災若能使用家具固定器具將家具與牆壁互相固定，便能減少地震時家具傾倒機率或位移程度。

(E) 受困時可利用身邊的物品製造規律的敲擊聲告知救難人員有人受困，並在該人員接近時再以口頭告知位置與狀況，大聲呼叫雖也可以吸引救難人員注意，但需消耗較多體力，故較不合適。

Reading

地震經常沿著斷層帶發生，如在北美洲和南美洲的西岸、亞洲太平洋沿岸以及地中海周邊。歷史上一個著名的例子是 1906 年突然侵襲舊金山地區的致命地震。地震觸發的火勢造成了最龐大的破壞。城市連燒了三天，超過一萬棟建築物被毀壞。數百人喪命，超過數千人無家可歸。1989 年，北加州又發生一起芮氏規模 7.1 的地震，造成近 70 人死亡。

臺灣也位處地震多發區域，其地震之頻繁可謂眾所皆知。例如，2018 年 2 月 6 日，一場 6.4 級的大地震襲擊花蓮，震央位於鄰近的海岸線附近。在主震之前先來了幾次小地震，之後又發生一連串餘震。好幾座建築物傾斜，其他的也嚴重受損。儘管人們奮勇地在嚴重損毀、極度不穩並呈現危險傾斜且有徹底倒塌風險的建築物裡營救身陷其中的受困者，但悲劇的是，還是造成了大量的生命逝去。有許多居民和遊客傷亡。

地震有可能毀壞橋樑和高速公路，中斷了供水、電力和通訊。更糟的是，地震會使許多人無家可歸，甚至造成人員傷亡。為了保護自己的家園和性命，生活在地震多發區域的人們必須建造更堅固的建築物和道路。發電廠和醫院應要建離地震斷層帶越遠越好。當地震來襲時，人們應該疏散到開闊空間。如果無法做到，他們應採取保護措施，像是在堅固的桌子下避難。

混合題

▶ 解答

1. D　2. A　3. C、E　4. as far away as possible from earthquake fault lines

▶ 解析

1. 本文主旨為何？

(A) 臺灣和美國都位於地震帶。

(B) 主震發生前後通常會發生較小的地震。

(C) 歷史上發生的大地震大多都造成了悲慘的死亡。

(D) 地震會導致人員傷亡和建築物毀損。

✎ 本題測驗能否理解全文文意並歸納出主旨，作答線索在全文內容。由第一、二段分別說明美國與花蓮發生過的地震傷亡事件，與第三段談論地震可能帶來的影響與破壞，強調地震可能帶來的影響不容小覷，故選 (D)。

2. 根據本文，下列何人**不是** 2018 年花蓮地震的目擊者？

(A)「報導說震央位於花蓮東部山脈。直到看到新聞我才知道距離有多近。幸運的是，我的家人沒有受傷。」

(B)「我無法判斷這是否只是我的錯覺。感覺在主震過後又震動了好幾次。」

(C)「我很遺憾聽到有災民受困在建築物內，且還有一些人在地震中喪生。真是慘痛的損失！」

(D)「救援隊已經盡力了。如果你看到在嚴重傾斜的建築內引導受害者是多麼的困難，就會瞭解了。」

✎ 本題測驗能否整合文章細節訊息的能力。作答線索在第二段，由第二句可得知「2018 年的花蓮地震震央在海岸線附近」，並非在山區，故選 (A)。

3. 請從下列 (A) 到 (E) 中，選出文章中**未**提及的選項。

(A) 地震可能造成的破壞。

(B) 世界上的幾個地震多發區域。

(C) 大地震發生後應採取的適當措施。

(D) 臺灣和美國發生的大地震。

(E) 地震多發國家所使用的預警系統。

✎ 本題測驗能否理解文意並掌握文章細節，作答線索在全文。(A) 全文內容都在談論地震造成的破壞；(B) 第一段第一句即列舉了幾個地震多發的區域；(D) 第一段與第二段分別描述了臺灣和美國曾發生過的大地震；本文中提到了地震時的措施，並未提及 (C) 地震後的措施；而 (E) 則並在本文中被提及，故選 (C) 和 (E)。

4. 為確保市民的安全，Sowa 市市長決定要把新的發電廠興建在**離地震斷層帶越遠越好 (as far away as possible from the earthquake fault lines)**。因此，市長選擇了地點 B。

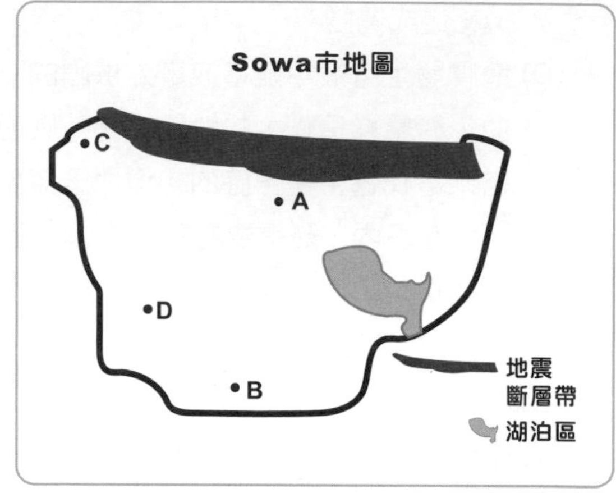

✎ 本題測驗能否理解文意並正確判讀圖表。作答線索在第三段第四句，表示「發電廠應要建離地震斷層帶越遠越好」，故本題詞組選擇填入 as far away as possible from earthquake fault lines。

Nearly 60% of the Earth's Vertebrate Wildlife Has Gone 地球上近6成的野生脊椎動物已消失

Fun Facts

▶ 解答

A、D、E

▶ 小故事

石虎在 2008 年正式被列為瀕臨滅絕的物種，且在臺灣可能只剩不到 500 隻。人們可以採取下列哪三種行動來保育石虎？

(A) 停止棲息地的砍伐與破壞，以保護牠們的家園。

(B) 把像貓咪一樣可愛的石虎帶回家並細心照顧牠們。

(C) 開車快速通過牠們的棲息地，以避免打擾牠們。

(D) 避免使用陷阱與毒餌，以免威脅牠們的生存。

(E) 不丟棄或棄養動物，以降低石虎的危險。

正確：

(A) 減少石虎棲息地的開發，即不砍伐森林、不將溪流鋪上水泥以及不汙染環境，就是對石虎以及其他淺山生物的最大保護。

(D) 獸鋏以及毒餌都會嚴重傷害野生動物，包含石虎，應該絕對避免這樣的行為，以維護野生動物的生存權。

(E) 遊蕩的犬貓易與石虎爭搶棲地和食物，甚至會獵捕石虎，對石虎來說都是非常大的生存威脅。當個負責任的飼主，不棄養、不放養，對保育野生動物來說是非常重要的。

錯誤：

(B) 石虎雖然很可愛，但在臺灣已被歸類為第一級保育類動物，故不可擅自將石虎帶回家中飼養，以免觸法，也泯滅了石虎的野性。

(C) 開車經過石虎棲息森林時應減速慢行並留意車前視線，以降低「石虎路殺事件」的發生，將不小心傷害到石虎的可能性降到最低。

Reading

❶根據世界自然基金會 (WWF) 的報告，過去幾十年對野生動植物而言是場災難，許多物種經歷了數量下降或甚至走向滅絕。❷數量下降對哺乳動物、魚類、鳥類和其他有脊椎的動物來說是特別具有毀壞性的。❸統計數據顯示，自 1970 年以來，地球上已有將近 6 成的野生脊椎動物消失了。❹更令人擔憂的是，世界自然基金會警告說這一趨勢並沒有減緩的跡象。

不出所料，人類活動就是動物消失的主要原因。無論是為了食物還是金錢，狩獵殺害了大量的動物。雖然法律禁止瀕臨滅絕動物身體部位的貿易，例如象牙和犀牛角，但黑市仍繼續滿足對此類產品的需求。

人口快速增長也推動了對可用土地的需求。森林遭到清空，以便騰出空間給不斷擴大的城市和道路，這意味著鳥類、哺乳動物和爬蟲類的自然棲息地也因此被摧毀殆盡。覓食和繁殖空間受到剝奪，那些無法適應不斷變化的環境條件的物種註定會滅亡。

而且，海洋以及許多湖泊和河流，都被汙染物塞滿，包括塑膠、化學製品和未經處理的廢棄物。再加上水溫上升，打造出了不再適合許多水生物種的條件。即使在那些可以存活下來的物種裡，又有很多物種因為過度捕撈而迅速地減少。

❺然而，雖然局勢嚴峻，但希望仍舊存在。❻保育工作已成功挽救了許多瀕危物種，把牠們從滅絕的邊緣中拯救出來。❼不過，儘管一些保育計畫的成功，人類還是需要採取更多立即與更明確的行動來減緩或扭轉野生動物數量的下降。❽為了維持環境，我們必須重新思考我們的輕重緩急和消費模式。

混合題

▶ 解答

1. C　2. (A) ❹；(B) ❻
3. (A) Rapid Human Population Growth；(B) overfishing

▶ 解析

1. 根據世界自然基金會的報告，下列何者不在消失中的動物的名單上？
   (A) 海龜 (脊椎動物)
   (B) 大象 (脊椎動物、哺乳動物)
   (C) 蝸牛 (無脊椎動物)
   (D) 鳥 (鳥類、脊椎動物)
   ✎ 本題測驗能否理解文意並選出與文意相符的圖片。作答線索在第一段第二句，可得知「哺乳動物、魚類、鳥類和其他脊椎動物都是正在消失的動物」，故選未提及的 (C)。

2. 第一段與最後一段的句子已標示為❶到❽。寫下該句的編號來回答以下兩個問題。
   (A) 在第一段中，哪句最能指出野生動物數量的可能進展？
   ❹
   (B) 在最後一段中，哪句**不是**作者對野生動植物保育的看法？
   ❻
   ✎ 本題兩小題測驗能否理解文意後加以舉證以及因果分析的能力。
   第一段❶～❹句子中，作者引述世界自然基金會報告中的數據以及資料，說明一些野生動物消失的已成事實，而由❹可知世界自然基金會對動物數量下降的趨勢並沒有減緩這件事提出警示，即是未來可能進展的發表，故 (A) 題選❹。
   最後一段❺～❽句子內，❺中作者提到 hope，表達出仍有希望的評論；❼和❽則使用了 people should take action、we must rethink 等字眼，提出呼籲與訴求，皆是作者個人表達對野生動植物保育的看法。反之，❻為描述保育工作的現況，故 (B) 題選❻。

3.

野生動植物消失的原因

I. 人類活動
- 為了食物獵捕
- 為了金錢獵捕 (例如象牙和犀牛角)

II. (A) 人口快速增長 (Rapid Human Population Growth)
- 清空森林
- 擴大城市和道路
- 破壞自然棲息地

III. 水汙染及與水相關的活動
- 塑膠、化學製品和未經處理的廢棄物
- 水溫上升
- **(B) 過度捕撈 (overfishing)**

本題測驗能否歸納文章重點以及因果分析的能力，需將各段點出造成動物消失的原因通盤理解，再依文章架構分層條列原因以及破壞行為。

作答線索在第三段至第四段，第三段第一句提及「人口快速增長」造成人類對土地的無盡需求，因此開始清空森林、擴大城市等，又空格 (A) 在此表中做次標題，字首須按照標題規則大寫，故空格 (A) 應填入 Rapid Human Population Growth。

空格 (B) 則可由第四段最後一句提及，又有很多物種因為「過度捕撈」而迅速地減少得知，故空格 (B) 應填入 overfishing。

The Rise of Robot Co-Workers 機器人同事崛起

Fun Facts

▶ 解答

B

▶ 小故事

「恐怖谷」是日本機器人學家森政弘於 1970 年提出的理論。根據該理論，當機器人在很多方面與人類非常相似，但又不完全逼真時，人類會有什麼樣的情緒？

(A) 人們會害怕對機器人產生喜歡的情感。

(B) 人們會感到不安、不自在，甚至毛骨悚然。

(C) 人們會對自己作為人類的存在感到懷疑與恐懼。

(D) 人們會害怕跟不上機器人的發展趨勢。

根據日本機器人學家森政弘提出恐怖谷理論，當機器人還「不夠擬人」的時候，它的「人類特質」會被突顯出來，當人們特別注意與自己相像的這些特質時，便會對機器人的好感度提升，所以多數卡通裡的機器人角色，人們大多都覺得很可愛；反之，當該角色變得「非常像人」時，人們反而會特別去注意到它「跟人類不同的地方」，像是僵硬的肢體行為與表情、電腦化的頭部，就會進而產生與人類很像，但又不太尋常的詭異感，因此對機器人的好感度就會驟降，故選 (B)。

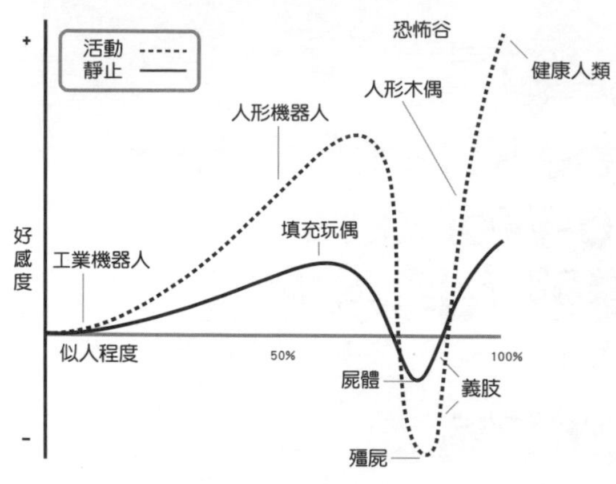

▲ 恐怖谷理論圖解說明

Reading

由於新技術的興起，我們很快就有可能必須與機器人一起共事。雖然這聽起來像是科幻電影中的場景，但專家表示，機器人同事終將成為工作場所習以為常的一部分。

事實上，有些機器人早已開始與人類合作。例如，當人類生命受到迫在眉睫的威脅時，美國士兵可以請拆彈機器人來處理。有些士兵與這些機器人變得非常親密，還為它們取了名字，甚至當它們被炸彈炸毀時為它們舉行喪禮。

機器人在製造場所也變得越來越普遍。近年來，北美洲公司工作場所的機器人數量已增加了近 50%。部分專家推測，我們可能很快就會看到特定工業場所裡的機器人數量超過人類的場景。

儘管人們越來越擔心人類將會被機器取代，但專家表示，人類不應該擔心機器人會接手他們所有的工作。雖然機器人確實擅長例行性和重複性的任務，但它們在同時做多件事的能力和感知能力方面仍然是落後的。這意味著單調的或危險的任務可能會被分配給機器人，讓人類能夠專注於需要企劃、談判或同理他人等技能的工作。

同樣重要的是要記住，機器人擁有的能力有限，且通常在它們專注於單一任務時表現最佳。與人類不同，機器人不會主動協助需要幫助的同事，除非程式有指示它們這樣做。

最重要的是，專家強調人們應該將機器人視為助手，而不是取代者。

混合題

▶ 解答

1. C、D、F　2. A　3. probable/Probable.
4. C

▶ 解析

1. 請從下列 (A) 到 (E) 中，選出根據文章內容目前不會被機器人取代的職位。
   (A) 工廠員工。
   (B) 拆彈小組。
   (C) 公關顧問。
   (D) 業務。
   (E) 打字員。
   (F) 醫療保健專業人士。
   ✎ 本題測驗引申推論，依據文意推論符合情境敘述之選項。(A) 可由第三段「機器人在工廠以及製造場所越來越普遍」得知可被取代；(B) 可由第二段第二句「機器人被美國士兵用來拆解炸彈」得知可被取代；而其他選項作答線索在第四段第三句至第四句，點出「機器人擅長例行性、重複性、單調的或危險的工作，而不擅於同時做多件事和感知能力不及人類」，(E) 是重複性的工作因此也可被取代，故選 (C)、(D)、(F)，需要企劃、談判或同理他人的工作。
2. 根據本文，下列哪張圖表最能描述製造業中人類工作者和機器人數量的未來趨勢？

(A) 機器人數量「將會超過」人類工作者。

(B) 機器人數量「持續低於」人類工作者。

(C) 機器人所占的比率「有增長，但仍低於」人類工作者。

(D) 機器人數量「以前超過」人類工作者，但未來人類工作者會多於機器人。

本題測驗能否理解文意並正確判讀圖表。作答線索在第三段，由第一句提及「機器人在製造業變得越來越普遍」，以及最後一句提及「我們很快就會看到機器人數量超過人類工作者的場景」可知機器人數量未來會超越人類工作者，只有 (A) 圖表符合此未來趨勢，故選 (A)。

3. 本文中哪一字為「可能是真的或可能發生」之意？

probable/Probable. (很可能發生的)

本題測驗能否利用上下文理解文章中的生字。作答線索在第一段，說明「因為新技術的興起，未來我們是很有可能會跟機器人一起工作的」，故選擇填入 probable 或 Probable. (很可能發生的)。

4. 根據本文，機器人最可能在未來的工作場所扮演什麼角色？

(A) 它們對人類工作者來說是像炸彈一樣的威脅。

(B) 它們是人類工作者面臨的主要風險。

(C) 它們是人類工作者的隊友。

(D) 它們是人類工作者的取代者。

本題測驗能否理解文意。作答線索在最後一段，講述「人們應該視機器人為工作時的助手，而非取代者」，可推知機器人可以與人類共同分擔工作，為人類的隊友，故選 (C)。

A Closer Look at AR and VR
深入一探擴增實境與虛擬實境

Fun Facts

▶ 解答

B

▶ 小故事

5G 是新一代蜂巢式網路，可以推進各項技術發展。下列哪一項不是使用 5G 的好處？

(A) 使用者在使用 AR、VR 甚至 XR 時可以獲得更好的體驗。

(B) 使用者可以在簡訊中輸入超過 500 個單詞。

(C) 醫生可以藉助其低延遲率進行遠端手術。

(D) 與 4G 相比，它為使用者提供了更快的下載和上傳速度。

5G 的全名為第五代行動通訊技術，是新一代的行動通訊技術，其速度約是 4G 的 100 倍，也有著極低的延遲率 (回應時間)。這項新技術的發展在未來影響的將不只有科技業，也能推進許多行業的科技發展，像是 AR、VR 和 XR 技術、遠端手術、自動駕駛汽車、無人機等更進階的應用。唯有簡訊字數不在 5G 的增強範圍內，故選 (B)。

Reading

我們現在生活在網路世代，且科技毫無疑問地將在我們的生活中扮演越來越重要的角色。AR (擴增實境) 和 VR (虛擬實境) 是網路技術的兩個絕佳案例。

在 VR 裡，使用者通常必須配戴看起來結合了眼罩和眼鏡的專業裝備。該裝置內含一個模擬器，可以投射出一個非常逼真但卻是完全人造的世界。VR 體驗就像進入一個人最喜歡的動畫或遊戲，使用者可以在其中觀賞或甚至與虛擬角色互動。例如，一款廣受好評名為《戰慄時空：艾莉克絲》的 VR 遊戲帶領玩家進入《戰慄時空》的反烏托邦世界。然而，VR 的一大缺點在於設備本身。一些使用者反映他們對投射功能不太滿意，抱怨虛擬世界缺乏真正的現實感。還有一些案例是人們使用 VR 設備後感到頭暈目眩。

相比之下，在 AR 裡，現實世界只不過是由電腦生成的元素進行即時修改或擴增。這些元素可能包括從聲音到影像或圖像的一切事物。AR 的一個高人氣實例是一款在全球取得巨大成功的 AR 遊戲《寶可夢 GO》。在這款遊戲裡，玩家在他們的行動裝置上使用 AR 技術尋找、捕捉和訓練各種寶可夢怪獸。這些怪獸全都出現在真實世界的位置，例如公園、紀念碑和商店。

不過，這種網路科技的範疇並不只有擴展至遊戲。研究人員已正在探索多種能將它有效運用在旅遊業、建築和醫學等各種其他行業的方法。舉例來說，AR 已應用於多種軍事用途。當然，像是 AR 和 VR 的網路技術將會幫助人們以不同又有趣的方式體驗這個世界。

混合題

▶ 解答

1. (A) dizziness；(B) elements　2. military
3. (1) AR；(2) VR

▶ 解析

1. VR 設備讓使用者進入一個完全模擬但非常逼真的人造世界。然而，一些使用者反映在使用該設備後出現 **(A) 頭暈症狀 (dizziness)**。相比之下，AR 技術不需要使用者配戴頭戴式耳機。它透過像是視覺和聽覺輔助等電腦即時改善的 **(B) 元素 (elements)**，來擴增現實世界。

   ✎ 本題測驗能否依據上下文脈絡，從指定的段落中選出一個單詞，並運用語法知識做適當字形變化。根據第二段最後一句提及人們使用 VR 裝置後感到「頭暈目眩」，可知 (A) 應選擇該句的形容詞 dizzy (暈眩的)，並根據本題空格在動詞之後，將之變化成名詞 dizziness；根據第三段第一句及第二句提及在 AR 裡，現實世界只不過是由電腦生成的聲音或影像「元素」進行即時修改或增加，可知 (B) 應選擇該句的名詞 elements (元素)，本題空格需填入名詞，故直接填入 elements。

2. 將文章內有關 AR 及 VR 的資訊填入空格中。

	擴增實境	虛擬實境
設備	使用者的行動裝置	專業裝備
應用	遊戲和**軍事 (military)** 產業	遊戲

範例	《寶可夢 GO》	《戰慄時空：艾莉克絲》

本題測驗能否掌握並歸納文章細節訊息。VR 和 AR 的應用可以在第二段與第三段找到，而最後一段特別提及了 AR 的其他應用，由第三句可知「AR 已應用於多種軍事用途」，故選擇填入 military。

3. 根據本文所給資訊，將 AR 和 VR 與正確的圖片配對。

真實世界 **虛擬世界** **虛擬角色**

(1) 在真實世界裡的虛擬角色 **(2) 在虛擬世界的虛擬角色**

AR

VR

本題測驗能否理解文意並選出與文意相符的圖片。(1) 作答線索在第三段，可得知「與 VR 不同，AR 是在真實世界中加入一些由電腦生成的虛擬元素」，為虛擬角色與真實世界的結合，故 (1) 選擇填入 AR；(2) 作答線索在第二段第二句至第三句，可得知「VR 的定義是透過模擬器投射出一個完全虛擬的世界」，為虛擬角色與虛擬世界的結合，故 (2) 選擇填入 VR。

The Pros and Cons of Drones
無人機的優缺點

Fun Facts

▶ 解答

A、C

▶ 小故事

下列哪兩項關於無人機在臺灣做個人使用的敘述是正確的？

(A) 重量少於 250 克的無人機無需註冊即可飛行。

(B) 在移動的車輛或船隻上操作遙控無人機是被允許的。

(C) 無人機應該遠離鐵路、機場、公路以及高架大眾運輸系統。

(D) 使用無人機飛越人群聚集處上空拍照是被允許的。

(E) 不需要有無人機操作證，就可以在夜間飛行無人機。

(A) 和 (C) 為正確的飛行無人機守則。(B) 則是不允許在移動的車輛或船隻上操作遙控無人機；(D) 則是不可飛越人群聚集處上空，除非考取特定高級操作證；(E) 也是需要考取特定高級操作證，否則不可於夜間飛行無人機，故選 (A)、(C)。

Reading

無人機被用於執行各式各樣的任務。然而，對於它們的優點和潛在的缺點也存在許多爭議。

無人機是遙控飛行載具，經常用於高空攝影以及探索難以到達的地方。新聞組織可以派無人機去捕捉對攝影師來說可能難以獲得的圖像。此外，無人機在現代戰爭中也扮演著至關重要的角色，執行原本可能危及飛行員生命的任務。警察部門和保全公司也使用無人機實施監控，以確保其小隊成員的安全。

無人機也具有改變許多行業營運方式的潛力。例如，澳洲有些公司已樂意採用無人飛行載具 (UAV) 以遞送像是零食和飲料的商品。亞馬遜 (Amazon) 等其他公司也利用無人機代替它們傳統的卡車車隊來運送包裹。無人機送貨比其他交通運輸方式還要快很多，尤其是在道路交通堵塞時。這可以節省時間和金錢。

另一方面，無人機也沒有倖免於挑戰或反對。例如，如果所有者或操作者不夠謹慎，無人機可能會被駭入或遭竊。對於如何處理像是無人機失靈或電力故障等機械問題，也存在許多疑慮。在軍事環境中，無人機襲擊出差錯可能甚至造成無辜市民的逝去。除此之外，有些人因為侵犯隱私的問題而反對無人機。其他可能的問題包括噪音汙染以及空中過度擁擠。

然而，儘管優劣並存，人們仍繼續使用無人機，且其產業也持續成長。畢竟，使用者有責任去確保該技術被用來做好事而非作惡。

混合題

▶ 解答

1. C　2. C、E
3. (A) unmanned；(B) deliver

▶ 解析

1. 下列何者最能描述作者對無人機未來發展的態度？
   (A) 保留的。　(B) 猶豫的。
   (C) 中立的。　(D) 悲觀的。
   ✎ 本題測驗能否理解文意並判斷作者的態度。作答線索在於全文內容，第一段為文章的引導，第二段至第三段為無人機目前應用及其優點，第四段為無人機潛在的缺點，最後一段為作者對無人機中立的評價，由全文可推斷作者對於無人機發展的態度是中立的，故選 (C)。
2. 請從下列 (A) 到 (F) 中，選出符合作者於文章內提及無人機的正確敘述。
   (A) 無人機可能會造成噪音和空氣汙染。
   (B) 天氣條件可能會影響無人機飛行。
   (C) 無人機可能會引起人們對個人資訊洩露的擔憂。
   (D) 使用無人機包裝產品比傳統方法更有效率。
   (E) 許多公司願意使用無人機，因為它們是符合成本效益的。
   (F) 無人機對普通人來說太昂貴了無法購買。
   ✎ 本題測驗能否理解文意並掌握文章細節。作答線索主要在第三段與第四段，(C) 可從第四段倒數第二句得知「有些人因為侵犯隱私的問題而反對無人機」，因此會引起個資洩漏的擔憂；(E) 可從第三段最後一句得知「無人機的使用可以節省時間和金錢」，因此是符合成本效益的，故選 (C)、(E)。其餘選項皆不可選，(A) 可從第四段最後一句得知「會造成噪音汙染」，但無提及空氣汙染；本文並無提及 (B)；(D) 可從第三段最後兩句得知「用無人機遞送包裹比其他交通運輸方式還要快很多」，並非包裝產品；本文並無提及 (F)。

3. 無人機，也稱為 **(A) 無人 (unmanned)** 飛行載具，不需要飛行員，而是由地面人員控制。

   無人機在 **(B) 遞送 (delivery)** 包裹方面有無窮的潛力，因為它們比起其他運輸方式更具有速度優勢。

   ✎ 本題測驗能否依據上下文脈絡，從文章第三段中選出一個單詞，並運用語法知識做適當字形變化。空格 (A) 為統整作者在本文針對無人機的描述，第三段第二句提到無人機是無人飛行載具 (unmanned aerial vehicles)，故空格 (A) 可選擇填入第三段第二句的 unmanned (無人駕駛的)；空格 (B) 則是說明用無人機運送包裹的優勢，由第三段第四句提到用無人機運送包裹比用其他運送方式更省時和省錢，故空格 (B) 可選擇該句的名詞 delivery (遞送)，並根據本題空格在介系詞 to 後，將之變化成原型動詞 deliver。

The Suffering of Refugees
難民煎熬受苦

Fun Facts

▶ **解答**

1. D　2. B

▶ **小故事**

1. 截至 2022 年底，下列哪個國家產生的難民最多？
   (A) 南蘇丹。　(B) 阿富汗。
   (C) 烏克蘭。　**(D) 敘利亞。**

   ✎ 根據聯合國難民署 (the UN Refugee Agency) 2022 年的統計數據，全球難民最多來自敘利亞，其次是烏克蘭、阿富汗、南蘇丹與緬甸等國。

2. 截至 2022 年底，下列哪個國家收容的難民人數最多？
   (A) 哥倫比亞。　**(B) 土耳其。**
   (C) 德國。　(D) 英國。

   ✎ 根據聯合國難民署的統計數據，2022 年接收最多難民的收容國是土耳其，其次是伊朗、哥倫比亞、德國與巴基斯坦。

Reading

難民，或流離失所者並不是什麼稀少的存在。綜觀歷史，普通民眾都在承受著衝突或戰爭的衝擊。因此有許多人在暴力或迫害的驅使下被迫逃離祖國，到外國尋求安全和庇護。不幸地，如今世界上還有更多的難民。

這場日益嚴重的全球難民危機的根源可以追溯到 2011 年和 2012 年發生在中東和非洲的事件。「阿拉伯之春」開始進行時是和平的支持民主運動，但最終演變成敘利亞和利比亞的可怕戰爭。此外，該地區各個伊斯蘭教國家內戰頻繁爆發。這些衝突已導致數百萬敘利亞人、伊拉克人和索馬利亞人離鄉背井，成為難民。

許多難民渴望在歐洲或北美洲開始新生活。然而，前往陌生的國家很困難，而且通常很危險。其中有些難民為永遠不會抵達的交通運輸支付大筆費用。還有一些人在載輸途中死於意外。一名敘利亞小男孩在家人試圖從土耳其抵達希臘時在地中海溺斃的照片震驚了世界，也讓世界同悲。然而，這場悲劇也提高了人們對不斷惡化的難民危機的意識。

令人難過的是，並非所有國家都會熱烈歡迎難民。反移民情緒導致某些政府限制難民入境。部分難民可能成為人口販運的受害者。即使是歡迎難民的國家，通常也難以應付如此大量的非公民湧入。許多難民被禁閉在偏遠的難民營中，且與當地社區隔絕。在這種情況下，即使難民已在新的國家重新定居，他們所面臨的困難通常也會持續。他們可能很難適應新地方的生活。

做一個難民絕非易事。然而，只要有戰爭，就會有人被迫離開家園去尋求和平與安全。這就是全球難民危機日益嚴重的原因之一。此外，難民危機也提醒我們，爭取人權的抗爭仍是個持續存在的旅程。

混合題

▶ 解答

1. B　2. (A) human trafficking；(B) adjusting to life in a new community
3. B、E

▶ 解析

1. 作者對難民危機抱持什麼樣的態度？
(A) 樂觀的。　**(B) 擔憂的。**
(C) 開心的。　(D) 不關心的。

✎ 本題測驗能否理解文意並判斷作者的態度。作答線索在全文，由第一段最後一句使用 unfortunately 與第四段第一句使用 sadly 可得知，作者的態度是關心且擔憂的，故選 (B)。

2. 將文章內有關難民們所面臨的挑戰的資訊填入空格中。

抵達外國後的困境	➔	• 被限制入境。 • 受 **(A) 人口販運 (human trafficking)** 所害。 • 被關在偏遠的難民營裡。
定居後的困境	➔	• 很難 **(B) 適應新社區的生活 (adjusting to life in a new community)**。

✎ 本題測驗能否掌握並歸納文章細節訊息。作答線索在第四段，空格 (A) 可從第二句至第三句得知「有些政府會因為反移民情緒而限制難民入境，導致有些難民可能會成為人口販運的受害者」，故空格 (A) 選擇填入 human trafficking；空格 (B) 可從最後兩句得知「即使難民重新定居後，可能也很難適應新社區的生活」，故空格 (B) 選擇填入 adjusting to life in a new community。

3. 請從下列 (A) 到 (F) 中，選出以下圖片可正確對應本文文意的選項。

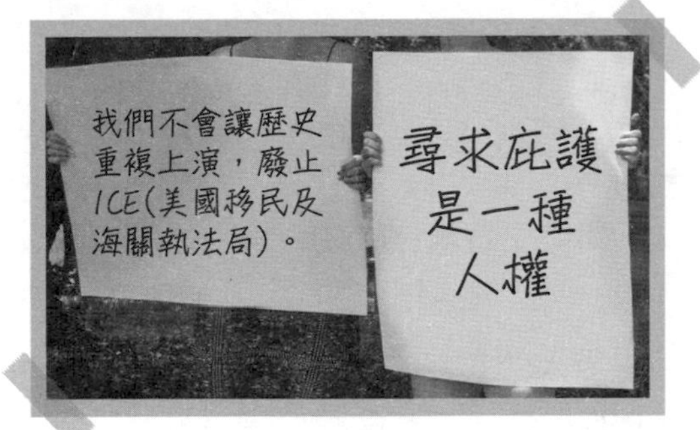

(A) 應禁止所有難民進入，以維持公民素養。

(B) 全世界的戰爭都應被終止，以減少難民的數量。

(C) 一個國家很難處理如此大量湧入的難民。

(D) 歷史上的民主運動皆是由右翼領導的。

(E) 難民應享有得到重新安置的基本人權。

(F) 政府應該認真對待人們的反移民情緒。

本題測驗能否理解文意並根據圖片選出與文意相符的敘述。左邊海報講述「我們不能讓歷史再度上演…」，可對應到第二段第四句與最後一段第二句，表達戰爭讓許多人都被迫離鄉背井變成了難民，符合敘述 (B)；右邊海報講述「尋求庇護是一種人權」，可對應到尾段最後一句，表達難民危機暗示了人權的不公，也造成難民在尋求庇護過程的種種困難情況，符合敘述 (E)，故選 (B)、(E)。

Is "Cold Hard Cash" Still King? 「實體現金」仍是王道嗎？

Fun Facts

▶ 解答

1. (1) C；(2) F；(3) E；(4) B；(5) D；(6) A

▶ 小故事

將正確的貨幣符號與使用國家配對

(1) €：Euro (EUR) 歐元，為歐元區國家 (如法國、德國等) 使用之貨幣，故選 (C)。

(2) ₹：Indian rupee (INR) 印度盧比，為印度使用之貨幣，故選 (F)。

(3) ¥：Yen (JPY) 日圓，為日本使用之貨幣，故選 (E)。

(4) £：Pound sterling (GBP) 英鎊，為英國使用之貨幣，故選 (B)。

(5) ฿：Thai baht (THB) 泰銖，為泰國使用之貨幣，故選 (D)。

(6) ₩：South Korean won (KRW) 韓元，為南韓使用之貨幣，故選 (A)。

Reading

你聽過「實體現金」一詞嗎？與支票和信用卡不同，它指的是硬幣或紙鈔形式的實體貨幣。許多人偏好收到現金，又稱法定貨幣，而不是非現金形式的支付。而且，在危機和災難期間，信用卡或其他數位支付方式結果可能是無效的。因此，就像俗話說的「現金為王」。事實上，有些人甚至在家裡囤放現金，因為他們不信任銀行，而且這會讓他們有安全感。

這是否意味著無現金支付無法撐過危機嗎？不必然是這樣。例如，新冠肺炎疫情無意間加速了無現金支付方式的採用。這是因為紙鈔和硬幣經常數度轉手，可能會促進疾病的傳播。因此，世界各地許多商店都開始採納信用卡或行動支付應用程式。在極端狀況下，一些企業停止接收實體貨幣。反之，他們實現完全無現金化，要求顧客使用簽帳金融卡、信用卡付款或線上或行動支付系統。

雖然無現金社會的願景逐漸獲得大眾認可，但現金會繼續存在仍有其充分理由。首先，現金對於那些重視隱私的人來說仍是最佳選擇。此外，總會有人更相信現金，或就是欣賞它的便利性。使用現金時，人們不必擔心有未支付的帳單或貸款，因為現金交易都是當場完成的。現金在非法活動中也是更受喜愛的選項。此外，有些人可能因為無法上網，而難以使用線上或行動支付系統。

也許合乎邏輯的結論是，儘管現金可能不再像以前那樣占主導地位，但它仍將保有其重要意義。畢竟，在情勢動盪時，手頭有一些現金是有用的。

混合題

▶ 解答

1. B　2. access　3. A、B、E

▶ 解析

1. 下列句子最適合放在哪一個段落？
「此外，新冠肺炎的封城限制使被困在家中的人們轉向線上購物。電子商務的擴張也促使消費者轉向數位管道。」
(A) 第一段。　**(B) 第二段。**
(C) 第三段。　(D) 第四段。
✎ 本題測驗能否理解文意並掌握文章脈絡，將句子放入文章正確的段落中。作答線索在第二段第三句說明「新冠肺炎疫情加速了無現金支付方式的採用」，可得知第二段是在探討疫情對數位支付帶來的影響，對應本題所給句子敘述的「疾病帶來的封城限制與消費者轉向數位管道」，故選 (B)。

2. 有些人在採用行動支付系統時遇到難題，因為他們要麼沒有特定的設備可使用，要麼無法<u>**連上 (access)**</u> 網路。
✎ 本題測驗能否依據上下文脈絡，從指定的段落中選出一個單詞，並運用語法知識做適當字形變化。根據第三段最後一句提及有些人因為無法「連」網路而無法使用線上或行動支付系統，可知本題空格應選擇該句的名詞 access (途徑)，並根據本題空格在助動詞 cannot 後，將之變化成原型動詞 access。

3. 請從下列 (A) 到 (E) 中，選出符合本文對更喜歡使用實體現金的人的論述。

(A) John 說：「我喜歡它，因為付款過程不會涉及個人資料或詳細情況。」

(B) Mary 表示：「我更喜歡它，因為這種付款方式有助於防止人們超支或積欠債務。」

(C) Jane 主張：「我喜歡它，因為當每筆交易都可被數位追蹤時，它會降低犯罪風險。」

(D) Jerry 說：「流通中的貨幣在其使用週期內被許多人使用過，可能成為傳播細菌和病毒的媒介。」

(E) Joan 表示：「在任何時候有一些現金在身邊，會給使用者帶來一種安全感。」

本題測驗能否理解文意並掌握文章細節。作答線索在全文，(A) 可由第三段第二句得知「現金對重視隱私的人來說是佳選擇」；(B) 可由第三段第四句得知「使用現金就不必擔心會有未支付的帳單或貸款」；(E) 可由第一段最後一句與最後一段最後一句得知「有一些現金在身邊可以為某些人帶來安全感」，故 (A)、(B)、(E) 為喜歡使用實體現金的人之論述。另外 (C) 可由從第三段倒數第二句得知「現金是非法活動中更受喜愛的支付方式」；(D) 可由第二段第四句得知「現金因為使用時會經手非常多人，故很可能會促進疾病傳播，所以新冠肺炎疫情期間就減少使用現金了」，皆非喜歡使用實體現金的人之論述，故不選。

Will Taiwan Benefit from the U.S.-China Trade War?
臺灣會從美中貿易戰中受益嗎？

Fun Facts

▶ 解答

(1) B；(2) D

▶ 小故事

將動物與他們常代表的市場狀況進行配對。

股價飆升，且投資者看好市場未來。	股價暴跌，且投資者不看好市場未來。
(1) 牛市	(2) 熊市

(A) 馬 (horse)。　(B) 牛 (bull)。

(C) 豹 (leopard)。　(D) 熊 (bear)。

牛市 (bull market) 又稱多頭市場，指的就是股價持續上漲超過 20%，且投資人對整體市場有信心並紛紛入場的情況；熊市 (bear market) 即是空頭市場，表示股價持續下跌超過 20%，整體買氣不佳。而牛與熊這兩種動物被用來形容股市的原因眾說紛紜，從牛與熊攻擊對手的方式、中古世紀英國的野蠻遊戲牛與熊是死對頭、證券交易所熱絡的報價訊息 (bull) 和低迷時的空無一物 (bare) 諧音，再到以牛群與冬眠的熊比喻證券交易所的市場狀況，已變得不可考。

◀ 華爾街銅牛 (Charging Bull) 是代表華爾街金融區的重要地標，創作背景為 1987 年美國股市崩盤，象徵著期望美國股市景氣上升，期待牛市到來。

Reading

美國和中國擁有世界上最令人敬畏的經濟。無論這兩個超級強權間發生什麼事，都不可避免地影響世界其他地區。兩國在 2018 年 7 月開始的貿易戰堪稱「龍爭虎鬥」。

臺灣這個小島國被夾在這爭吵不休的兩大巨擘之間。該國多年來一直是美國和中國的密切貿易夥伴，並且透過製造和出口商品到這兩個國家而繁榮起來。有些人表示，臺灣會在這場貿易戰中被徹底擊垮，而其他人則主張臺灣最終可能會從這場衝突中獲利。

在 1990 年代，許多臺灣企業將製造業搬移到中國，憑藉著那裡更廉價的勞動成本獲利。然而，隨著貿易戰導致中國的勞動成本上升以及美國對中國進口商品加徵關稅，在中國製造逐漸變得昂貴。因此，許多臺灣企業選擇將工廠遷回臺灣，為臺灣創造潛在的經濟成長和就業機會。此外，臺灣經濟部發起的「歡迎回臺投資方案」為這些返回臺灣的企業提供像是補助金、低利息銀行貸款以及稅務諮詢等激勵措施。

而且，有些跨國企業也選擇在臺灣投資，因為臺灣對智慧財產權的保護更加健全。例如，谷歌 (Google) 在臺灣興建了亞洲最大的研究與發展中心。微軟 (Microsoft)、亞馬遜 (Amazon)、蘋果 (Apple) 和國際商業機器股份有限公司 (IBM) 等其他國外大企業也計畫在臺灣拓展他們的總部，因為臺灣更能讓他們免於擔心數據中心的安全性問題。

希望美中貿易戰能夠盡快得到圓滿解決。而在此同時，無論情勢如何發展，臺灣應要竭盡所能從這個「危險機遇」中獲利。

混合題

▶ 解答

1. A　2. B、E
3. (1) manufacturing/labor；(2) tariffs；(3) protection；(4) security

▶ 解析

1. 根據本文，下列哪張圖表最能描述多年來在中國經營的臺灣工廠數量變化？

(A) 自 1990 年代開始後有明顯增加，而 2010 年代開始減少。

(B) 自 1990 年代開始就大幅減少，之後逐年穩定增加。

(C) 自 1980 年代開始有明顯增加，隨後逐年皆穩定增加。

(D) 自 1980 至 2000 年代就不斷減少，直至 2010 年代才開始遽增。

✎ 本題測驗能否理解文意並正確判讀圖表。作答線索在第三段，第一句至第二句提及「在 1990 年代，因為中國勞動力更便宜，許多臺灣企業將製造廠搬移到中國，而美國因為貿易戰的關係增加了中國進口商品的關稅」，由第一段最後一句可知「美中貿易戰爆發於 2018 年 7 月」，可知在中國經營的臺灣工廠數量會於 1990 年代增加，並於 2010 年代開始減少，故選 (A)。

2. 請從下列 (A) 到 (E) 中，選出本文中為「意見」，而非「事實」的選項。

(A) 近期在中國的製造業開銷已增加。

(B) 臺灣最終可能會從兩個大國之間的衝突中受益。

(C) 谷歌在臺灣建立了它在亞洲最大的研究與開發中心。

(D) 臺灣政府發起了一項「歡迎回臺投資方案」，以吸引企業歸國。

(E) 有些人聲稱臺灣會在此貿易糾紛中被擊垮。

✎ 本題測驗能否理解文意並掌握文章細節，並分辨文章中的陳述為意見或事實，作答線索在第二段到第五段。事實即是根據真實發生的事進行陳述，意見則是以個人的信念、感受或評斷為根據。由第二段最後一句提及「有些人表示，臺灣會在這場貿易戰中被徹底擊垮，而其他人則主張臺灣最終可能會從這場衝突中獲利。」，可知 (B) 和 (E) 皆為某些人的推測與意見，並非對事實現況的陳述，故選 (B) 和 (E)。其他選項皆為事實之敘述，故不選。

3. 將文章內有關為何臺灣與跨國企業搬移到臺灣的資訊填入空格中。

臺灣企業為何要揚帆回國？
➔ 因為中國 (1) 製造 / 勞動力 (manufacturing/labor) 成本增加。
➔ 因為美國對中國進口商品徵收高額 (2) 關稅 (tariffs)。
跨國企業為何來臺投資？
➔ 因為臺灣對智慧財產權有更強的 (3) 保護 (protection)。
➔ 因為臺灣的數據 (4) 安全性 (security) 比中國更高。

✎ 本題測驗能否掌握並歸納文章細節訊息。空格 (1) 和 (2) 作答線索在第三段，第一句及第二句提及「在中國的臺灣企業會搬回臺灣是因為貿易戰導致中國的勞動力成本上升，且因美國對中國進口商品徵收高關稅，所以在中國製造成本也越來越貴」，故 (1) 選擇填入 manufacturing (製造) 或 labor (勞動) 皆合適、(2) 選擇填入 tariffs (關稅)；空格 (3) 和 (4) 作答線索在第四段，由第一句講述跨國企業選擇轉向投資臺灣是因為臺灣對智慧財產權的保護更加健全，故 (3) 選擇填入 protection (保護)，而由同段最後一句講述臺灣更能讓跨國企業免於擔心數據中心的安全性問題，故 (4) 選擇填入 security (安全性)。

題本與解析本不分售
211-87236G